THE Jerusalem DONKEY LEGEND

BOOK ONE OF THE ACHSAH LEGACY

ANNE CHURCHILL

The Jerusalem Donkey Legend: Book One of The Achsah Legacy
Copyright © 2013 by Anne Churchill. All rights reserved.

First Print Edition: February 2013
Churchill Enterprises, Inc.

ISBN# 978-0615762753

1   2   3   4   5   6   7   8   9   0

Editor: Epiphany Imprint, Nancy Nichols
Cover Design and Formatting: Streetlight Graphics
Cover Photo: Martin Jelinek
Additional Models: Rebecca Ann Hoos riding Crimson Cross
            Danielle Durette Tursky riding Inki

THE JERUSALEM DONKEY LEGEND

BOOK ONE OF THE ACHSAH LEGACY

ANNE CHURCHILL

AUTHOR'S NOTE

Biblical scriptures "Resource Notes" located at the end of the book.

Find out more at my website:
www.thejerusalemdonkeylegend.com

This book is dedicated to those who struggle to find their way.

PROLOGUE

———·•·———

FRANCE
1943

PURE, WHITE SNOWFLAKES FELL SOFTLY on the windshield and dissolved instantly. The man eyed the unmarked, tall ornamental iron gates and looked again at the piece of paper in his hand. The directions, hastily written, had been easy to follow. He was certain he was at the correct driveway. Opening the car door, he stepped out and walked to the gates, the crunching sound of his boot heels on gravel loud in the quiet November night. He pushed open the heavy gates and returned to his car. He put his foot on the gas and switched on the Renault's windshield wipers.

The tree-lined gravel drive gently sloped upward and after half a mile, the Chateau de Vignon came into view, its massive Baroque structure imposing in the dark night. The Chateau, just outside of Grenoble, France, sat atop a hill in the foothills of the Alps. No lights burned; the house was silent. He parked the car and turned off the

1

engine. Using the rearview mirror, he adjusted his Basque beret, then opened the car door and stepped out.

The man walked up the wet, worn stone steps and rang the bell. He rubbed his hands together in front of his mouth and blew, his hot breath warming his cold fingers. Hearing no footsteps, he rang the bell again and waited. Several seconds passed and then he heard a woman's gruff voice, heavy with irritation.

"What do you want?"

"I saw a Bohemian Waxwing today," said the man.

There was a click and the wide oak door creaked slowly open, revealing an old woman with short, curly white hair wearing a faded, slightly tattered blue robe. In her left hand, she clutched a rolled glass oil hurricane lamp.

"Yes?" she asked sternly, eyeing him suspiciously.

"Are you Edmae Chavel?" asked the man, reaching into his coat pocket. He withdrew a piece of folded white paper, lightly stained with blood.

"I am Edmae Chavel," answered the old woman, her cold calculating eyes darting to the piece of paper in his hand, and back to his face.

"I was instructed to give this to you," said the man, handing it to her.

Edmae took the piece of paper from him.

"Come in," she instructed, stepping aside for him to pass.

The man stepped over the threshold into the gloomy darkness of the hall, the only light was from the flame dancing in the hurricane lamp. Two big, black dogs sat alertly on the tile floor behind Edmae.

"Which one of my granddaughters is this from?" Edmae asked coolly.

"Gabrielle," answered the man, his voice soft. "There was an unfortunate incident tonight—she was wounded."

"*Where is she?*" demanded Edmae.

The man shook his head. "I don't know where they've

taken her, but she's safe and her wound isn't fatal. She will be fine."

"Isaac, please show our guest to the kitchen," ordered Edmae. "Then meet me in the library."

A tall, well-built young man, with long, unruly black hair that framed his narrow, oval face stepped from the shadows.

"Follow me," he said, his voice deep, his accent American, striding past the man down the hall.

Edmae unfolded the note and stared down at Gabrielle's familiar handwriting.

Nana,

I'm okay. Gestapo raided the meeting tonight at Vitor Lessard's. I escaped but Angelina's been captured. She had one of the Achsah codices with her.

Gestapo now has it!

Gabbie

Edmae fumed silently at her twenty-one-year-old granddaughter, Angelina, for disobeying her orders in removing one of the Achsah codices from the vault. She crumbled the note, shoving it into the pocket of her robe and she crossed the hall.

"Crosby, Pelham—come," she called, pushing the library door open. The two Bouvier des Flanders trotted in after her, their nails clicking on the bare floor. She walked towards an elegant Louis XV writing desk positioned at one end of the walnut paneled room and collapsed down into a plush upholstered arm chair in front of the desk. Other than the desk, two chairs, a sofa and a small table, the room was sparsely furnished, the walnut parquet floor naked of rugs. The fire burning in the massive fireplace threw dancing shadows across thousands of books, helping to warm the large, nearly empty room.

Edmae closed her eyes and thought about her oldest daughter, Monique, and her husband, Phillip Bonet, wondering if they were still alive. There had been no news or communication from Paris in over a year. When the Germans invaded France in May of 1940, Monique had sent her six daughters, Angelina, Gabrielle, Zara, Caroline, Chloe and Lydia to Grenoble to live with her.

Crosby and Pelham, lying in front of the fireplace, lifted their heads.

"Ruth has prepared food for the gentleman," said Isaac, coming to a stand beside her chair. Ruth Brossier was the housekeeper.

Edmae opened her eyes and stood up. Reaching out, she picked up the two oil lamps sitting on the Louis XV writing desk, handing one to Isaac.

"Follow me," she ordered.

Isaac nodded and followed her across the room to a corner. Edmae bent over, and thrust the fingers of her right hand between two books on the lowest shelf. They heard a sharp metallic sound. She straightened and reaching up to a higher shelf, she removed a leather bound black book, clasped it to her chest and stepped back. Indicating with a nod of her head, she told Isaac, "Reach here and pull."

Isaac did as she instructed and the book shelf swung open on its hinges, revealing a passage. Edmae stepped through the secret door and Isaac followed her down the narrow, circular stone staircase to a cavernous hall with a low ceiling and stone walls. Branching off in multiple directions were several long corridors. Holding her hurricane lamp before her, lighting her way, Edmae turned right and they walked down a long corridor until they reached a cedar door with three iron locks. Edmae stopped in front of the door and passed her glass hurricane lamp to Isaac. She opened the book and removed three large iron keys from its hollowed interior. She inserted them into the locks and turned to look at Isaac.

"All three keys must be turned at the same time," she instructed.

Isaac put both lamps on the stone floor and stepped closer to the door, his left hand closing around the top key, his right hand closing around the middle key.

"At the count of three," instructed Edmae. "One . . . two . . . three—*turn*."

They heard what sounded like the clanging of gears and three dull clinks. Edmae pushed and the heavy door swung open. They picked up the oil lamps and stepped over the threshold into a massive stone room, the floors covered in Persian rugs. Floor to ceiling cedar cabinets lined one wall and on the other wall hung dozens of oil paintings in heavy gilded gold frames. Lined across a gilded pine table were dozens of candlesticks made of bronze, copper, silver and gold in varying shapes and sizes. A carved antique sideboard displayed a collection of sculptures in bronze, copper and marble. A walnut framed settee upholstered in glazed wool and embroidered in gold silk sat facing a pair of gilded walnut Chippendale chairs upholstered in scarlet damask.

"This past year, I noticed items disappearing from the house. I assumed you'd been selling things," said Isaac eyeing Edmae.

Edmae smiled wryly. "When this chateau was built by my ancestor in 1624, it was designed as a fortress for hiding treasures. This room is one of many secret vaults." She shuffled forward.

Isaac followed Edmae to the far end of the room. They stopped in front of the first cabinet.

"Hold this," said Edmae, handing Isaac the glass hurricane lamp again.

Edmae removed a long gold chain from around her neck. Dangling on its end was a bronze cross. She inserted the long end of the cross into the cabinet lock, turning her wrist counter clockwise, pulling open the tall doors. The shelves of the cedar cabinet were full of what looked like old books.

"What are these?" asked Isaac.

"They're ancient hand-written manuscripts called codices," replied Edmae. Looking at the top shelf, she gasped, the blood draining from her already pale face.

"*Oh dear God,*" she cried, her voice full of fury. "Angelina took the most important codex!" She closed the cabinet doors, removed the cross key, and returned the necklace to her neck. Jerking the oil lamp from Isaac's hand, she turned on her heel and hurriedly headed for the door.

"I'm sending you to Lyon tonight," she announced sharply over her shoulder. "Zara needs to know Gestapo has the *Arimathea Codex*!"

THE CITY OF LYON, France was founded as a Roman colony in 43 B.C. The Roman General Marcus Vipsanius Agrippa, father-in-law of the Roman Emperor Tiberius, recognized its strategic importance and made the city the starting point for Roman roads throughout the region. In 1943, the city was a major rail center and industrial zone, giving it key significance to the German war machine.

After driving two and a half hours on dark, winter roads, Isaac found himself standing outside the building Zara Bonet had been living in for the past seven months. He looked right, then left, and he quickly headed for the building's front door. He passed through the door, and climbed two flights of stairs, walking to the second door from the top of the landing. He rapped once, waited a second, then knocked four times consecutively and said in a low voice, "Homakbi." It meant purple, Zara's favorite color, in Choctaw.

The door opened.

"Isaac Leitner," said Zara, smiling warmly. Unlike her two older sisters who were tall, voluptuous, dark and sultry looking, Zara was petite with naturally curly blonde hair and bright blue eyes. Like Angelina and Gabrielle, Zara was in the Resistance. She worked at Ecole de Sante Militaire, Gestapo headquarters, as a secretary, passing vital information to the Resistance and the Maquis. She stepped aside, opening the door wide.

"What brings you to my doorstep on this cold Sunday night?"

"Your grandmother sent me," said Isaac, walking past her into the small, eclectically decorated living room.

Zara closed the door behind him.

"You've grown—a lot," she said appraisingly, looking him up and down. Isaac, now sixteen, no longer looked like the frightened boy who had arrived at the Chateau fifteen months earlier. He was tall, his shoulders broad. His face had lost its boyish roundness, and was more angular, his cheek-bones prominent, his jaw squared.

"There's been an incident," Isaac said, withdrawing an envelope from inside his leather jacket. He handed it to her.

Zara took the envelope from him and walked slowly over to a long, muslin upholstered eighteenth-century French provincial sofa. Sitting down on the comfy down cushions, she tucked her bare legs underneath her and pried open the envelope.

Isaac settled himself down onto a crushed velvet club chair and watched her. She was wearing a floor-length black chiffon robe over a short, pink silk chemise with black lace trim that hit her at mid-thigh. Her shoulder-length hair was parted on the side, soft curls framing her oval face. She twirled a lock of hair around her finger as she read. Finished, she pushed her hair back and uncurled her legs. Leaning forward, she held the note over a burning candle sitting on the coffee table. The flame ignited the paper and she dropped the burning note into a bowl, watching it burn.

"What is so important about this Arimathea Codex?" Isaac asked.

Zara met his gaze. "I can't tell you."

"You can't or you won't tell me?"

"Both," replied Zara honestly.

"Damn it, Zara, I've a right to know!" growled Isaac, his dark eyes blazing with rage. "Your grandmother is holding my brothers hostage and she threatened to turn them over to the SS if I didn't return with that codex."

Zara shook her head vigorously, her blonde curls swaying. "Nana wouldn't turn Aaron and David over to the SS, Isaac," she said assuredly, her voice firm. Isaac and his two younger brothers, Aaron and David, were Jewish Americans. Their father, a professor at Berkeley University in California, and childhood friend of her father, had accepted a teaching position at the University of Paris and had moved his family to France in early 1940. After the disappearance of their parents in 1942, her mother, Monique Bonet, had arranged for the three Leitner boys to be smuggled out of an internment camp in Paris to the Chateau de Vignon.

"It's late and I have to be up in a couple of hours," announced Zara, standing up. "We'll talk further tomorrow." She disappeared into her bedroom, reappearing a minute later carrying a pillow and wool blanket. She laid them on the sofa and turned to Isaac.

"Promise me that you won't leave this apartment while I'm at work," she said in a soft voice.

Isaac glared at her and said nothing.

"Give me your word, Isaac," implored Zara.

Isaac nodded and muttered in Choctaw, "Okeh."

ANGELINA BONET, HER HANDS HANDCUFFED behind her, shifted on the hard wooden chair trying to find a measure of comfort. She was cold and frightened. Her shoulders, back and arms ached. Her right foot kept cramping. She was in a small windowless room with smooth concrete curved walls in the bowels of Montluc prison, the same prison Jean Moulin, the backbone of the French Resistance, had been housed until he was tortured to death six months ago. The only light in the room came from a bare overhead bulb in the ceiling. At the end of the room, attached to the ceiling of the chamber, was a cable and pulley system. On the opposite wall were several large metal rings from which chains of varying lengths hung.

Angelina heard the door open. Looking over her right shoulder, she saw two tall German officers dressed in grey-green uniforms with the distinctive SS insignia on their collars. Fear slithered like a snake through her insides, filling the pit of her stomach with dread. She knew the way to conquer fear and she began reciting the words silently.

The Lord is my shepherd; I shall not want. He makes me to lie down in green pastures; he leads me beside still waters. He restores my soul; he leads me in the paths of righteousness for His name's sake. Yeah, though I walk through the valley of the shadow of death, I will fear no evil; for You are with me; Your rod and Your staff, they comfort me.

The two officers walked around the dark wood table and sat down in front of Angelina. The taller of the two, powerfully built with pale blonde hair, was clearly in charge.

"My name is Fritz Keppler," he said in French. "This is Josef Eichmann," indicating the brown-haired man next to him.

Josef Eichmann opened a brown folder, laid it on the table, and with his long, manicured fingers slowly pushed the file across the table.

Fritz's blue eyes scanned the folder. His gaze shifted to Angelina.

"You are twenty-one—is this correct?"

Angelina nodded. "Yes."

"You have five younger sisters, Gabrielle, age nineteen; Zara, age eighteen; Caroline and Chloe, twins, age thirteen; and Lydia, age eleven. Correct?"

"Yes."

"You are a student at the University in Grenoble?" Fritz asked.

"Yes."

"Are you involved with the Resistance?" asked Fritz, his voice stiffened.

"*No*," replied Angelina, trying to keep her voice even. "As I told the other officer who questioned me—I didn't know any of those people at Vitor's!"

Fritz eyed her skeptically. "You don't know who your boyfriend's friends are?"

"Vitor and I haven't dated that long."

"You're lying," Fritz said coolly. "I don't like being lied to."

Angelina swallowed. Her legs were trembling underneath her dress, her heart racing at an explosive rate.

"I'm telling you the truth," she said coolly, glaring at him.

Fritz stood up abruptly, walked around the table, and stood facing her, his eyes assessing her with interest. "Your boyfriend told us differently."

"I don't know what you're talking about," Angelina said angrily.

Fritz backhanded her, the blow jolting her sideways in the chair. "You're lying."

"I'm not," implored Angelina, tears filled her eyes.

"Tell me the truth—what is your involvement with the Resistance," demanded Fritz.

Angelina shook her head adamantly. "I'm not involved!"

Fritz hit her again, harder. "You're lying?"

"I'm not lying," Angelina retorted, meeting his icy stare, hot, angry tears sliding slowly down her face.

Fritz folded his arms across his chest. He turned his head to the younger officer. "Josef . . . earlier . . . how long was she questioned?"

Josef's gaze shifted to the folder, then up to Fritz's face.

"For over five hours," he answered in a honey-tongued voice.

Fritz eyed her, his blue eyes cold. An icy smile spread across his handsome features. "I tire of your unwillingness to answer our questions honestly."

"I'm telling you the truth!" cried Angelina.

Fritz jumped forward suddenly, his right hand around her neck, his face inches from hers.

"I know you're lying," he growled, his tone menacing.

"I'm not," croaked Angelina. "I swear it!"

"We shall see," snapped Fritz, his grip tightening around her throat.

"*I swear*," gasped Angelina.

Fritz jerked her up out of the chair, dragging her around the table, pulling her to the end of the room. He undid her handcuffs, tossing them to the concrete floor and he put her wrists into medieval-looking iron shackles lined with tiny spikes. Using the cylinder screw key, he tightened them around her wrist until the spikes cut into her flesh.

"How long have you been involved with the Resistance?" he asked, pulling on the cable, lifting her arms over her head.

"I've nothing to do with the Resistance!" Angelina stuttered.

Fritz pulled on the cable again, lifting her body three feet off the ground.

Angelina shrieked in pain. A gripping, intense pain engulfed her as the spiked, jagged cuffs bit through her flesh and blood dribbled down her forearm.

"Are you ready to confess?"

Angelina could hardly breathe. "I've . . . nothing . . . to confess . . . to," she stammered through tears.

Fritz punched her in the stomach.

Angelina cried out in pain. Her cries echoed off the walls, ringing loudly in her ears.

"Do you know why the walls of this room are curved," said Fritz with a satisfied smile. It was not a question. "So your screams are reflected back." He punched her again.

Angelina gulped air, her face contorted in sheer agony.

"Tell me the name of your network and the name of the wireless operator?" demanded Fritz.

"I don't know . . . what . . . you're . . . talking about," panted Angelina. Blood streamed down her arms, soaking her blue dress in bright red liquid. She struggled to breathe through the throbbing, excruciating pain blazing through her body and mind.

"I don't want to hurt you, Angelina, but I must have answers," said Fritz. "I want to hear you admit the truth. If you do, the pain will stop."

"*I don't . . . know . . . anything . . . I swear,*" groaned Angelina in anguish, her breath coming in gasps, her voice barely audible.

Fritz stared at her, his blue eyes slid admiringly from her face down her curvaceous body, and back up to her face. He turned, walked over to Josef Eichmann and putting his hand on the younger man's shoulder said, his tone commanding, "It's late, Josef. Go home."

Josef pushed back his chair, jumping abruptly to his feet. He clipped his heels together, saluting Fritz with the Nazi arm extension and he marched quickly out of the room, pulling the solid door closed behind him.

"You're beautiful," Fritz said, his voice low. "It would be a shame to damage such beauty." He slowly unbuttoned his uniform tunic. Shrugging out of it, he hung it with care on the back of the wooden chair. His crisp white undershirt hugged his broad, muscular chest, shoulders and well-defined arms.

"It doesn't have to be like this, Angelina. Just answer my questions honestly," he said, walking over to where she hung, her feet dangling in mid-air beneath her, and he stared up at her.

"Tell me . . . where . . . I can find . . . the wireless operator?"

"*I don't know!*" whimpered Angelina. She felt her mind surrendering to the sickening, overpowering pain.

"Vitor's not strong like you. He was *persuaded* to tell me many things." Fritz released the cable. Angelina dropped to the ground, her knees buckled and she slumped limply onto the cold, abrasive floor, her back against the concrete wall. He stood over her, staring down at her with a salacious smile on his face.

"Vitor told me that you're highly knowledgeable about explosives. That you have an exceptional talent for shooting, riding horses and cutting communication lines," he said, a hint of respect in his voice. He knelt down and brushed her tears from her cheeks with his fingers.

"He also said that you're multi-lingual, you speak English fluently and that it is *you* who arranges the safe houses for the British spies in the region."

"Vitor's made me into something I'm not," quipped Angelina, trying to sound ambivalent, her mind frantically raced over everything Vitor Lessard knew about her and her sisters, especially her younger sister, Zara. Zara, using forged documents and the name Madeline Stein, was working at Gestapo headquarters. Vitor, like everyone else in Grenoble, thought Zara was away at boarding school in Switzerland.

Fear and panic gripped her—had Vitor seen Zara at Gestapo headquarters? She met his gaze with steeled determination. Her lips, pouting with indignant innocence, curled into a weak smile.

"I do know how to ride and shoot, but I don't know anything about explosives—*I swear.*"

"You're a good liar, Angelina. I want you to work for me," said Fritz, in a soft voice. "If you do this, I'll see to it that your grandmother and younger sisters aren't shipped off to a Labor camp. And your parents, who are at Auschwitz and still alive—I'll arrange for them to be moved. I'll take care of *you* and your family." He ran his fingers through her long hair.

Angelina studied him warily. He was handsome but his eyes were devoid of light and chillingly cold, as if his soul was full of darkness and unimaginable cruelty.

"I'm just a—"

"You're part of a partisan network engaging in terrorist activities against Germany," snapped Fritz. "I could have you shot!" He cupped her chin, staring intently into her eyes.

"You have courage. You're spirited and I'm intrigued. I find you enticing," he murmured, lust radiating in his eyes. "I want—"

"I'll *never* turn against France or *help* Germany," Angelina said with conviction, glaring at him, her brown eyes blazing.

Fritz reached out for the cable, pulling it until her arms were lifted over her head, leaving her sitting on the floor with her arms stretched up, her back arched. He tied and secured the cable.

Angelina moaned, the pain from her lacerated, cuffed

wrists excruciating.

"I always get what I want, Angelina," he growled, his voice low and menacing. Grabbing a handful of her silky dark hair in his right hand, he yanked her head back.

Angelina grimaced, her face twisted in pain. She shut her eyes tightly, her pink lips pressed in a thin line to keep from crying out. Feeling and hearing the ripping of fabric, her eyes flew open.

Fritz was using his dagger, slicing through her dress. He released her hair and using both his hands, tore off her dress, exposing her soft mounding breasts. His eyes were bright with triumph. He ran his hands up the inside of her thighs, his eyes roving over her long, shapely legs and curvaceous body.

"Your skin is flawless and so soft," he breathed, his fingers tracing the outline of her silk underwear.

Angelina tried kicking him.

Fritz smacked her across the face hard. "Stay still or I'll hit you again."

He stood up and stared down on her, smiling sadistically. "You're exquisite," he said, unbuckling his belt.

DARK, HEAVY CLOUDS obscured the full moon, making the raw November night gloomier. Zara drew the heavy damask curtains and joined Isaac on the French provincial sofa.

"What did you learn about Angelina when you were at work today?" Isaac asked, staring unseeingly into the fire.

"She's in Montluc Prison. She's still alive," said Zara, her voice quiet. "That's all I was able to find out."

Isaac looked at her, his expression solemn. "Maybe you'll learn more tomorrow."

"I can't even imagine the hell she's going through in

that place," whispered Zara sadly.

They sat quietly, watching the dancing flames. After a long silence, Isaac asked, "You're sure the codex is in Josef Eichmann's office?"

Zara nodded. "I saw it in there this afternoon."

"Why didn't you take it?"

"There were too many people around. I would have been seen." Zara, her blonde hair pinned into large tunnel curls on the side of her head, reached up and started removing the pins, laying them in a pile on the round, chrome coffee table. She ran her fingers through her curly hair, shaking it out.

Isaac glanced over. "I'd like to help."

"I don't want you involved—it's too risky."

"Don't treat me like a child, Zara," Isaac said in a firm voice. "After you left, I joined the Resistance. I—"

"Why weren't you at the meeting on Sunday at Vitor's?"

"My brothers were sick," said Isaac. "I stayed home to care for them."

Zara stared at the fire deep in thought. After a long pause, she turned to Isaac and said, "Imprudent don't you think—scheduling a meeting at a place with no back door and no planned escape route?"

"Yes," agreed Isaac. "I'm surprised three people were able to get away."

"I learned today that Gestapo knew about the meeting the day before."

"That would mean our network's been infiltrated," said Isaac in dismay.

Zara nodded. "In all likelihood, someone's a traitor."

After an extended silence, Isaac asked, "How long do you think it will take you to steal the codex?"

"Maybe fifteen minutes," said Zara. "Some kind of distraction would be ideal."

"That—I can help you with," said Isaac confidently, meeting her gaze.

Zara frowned.

"What do you have in mind, Isaac Leitner?" she asked with skepticism.

"Let's just say its Indian ingenuity," replied Isaac, grinning sideways. His parents had met during their junior year at the University of Mississippi. His mother, a full-blooded Choctaw Indian, converted to Judaism on her marriage to his father. Growing up, Isaac had spent summers with his maternal grandfather, absorbing and learning the traditions and ways of the Choctaw.

"Truth is, I could use your help," Zara said frankly. "It's imperative that I get that codex back."

"I saw lots of codices in that cedar cabinet. What's so important about the Arimathea Codex?" demanded Isaac.

"My ancestor, who wrote that codex, was married to Joseph of Arimathea," said Zara, meeting his gaze, her blue eyes intense.

Isaac shrugged. "Who was Joseph of Arimathea?"

"You need to read the Bible, Isaac," replied Zara. "He was a disciple of Jesus. Joseph of Arimathea was granted permission by Pilate to take Jesus' body away. He helped prepare Jesus' body for burial."

Isaac stared disbelievingly at Zara, his brown eyes wide in astonishment.

Zara nodded. "*That* codex—it's *his wife's* diary!"

ANGELINA WAS DISORIENTATED, her mind grasping, clutching at fragments of wakefulness. She opened her eyes and she saw she was in her cell, lying on a thin, dirty straw mattress. The small room was filled with the muted light of approaching sunset. She wondered what day it was. Her mouth was bone dry. She licked her swollen cracked lips, the taste of blood in her mouth. Dried blood stains dotted her grubby, tattered prison uniform. Her body was bruised and broken from being beaten, the pain excruciating and intense each time she moved. She knew the night would bring a fresh round of interrogations. The fact that she hadn't been questioned about the Arimathea Codex meant the Nazis didn't yet know what they had in their possession. The thought brought her a small measure of comfort—but it was fleeting. The sobering reality was the Nazis would eventually decipher the two languages used in the codex. It was only a matter of time. Her recklessness had put her sisters and her grandmother in jeopardy and once the Nazis read the codex, no one in the family would ever be safe.

"I broke the Achsah family code," she whispered to the walls. *"Forgive me, Lord Jesus."*

With great effort, she pulled her knees up to her chest, wrapping her arms around her legs, and she cried softly. She heard the rattling of keys. Panic clawed at her thoughts. *"I am blessed and highly favored, regardless of my circumstances,"* she prayed in a faint, terrified voice. *"God's favor blesses me with courage and strength of will. On God I lean, rely and confidently put my trust. I will not fear. I will not be afraid. What can man, who is flesh, do to me?"*

She heard the metallic click of the bolt and the door opened. She clenched her eyes shut, pretending to be asleep. She felt rough hands grab her arms, yanking her to her feet. Her legs and feet were undamaged but standing upright took more strength than she had.

The two prison workers dragged Angelina down several flights of stairs to the cellar, into a small, windowless room with smooth, concrete rounded walls. Angelina glanced around the room. Unlike the other room she'd been in, this chamber was filled with torture devices. Meat hooks on chains hung from the ceiling. A wood bench with thick, wide leather straps stood against one wall. Next to it was an iron claw bathtub filled with water. Heavy iron forceps, whips, clubs of varying sizes, and a spiked ball attached to a chain, all tools of heinous torture, were lined up neatly on a small wooden table. Next to the table were three chairs, two men sat upright in two of the chairs, the third was empty. She recognized one of the men. It was Josef Eichmann, his SS uniform perfectly pressed, his black military boots shining.

"Join us," said the second man with a round face, dark hair and pale, hooded eyes. He didn't look like the typical tall SS officer. He was dressed in plain clothes and he sat with his legs crossed at the knees. In his lap, purring contently was a short-hair white cat with large yellow-green eyes.

The prison workers pushed her down into the empty chair and quickly left the room.

"My name is Klaus Barbie," said the man, calmly stroking the cat.

Angelina felt a new wave a terror spread through her, chilling her like a polar wind, turning her blood to ice. She'd heard of Klaus Barbie, head of Gestapo. He was a butcher, known for his brutality. He was the man responsible for the torture and death of French Resistance leader, Jean Moulin.

"You're the minx who bit off Fritz's appendage," said Klaus, his thin lips smiling in disdain. He had the eyes of a monster. He nodded at Josef Eichmann.

Eichmann rose to his feet and in one step, stood in front of her. Glaring down at her, brandishing a mallet in his right hand, he swung. The corner of the mallet connected with her forehead with a loud thud.

Angelina cried out in pain as she fell sideways out of her chair and crashed to the floor. From the gash on her forehead, a stream of bright crimson blood trickled down between her dark brows and eyes. dripping off the end of her nose.

Gripping her hair at the top of her head, Eichmann yanked her head up off the concrete floor. "The Fuhrer puts great emphasis on those who are racially pure and in perfect physical condition," he snarled, swinging the mallet again, hitting her in the jaw, breaking several teeth. "Fritz had just been accepted into the Lebensborn program—because of you, he's unable to participate."

Blood gushed from her mouth. Angelina wiped the back of her hand across her mouth, spitting out her teeth. She'd heard of the Lebensborn Project, a breeding program to promote Nazi eugenics, and implement by Heinrich Himmler, the SS leader.

"That's one less German prick," she hissed defiantly, glaring triumphantly up at Josef Eichmann through her swollen eyes.

Josef kicked her hard in the ribs, a crushing blow. Angelina yelped, gulping air, trying to breathe as indescribable pain vibrated through her chest. He stomped down on her right hand, and she heard the sickening crunch of her bones snapping beneath his heavy boot heel.

Angelina screamed, clutching her crushed, throbbing hand to her chest, tears poured from her eyes.

"I want the name of your group leader," said Klaus Barbie sternly, stroking the purring cat. "And I want the names of all the British couriers and where I can find the British wireless operator."

Angelina lay crumbled on the cold floor moaning in agony.

"Their names!" demanded Klaus. "*Their names*," he repeated in a menacing tone, pointing to the wooden bench.

Josef dragged her to the wooden bench, and strapped her on her stomach, her arms pinned at her side, her head turned so Klaus could see her face. Josef ripped open her uniform, exposing her bare back.

Angelina felt the sting of the whip across her back. She screamed, tears spilling from her eyes. Klaus smiled in evident enjoyment, her screams music to his ears. His demonic eyes danced with satisfaction. He licked his lower lip and motioned for Eichmann to lash her again.

Angelina closed her eyes, bracing herself for the next blow.

"Open your eyes or I'll have Josef hit you with the spiked ball," ordered Klaus.

Angelina quickly opened her eyes and stared into the face of true evil so singularly personified in Klaus Barbie. The whip cracked, slashing across her back, ripping her flesh. She cried out, her face twisting in anguish, the pain shooting through her brain and body.

Klaus's thin lips curved into a cold smile, his hooded eyes glimmering with delight.

The whip snapped across her back again. Angelina choked back sobs, trying to breathe through the searing pain, wet tears sliding down her cheeks.

"Josef's older brother, Adolf Eichmann, is interested in seeing the hand-written book you had with you," said Klaus, his voice calm and even. "We've learned it's very old and the pages are folded sheets of goatskin stitched together with leather."

Josef Eichmann returned to the chair sitting next to Klaus, facing her. He withdrew a pack of cigarettes, offering one to Klaus.

"Are there other books like it?" Klaus lit the cigarette, put it to his thin lips and inhaled.

"No," Angelina lied.

"My brother is convinced that the Fuhrer will want to see this ancient book. What language is it written in?" said Josef, his gray eyes scrutinizing her.

"I don't know," Angelina said firmly.

"What is this book about?" asked Josef.

"I don't know," spat Angelina.

"Your boyfriend told me you did know," insisted Josef.

"Under torture, Vitor would say anything," retorted

21

Angelina, her eyes meeting his cold stare.

Josef leaned forward, extending his arm, holding the burning cigarette to her cheek, the red-hot end seared into her skin.

Angelina shrieked in agony.

"In the end, everyone talks," Josef said with confidence. He smiled proudly. Angelina felt fear filling her heart and mind. Knowing she needed sustaining courage, she forced her mind to focus, and she began reciting silently.

The Lord is my light and my salvation; whom shall I fear? The Lord is the strength of my life; of whom shall I be afraid?

"*Answer my questions!*" Josef demanded.

Angelina met his gaze. Josef Eichmann was young, handsome and capable of savage brutality. She was confident Zara would find a way of getting the Arimathea Codex back. A plan was slowly forming in her mind on how she could buy her sister more time. She glared at him, her brown eyes blazing defiantly and boldly shouted,

"*I can do all things through Christ who strengthens me.*"

She started to laugh. Josef's face twisted in rage, his eyes seething with fury. Jumping to his feet, he grabbed her by the hair, yanked her head back off the bench, and he slammed his clenched fist into her face.

CHAPTER 1

UNITED STATES
2011

THE MARCH DAY HAD DAWNED gloomy with thick, heavy, dark clouds obscuring the sky and a cold biting wind that stung bare skin like needles. Darkness was descending by the time Paige Winston drove up the long driveway to her home, a large white T-shaped farmhouse. A hybrid of both old and new, the farmhouse stood in the northeast corner of the 700-acre farm that her brother-in-law owned. Having spent hours out in the elements repairing fences around the farm, she was looking forward to a long soak in a hot, steamy bath. Within seconds of opening the back door, she heard click—clack, click—clack, click—clack—Duke and Roscoe were coming to greet her.

"Hi guys," Paige said softly to the two canines. She removed her worn Australian Oilskin leather jacket and collapsed down onto a hard bench in the hallway.

Duke, a mixed breed rescue dog with the black and white markings of Border collie, howled happily, his black swifter-like tail moving rapidly, wagging his large Béarnaise Mountain dog body. Roscoe, a Rottweiler and also a rescue, hopped in excitement, his nub tail wiggled excitedly.

Paige gently stroked the two faces nudging her. "What have you done all day?" she asked softly.

In answer, Duke howled again. Izzie, a fluffy, black and white cat trotted over, jumped up on the bench beside Paige, and started meowing in her kitten voice.

Paige reached down and pulled off a Muck boot. She was struggling with the second one when she heard the ringing of her cell phone. She thought about letting it go to voice mail. She had the cats and dogs to feed, emails to read, bills to pay and dinner to prepare. Begrudgingly, she reached for her phone.

"Hello?"

"Hi," said Nancy LaPlace, one of her closest friends. "What are you doing?"

"Just walked in the door," replied Paige, dropping her mud splattered boot down beside its companion.

"Why?"

"I was thinking about you," admitted Nancy, her husky voice warm and friendly. "I know how melancholy you get this time every year. Do you have any plans tomorrow?"

Paige leaned back against the wall, tilted her head back, and stared at the ceiling. She took a long, deep breath.

"None," she said, and after a short pause, asked hesitantly, "What do you have in mind?"

"The Bureau of Land Management is sponsoring a Wild Mustang, Wild Burro adoption this Saturday in Martin. There's a preview tomorrow night—let's go!"

"I saw the commercial this morning on WBBJ," said Paige, rising slowly to her feet, she ambled into the large, bright open room that served as kitchen and family room.

A decade earlier, the walls of several small rooms and a kitchen had been removed, creating one massive room. It was decorated in warm colors and a pleasing décor of contemporary and classic furnishings, giving the huge room an inviting, cozy feeling.

"I don't know," Paige grumbled in a sharp tone. She had no interest in wild mustangs or wild burros.

"Let's go," urged Nancy.

Paige sighed wearily.

"Come on—you might have fun," Nancy teased affectionately.

"Oh—*alright.*"

Nancy laughed softly. "I'll pick you up tomorrow around four. By the way—I've got *something* to show you."

"Okay. See you then." Paige hit the end call button and laid the phone down, walked to the refrigerator and swung the door open. She stared at its contents wondering what to fix for dinner. She didn't enjoy cooking and preferred fast and easy solutions to meals.

Roscoe and Duke bounded towards the back door barking excitedly. She heard the squeaking of the door opening. "Hi Mom! We're home," her daughter Jaden yelled.

"Hi, Sweetheart," said Paige loudly. Her soon-to-be seventeen-year-old daughter had blossomed into a pretty young woman. Only a couple of years ago Jaden had been scrawny arms and legs, wearing braided pigtails with braces on her teeth. Now she was tall, her legs lean and strong from years of playing soccer and hours spent in the saddle riding horses. The planes of her oval face were sharper, the childlike plumpness gone.

"How was Hippo therapy?" asked Paige, glancing around.

Jaden, dressed in blue jeans and black T-shirt, her golden-blonde hair falling long and wavy down her back, walked into the room followed by her best friend, Hannah Butler.

"Stevie came tonight. She's ten and totally horse crazy" she said, her green eyes sparkling. Jaden and Hannah served as volunteers at the Rein-Bow Riding Academy, a program where children with varying disabilities received therapy while riding a horse.

Paige smiled.

"That's the same age you and Hannah were when you met," she said, removing two large frozen pizzas from the freezer.

"I remember that day," mused Hannah in her posh British accent. Born in Israel, Hannah had lived in the wealthy neighborhood of Knightsbridge, London from age three until age ten. After her mother was killed in a car accident, her father, Arthur Butler, sent her to live with his parents in his home town of Jackson, Tennessee.

"I'd just arrived from England and was in the front yard playing when you rode by on your pony," she said, smiling fondly at Jaden. Her grandparents, Sheila and William Butler, lived down the street from the Winstons.

"I remember that day!" Jaden snickered lightheartedly. "My pony ditched me for *your* carrot!"

Hannah's full, pink lips parted and she laughed. Taller than Jaden, she had the lean, lithe body of a dancer. Her oval face was framed by long, mahogany-colored hair that fell to her waist. She sank gracefully down onto a stool at the kitchen island beside Jaden.

"When's dinner?" asked Jacob Winston, strolling into the room, his dirty blonde hair, flecked with gold and brown, was messy. His dark pants were speckled with dry particles of grain and dirt. His work shirt was untucked, the sleeves rolled up to his elbows revealing muscular forearms.

"Shortly," said Paige looking at her son. "How was work?"

"Busy for a Thursday," said Jacob, pulling off his boots. During the school year, Jacob worked at Martin Feeds two nights a week. Glancing at his mother, he asked, "Aren't you meeting Uncle Matt tomorrow?"

Paige shook her head. "No, he called today and we rescheduled for Monday." Matthew Winston, her deceased husband's older brother, employed her as his personal assistant. "Why?"

"Is he going to be here for our birthday?"

"He hasn't said." Paige looked at her twin teenagers. "Regarding your birthday gift, are you both fine with what we discussed?"

"Are you kidding?" cried Jaden in earnest, her eyes wide and bright. "What could be better than a trip to Lexington for the Kentucky Rolex Three Day!"

Jacob nodded, and he turned his attention to the two dogs dancing impatiently before him.

"Before I forget," said Paige. "I'm going with Nancy tomorrow to a BLM sponsored adoption."

"Are we adopting a Mustang?" asked Jaden, her tone hopeful.

Paige scowled at her daughter and said in exasperation, "Don't you think we have enough animals?"

"But we don't have a Mustang," argued Jaden.

"If Nancy adopts one, you can help her with hers," retorted Paige.

Jaden opened her mouth to say something and then changed her mind.

Paige threw a sideways glance at Jaden and asked, "What are you and Hannah doing tomorrow night?"

"We're going to see the new Twilight movie," Jaden said.

"Jacob, what about you?" asked Paige, turning to look at her nearly seventeen-year-old son who looked more man then boy, busy wrestling with the dogs.

"He's going with us," interjected Hannah, glancing around at Jacob, a friendly smile on her lips.

"Am I missing something?" Paige asked in surprise.

"Bethany Shevar is going with us," Jaden said in an

amused voice.

"Got it," Paige nodded in understanding. The popular cheerleader had developed a crush on Jacob and had asked Hannah to play matchmaker on her behalf.

After dinner, Paige excused herself and walked down the hall to her bedroom, located in the front part of the 100-year-old farmhouse. The beige-colored walls gave the room a cozy feeling. She felt drained from the long day. Pulling off her gray hooded Naval Academy sweatshirt, she dropped it on an oversized chair, walked into the bathroom and turned on the water. She felt a bump against her leg and looking down saw a calico cat named Gizmo.

"You're an odd cat," said Paige bending down and scratching under the cat's chin. Gizmo, another rescue, was not physically pretty. Her body was oversized and bulky, her head small in comparison. Her short legs bowed inward and her tail was thin and too long. Her calico coat, with its array of chocolate, black and fawn colors, reminded Paige of the finger painting artwork the twins used to bring home when they were in the first grade.

Gizmo meowed multiple times in answer.

Paige twisted her long auburn hair into a pony tail and using a banana clip, secured it on top of her head. In her early forties, she kept her five-eight frame in shape by running and light weight lifting. She turned off the water, removed the rest of her clothes, stepped into the tub and sank slowly down into the hot, soapy water.

She felt her tight, sore muscles relax immediately. She shut her eyes and let out a long, slow breath. Her mind started to wander, from chores left undone on the farm, to issues with one of Matthew's businesses—but in the midst of her varying thoughts, she felt her stomach clench tightly. The dreaded date in June was quickly approaching—Ron Chatum's parole hearing.

CHAPTER 2

PAIGE HEARD THE DOGS BARKING, glanced out her window, and saw a black Jeep Grand Cherokee slow and come to a stop. Duke and Roscoe trotted over and stood anxiously waiting at the driver side door, which remained closed—Nancy was not getting out.

Paige closed the back door behind her, walked to the Jeep, opened the passenger door and slid onto soft beige leather. "Hi," she said, inhaling the new car scent. "I see you've been car shopping."

"I see you've added to your petting zoo," teased Nancy, shifting her gaze from Paige to Roscoe. "Is he as mean as he looks?"

Paige chuckled. "He's a teddy bear."

Nancy gave the Rottweiler a skeptical look through the car window, his teeth exposed in a growl.

"Could have fooled me," she said sarcastically. She handed Paige a French fashion magazine. "A friend sent this to me. Look at the page I earmarked."

Paige opened the magazine. Her eyes widened in amazement. "*Oh—my!*" The young woman's face looking at her from the glossy page looked like Jaden's best friend—

Hannah Butler. There were slight differences. The model's hair was lighter, her face was less angular, and her lips were thinner.

"Do you suppose she could be a cousin of Hannah's?" asked Nancy, her eyebrows raised questioningly.

"I suppose," said Paige with uncertainty. "Her mother, Henda, came from a large family." She ran a finger across the sleek paper, studying the brown-eyed beauty dressed in riding breeches and ivory silk shirt. She was standing beside a gray horse, her long reddish-brown hair blowing in the wind.

"Take the magazine. Show it to Hannah."

Paige shook her head. "If she's a relative, I doubt she would recognize her. She's had no contact with her mother's family in over seven years."

"Why exactly is that?"

"I don't know—Arthur's tight-lipped about it," replied Paige. "He refuses to talk about it. He insists that it's in Hannah's best interest."

Nancy frowned. "What does that mean? Does it have something to do with Henda's death?"

Paige shrugged.

Nancy threw a questioning, sideways glance at Paige. "Did the police ever learn anything more about the auto accident?"

"The motorcyclists who ran her off the road were never found," Paige said softly. Authorities found the burnt remains of Henda's Range Rover at the bottom of a hill with Henda in the driver's seat, dead. Miraculously, Hannah was found forty yards away, curled up in a state of shock, unscathed. "The accident remains unsolved." She closed the magazine.

"Have you talked with Hannah's dad recently?" asked Nancy tentatively. Nancy and Arthur Butler had dated in high school.

"No. Not in several months." Paige glanced at Nancy.

"Why?"

Nancy shrugged nonchalantly. "No reason—just curious when he was going to be back in Jackson."

Paige smiled. "I'll let you know."

———————

AFTER DRIVING AN HOUR Nancy turned off onto a winding gravel road, followed the posted signs and parked beside five other vehicles. Stepping from the vehicle they saw someone with the adoption program being interviewed by a WBBJ-TV reporter. They listened for a few minutes and then they walked to the barn where they were greeted by a man wearing a khaki-green uniform and a name tag identifying him as Tom. He explained to them that the mustangs were separated by age and sex. They strolled by the holding pens. Paige stared at the mustangs. Many had the classic Roman nose, all had long flowing manes.

"I'm surprised at how small some of them are," she said, turning to Nancy.

Paige and Nancy continued walking and they stopped at the first pen. Inside were six bays, all eating hay. Nancy read the card attached to the holding pen. "All fillies between the ages of two and three."

The next pen contained one bay wearing a black halter, also eating hay. "She's a six-year-old mare," said Nancy reading the card. "She's been worked with."

The last pen in the row, the largest, contained a dozen geldings of all ages and colors. One in particular caught Paige's eye.

"Look at him," Paige said admiringly, pointing to a copper-red chestnut gelding. His head was small and refined with a dished profile, suggesting Arabian in his bloodline. His neck, a desirable length, was connected to a well-sloped shoulder. His back was short and level, his hindquarters strong and powerful. Clearly the alpha, he carried himself with strength and grace as he moved the other geldings around the pen.

"Can you see what's in the pen behind this one?" Nancy asked intrigued. She craned her neck.

Paige shook her head. "All I see is the furry tips of ears."

"Let's go see," urged Nancy.

Paige opened a gate, stepped through and walked toward the pen behind the geldings. It contained six burros of varying heights. Five of them were the typical grayish-brown—but the smallest one was pinkish.

"Wow," said Nancy, coming to stand beside Paige. "They're so cute!"

"They are. I especially like that one," said Paige, pointing to the little blush-colored, knock-kneed burro that stood aloof, looking out beyond his metal cage.

Paige and Nancy moved around the outside of the pen toward the side where the burro stood. He was shaggy with big expressive brown eyes. Paige extended her arm between the gate panels and stroked his soft muzzle. He stood still. The other burros retreated to the farthest corner of the pen, their long ears forward, watching cautiously.

Paige reached into her pocket, brought out a carrot, and broke it into two pieces. She knelt down, and extended her arm, the carrot in her palm. The little blush-colored burro lowered his head, sniffed the treat, opened his lips and gently took the carrot half from her. When he finished chewing, he extended his nose looking for more. Paige gave him the second half. He ate it and then stepped forward.

"Nancy, check out the marking on the burro's back," Paige said, running her hand over the little burro's shoulder.

A Bureau of Land Management agent walked up to stand by Paige and Nancy. "Ever heard of the Jerusalem Donkey Legend?" asked the agent. He was wearing a khaki-green uniform and a badge identifying him as Gary.

Paige shook her head. "No."

"The legend is, that the donkey that carried Jesus into Jerusalem on Palm Sunday also followed him to Calvary, for the donkey loved the Lord," said agent Gary. "Appalled by the sight of Jesus on the cross, the donkey turned away but could not leave. The shadow of the cross fell upon his shoulders and back, forever marking him and all of his descendants."

"What an amazing story," Paige said sincerely. "What can you tell me about this little guy?"

"Let's see—what number is on his tag," said agent Gary, reaching for the oval tag hanging on a ribbon from the burro's neck. He glanced at his clipboard, "Says here the pink burro 2253 is two-years-old and he is gelded." Looking at Paige, he asked, "Are you familiar with donkeys?"

Paige shook her head. "I know about horses, but I'm unfamiliar with donkeys—never had any interest in them."

"Donkeys have an undeserved reputation for being stubborn and bad tempered," Gary explained. "When in reality, donkeys are unique creatures. They are highly intelligent, curious, gentle and extremely levelheaded. You just have to understand what makes them tick."

Paige looked into the soft brown eyes of the blush-colored burro and her heart filled with a fiery love. She turned to the BLM agent. "How do I adopt him?"

CHAPTER 3

S TEPPING INTO THE BARN ON Monday morning, Paige was greeted with its familiar, delightful fragrance—the combination of hay, horses, tack and manure, and a chorus of low knickers. The barn, designed with the local climate in mind, was picturesque and functional, staying cool in the summer and warm in the winter, its architecture reminded her of the barns in England. The walls were brick and the windows were large and shuttered. The ceiling soared. The center aisle was overly wide with brass lanterns outside twelve spacious box stalls.

Sliding back a stall door, Paige gave the occupant a good morning pat on the neck. "Good morning, Sophie," she said to the Paint mare.

In the next stall, a reddish-brown colored mare named Shiloh nickered eagerly, pawing anxiously at her door. Paige slid Shiloh's door open, rubbed her head and moved on to the next stall.

"Good morning, Bandana," she said patting the old brown Thoroughbred, the grandson of Secretariat. Paige had adopted him from New Vocations. He lowered his head over his stall guard and gave her a strong push.

Crossing the aisle, Paige slid back the door to Maddie's stall. The young mare, a rescue, nickered a greeting. She opened Gatsby's stall door, and the copper-colored mare tossed her head. Next she opened the stall doors for Armani and Timber, Matthew's big hunt horses. The last door to be opened contained the little pink burro.

"Good morning," Paige said softly. She glanced around the burro's stall and was pleased to see that he had eaten all of his hay. The little burro stood in a corner watching her, his fluffy long ears forward. She smiled tenderly at him and said, "I've no idea what to name you."

Paige finished feeding the horses, and her cell phone rang. She answered and she heard the warm, familiar voice of her brother-in-law, Matthew, informing her that he would be at her house in ten minutes. Grabbing her keys from the tack room, she called the dogs and headed for her truck. She beat him to the house and had a fresh pot of coffee ready when she heard him rap at the back door.

Paige opened the door, beckoning him in.

Matthew gave her a broad smile and said, "Good morning." At sixty he was a well-built, good-looking man, tall and broad shouldered. He was wearing his version of a working uniform: long sleeve cotton shirt, dark blue Wrangler jeans and baseball cap over short-clipped gray hair.

Paige poured coffee into two mugs, offering one to Matthew. "Just the way you like it," she smiled.

Matthew nodded and followed her down the hall to the office. The comfortable cluttered sitting room was filled with Paige's personality. The walls were covered with framed posters of famous equestrian partnerships, Rodney Jenkins on Idle Dice; Joe Fargis on Touch of Class; David O'Connor on Custom Made; and famous race horses, Ruffian, Secretariat, Red Rum, Arkle and others.

There were framed family photographs scattered liberally about the room and the built-in bookshelves were filled with books and other mementos.

Matthew lowered himself into a well-worn leather sofa. "What have you named your new donkey?"

Paige sank down opposite him into a soft, leather club chair. She shrugged.

"Jacob, Jaden and Hannah have suggested plenty of good names. I've tossed them out—none seem to fit him."

"I will be out of town the weekend of the twin's birthday, but I've arranged for their gifts to be delivered," declared Matthew, sipping his coffee.

Paige stared at him questioningly. Seeing the expression on her face, he quickly changed the subject.

"I'll be spending the month of July in Alaska fly fishing," he said. "Jacob will need to come to Montana in June."

Matthew owned a home in Bozeman, Montana and every summer Jacob flew out to join his uncle for a couple of weeks of fly fishing.

"I think he has a polo match the first weekend in June," said Paige. "I'll have him call you when he gets home from school. Does that work?"

"Yes." Matthew fixed his gray eyes on his sister-in-law, his expression serious. "Do you want me to fly back for Ron Chatum's parole hearing?"

Paige looked away from his gaze, her teeth clenched. She didn't want to think about the hearing. The thought of her husband's killer making parole was unbearable. She felt the anger and resentment explode within her.

"I don't know," she said finally. "I haven't made up my mind about what to do."

Matthew nodded again.

"If I decide to go, your being there would be comforting," Paige confessed, her voice taut with repressed fury.

"Let me know what you decide," Matthew said, and he turned the conversation to business matters.

36

MINTUES AFTER THE FINAL BELL SOUNDED, Hannah strolled out of the high school into the bright March afternoon sunshine, her backpack slung over her shoulder. She turned on her cell phone and it rang immediately.

"Hannah, are you still here?" Jaden asked, her voice hopeful.

"I'm just now heading to my car. Need a ride home?"

"Yes, *please*," insisted Jaden. "Wait for me. I'll be there in five minutes." She hung up.

Hannah climbed into her car and put the key into the ignition. The white Porsche 911 Turbo, a birthday present from her father, purred to life.

The passenger door swung open and Jaden jumped inside.

"I'm *so* glad I caught you," Jaden said, relief in her voice. "Jacob is taking Bethany home and I didn't want to ride with them. Bethany's fawning over my brother makes me want to gag."

Hannah laughed. "Bethany told me she'd asked Jacob to drive her home—I knew I'd hear from you."

"What does she see in my brother? He's such a tool!"

Hannah shrugged. "She says he's hot."

"Yeah, I hear girls say that," Jaden quipped, skepticism in her voice.

"When will your grandparents be home?" asked Jaden, changing the subject.

"April 2nd," said Hannah. Her grandparents, William and Sheila Butler, were in Australia.

"I've really missed them. It feels like they've been gone forever," she said.

"When's your dad coming to see you?"

"I talked to him last week. He told me he was coming in May," said Hannah, a hint of anger in her voice. Her father, Arthur Butler, CEO of an international banking

37

firm, resided in London. In the last eighteen months, he had come to Jackson only four times.

"That's less than a month away."

Hannah smiled thinly, a stony expression on her pretty face. She remained silent.

Arriving home, Hannah and Jaden changed out of their school uniforms into riding breeches and boots, returning to the Porsche within minutes. Pulling up to the barn, Hannah parked next to Paige's truck.

"Mom, we're here," yelled Jaden as she and Hannah walked down the aisle towards the tack room. Jaden ducked under Gatsby's stall guard and threw her arms around the mare's neck, inhaling Gatsby's horse scent.

Paige emerged from the tack room, wearing jeans and a long sleeve shirt, a baseball cap covering her auburn hair. She stopped outside the stall.

"Dr. Mincher was here today," she declared. "She said Gatsby's injury is healing nicely. You can start hand walking her."

Gatsby, Jaden's Holsteiner mare, had sprained a suspensory ligament and had been on stall rest for several months.

"*Yes!*" Jaden shouted happily, her green eyes gushing with joy. She ran her hand up the blaze on the mare's head, and whispered, "Soon girl."

Paige smiled. "Matthew said he is going fox hunting this weekend since it's the last weekend for it. So, both Timber and Armani need to be worked."

"I'll work Timber," Hannah volunteered.

"Jaden, you work Maddie. Jacob can work Armani," Paige said.

Hannah had Timber brushed and tacked in fifteen minutes. She was leading him out of the barn when Jacob arrived. He emerged from his Jeep wearing blue jeans with boots and a steel gray T-shirt under a Cabela's shirt.

Walking over, Jacob patted the big gray horse on his

neck. "Hi Timber," he said and he glanced at Hannah. "Want a leg up?"

Hannah nodded, smiling appreciatively. "Yeah, I'd love it."

Timber, standing 16.2 hands, wasn't easy to mount. Hannah gathered the reins in her left hand and bent her left leg for Jacob to grab. He easily hoisted her up into the saddle. Surprised by his strength, she looked down at him. His dirty blonde hair was disheveled, and his lips were curled in an alluring drop-dead crooked smile. His hand lingered on her thigh, igniting an electrical current that radiated through her entire body. Her heart was pounding, thundering uncontrollably and her pulse raced wildly.

"Thanks," she muttered, in a voice she didn't recognize.

Timber moved forward and Hannah felt overwhelmed by the confusing rush of feelings swirling through her. She could barely think straight. Jacob was her friend, a pal, a confidant. Someone she had grown up with. For the first time she recognized that he no longer looked like a boy—his boyishness had been replaced with broad, strong shoulders and the hardened muscles of a man.

Hannah chose the farthest corner of the ring in which to work Timber. Grateful for the simplicity of riding a horse, she focused on getting the big gray relaxed and soft. Thirty minutes later, she saw Jacob enter the ring riding Armani in dressage saddle. He had added leather chaps and removed his Cabala's shirt. His T-shirt enhanced his muscular biceps and forearms. He sat a horse beautifully.

Paige had been unwavering that both he and Jaden have a strong foundation in Dressage. Jacob was skilled at getting a horse settled and balanced, but he preferred equine activities that involved speed, like polo and foxhunting, or included a physical thrill, like cross country or rodeo riding.

Hannah was unable to forget the electrifying sensation

of Jacob's hand on her thigh. His presence continued to invade her thoughts, her mind was spiraling. She wanted to escape back to the barn to think. She finished the Dressage exercise and pointed Timber, who happily lengthened his stride, in the direction of the barn.

Without glancing in Hannah's direction, Jacob yelled. "See ya."

AFTER DINNER Hannah retreated upstairs to the bedroom she frequently occupied when she stayed with the Winston's. Her homework was scattered across the bed. She pushed it aside, reached for her iPod, and put in her earphones. She turned on Taylor Swift and thought about dinner.

Sitting across from Jacob had been uncomfortable. His eyes radiated with excitement as he talked about his upcoming trip to Montana and fly fishing with his uncle. She felt awkward when he glanced her way and she spent most of dinner looking down at her plate.

Lying on her bed, Hannah stared unseeingly at the ceiling. She felt tangled up inside, internally torn and disloyal. She was powerfully attracted to Jacob—but Bethany was her friend and she knew how badly Bethany wanted Jacob. Thinking about Jacob and Bethany together filled her with intense jealousy that tightened around her heart, strangling it like a vine. Bethany was gorgeous. She had long, lustrous red hair and porcelain skin, her figure was fabulous and proportionally curved in all the right places. Every guy in school lusted after her. How could she compete with Bethany? She groaned and rolled over on her stomach, her chin resting on her hands.

Hannah glanced at the clock on the nightstand and saw that it was getting late. Gathering up her homework papers, she tossed them into her backpack, walked downstairs, and dropped it by the back door. She stopped by Paige's room to say goodnight and then headed for the stairs. When she reached the landing, the bathroom door opened and out walked Jacob with a large towel wrapped loosely around his hips.

Hannah felt her mouth go dry—Jacob's body looked amazing. Her eyes moved from his hard, rippled stomach to his well-defined broad shoulders and arms. His wet blonde hair was uncombed and drops of water trickled down his tanned muscular chest.

"Hi," said Jacob, smiling nonchalantly.

"Ah—hey," stammered Hannah, her face reddening. She waved stupidly and darted hastily into her room, and quickly closed the door.

CHAPTER 4

WHEN PAIGE OPENED HER EYES, her room was filled with light. Glancing over at her bedside digital clock, she saw it was 6:45 a.m. She wiped the sleep from her eyes, and she stared at the ceiling, reflecting on her dream. A tickling curiosity crept over her, and she sat up abruptly, swung her legs off the bed and headed for her walk-in closet.

The left side of the closet was floor to ceiling storage, drawers and shelves. The right side had ample hanging space for all her clothes. At the back of the closet, on the highest shelf, she spotted it. A box marked with the initials *RW*. She grasped the step stool kept in the closet, stepped upon it, reached up and grabbed the box with both hands. She carried the box into the bedroom and sank down into a club chair beside the bed, setting the box on the ottoman in front of her. The flaps were not sealed and the box opened easily. Reaching inside, she picked up a leather bound book, laid it on her lap and dropped the box on the floor. She was staring at the book so intently she didn't hear Jacob enter her room.

"Wow!" Jacob's deep voice was voice full of surprise. "I

thought you threw that out after Dad died?"

"I couldn't," said Paige, her voice barely audible. "Your dad gave it to me the day you and your sister were born."

"What made you look for *that* book?" Jacob prompted with a nod.

"I wanted to know what the book said about donkeys," said Paige softly. Staring at the book in her lap, she ran her hand lovingly over the soft, smooth leather. She opened the cover and seeing Robert's familiar handwriting, felt the raw sting of tears. Her throat tightened as tears trickled down her cheeks.

"I miss your dad so much," she whispered, her lower lip trembling. It had been almost seven years since Robert Winston had stopped to help a stranded motorist. Ron Chatum, high on meth at the time, robbed, shot and killed her husband for the forty dollars in his wallet.

"Your dad was wonderfully imperfect and totally perfect for me," muttered Paige.

"I miss him too," said Jacob in a low voice, sitting down on the ottoman in front of his mother's chair.

Paige stared at her son, sitting on the ottoman facing her, dressed in his school uniform. The boyish roundness of his face was gone. His cheekbones were sharper, his jaw more sculpted and squared. He had his father's beautiful eyes. She knew Jacob missed his father and she felt guilty for her teary breakdown.

"I had this amazing dream," Paige said. "In the dream, I was in a large meadow trying to catch our new burro when I saw what looked like a man riding a fiery-red chestnut horse. His body was bathed in a golden, white light. His face was brilliant, beyond description. As he approached where I was standing, the man on the horse spoke in a soft reassuring voice and he said:

In the beginning was the Word, and the Word was with God, and the Word was God.

43

*By the word of the Lord the heavens were made,
and all the host of them by the breath of His mouth.*

*For it is with your heart that you believe and
are justified, and it is with your mouth that you
confess and are saved.*

*Every word of God is pure; He is a shield to those
who put their trust in Him.*

*For the word of God is living and active. Sharper
than any double-edged sword, it penetrates even
to dividing soul and spirit, joints and marrow; it
judges the thoughts and attitudes of the heart.*

"And then the man wheeled the large chestnut horse around, and as he rode away, I heard him say, 'Blessed is the one who reads the words and takes to heart what is written.' Then there came a great wind and he disappeared and I found myself standing amongst a herd of little burros—all of them had the mark of the cross."

Jacob, still as a statue, said nothing.

Paige sighed, her eyes flicked downward, reading what Robert had written in the book when she heard Jacob's deep voice reciting his father's writing from memory.

*Your word is a lamp to my feet and a light to my
path.*

And his voice trailed off.

Paige's head jerked up, her eyes meeting her son's. "You're so like your father," she whispered, closing the book in her lap. "How did you get to be so wise at almost seventeen?"

Jacob's eyes flicked to the book in her lap and he

smiled. He stood up, turned and said over his shoulder as he walked from the room, "See you after school."

Paige rose slowly to her feet. The piercing ring of her cell phone startled her and the book slipped from her grasp and fell to the floor. She knelt down to pick it up, her eyes unthinkingly drawn to an open page, suddenly—the perfect name for her little burro came to her—*Gabriel*.

HANNAH STARED OUT the classroom window. It was a bright, glorious Tuesday afternoon, but she felt gloomy. She fidgeted in her seat, glanced down at her watch and sighed in displeasure. She was anxious for her last class to end and the school day to be over. It had been a long day. She heard the bell chime. She jammed her books into her backpack, sprang to her feet and hurriedly headed for the parking lot and her car.

Jaden was in the parking lot, waiting for her, leaning against the sleek white Porsche. "Why weren't you at lunch?"

"I was working on a project." Hannah unlocked the car door and climbed in.

"Is that why you left the house so early this morning," asked Jaden, sliding into the passenger seat.

"Yes," Hannah lied. She'd purposely left before Jacob returned from morning feed duty. She couldn't face him, having acted like a clumsy, mindless idiot the night before. During the school day, she had successfully avoided him, Jaden and their friends.

"Mom left a message asking me to stop by the bank," said Jaden. "Is that okay?"

"Sure," replied Hannah, her voice tense.

"What's up? You look upset," said Jaden.

"I'm just tired. I didn't sleep well last night and I've got a headache."

Jaden looked at Hannah with concern. "Are you having bad dreams again?"

"Nothing like that," said Hannah, with a slight shake of her head. Her nightmares were less frequent, but they occasionally haunted her, and they were always the same—about the night her mother died.

Hannah turned the Porsche into the BancorpSouth parking lot and pulled into the only available space.

"I won't be long," promised Jaden, scrambling out of the car.

Hannah leaned her head back against the head rest. She heard Colbie Caillat singing, *"I don't know but I think I maybe fallin' for you,"* and immediately, she started thinking about Jacob. She sighed wistfully as the song ended. She reached out to change the channel—and she saw them—Jacob and Bethany across the street at Arby's. They were walking hand in hand towards the Jeep. Jacob opened the passenger door for Bethany. Instead of climbing into the Jeep, Bethany turned, entwined her arms around Jacob's neck, pressing her body into his, kissing him on the lips. Hannah saw Jacob's hand in Bethany's hair, his other hand, at the small of her back, pulling her closer, returning her kiss. White-hot jealousy exploded within her, searing her insides. Her heart ached with intense, burning envy.

The passenger door flew open and Jaden climbed in.

Hannah bit her lip hard to keep from dry heaving. She jammed her car into reverse.

Jaden shot Hannah a surprised look. "What's got your panties in a wad?"

"Nothing," grumbled Hannah tersely, refusing to look at Jaden. She immediately regretted her curt reply—she loved Jaden as a sister. She threw a remorseful look at her and said, "I'm sorry, Jaden. I'm having a really crappy day."

"No worries, Han," Jaden said in a tender voice, and she settled back into the soft tan leather seat.

They rode in silence for several miles.

"Any news from Lori about Black Tie Required?" Jaden asked, breaking the quietness. Lori and Bill Hoos, family friends and horse professionals, were her and Hannah's riding instructors. They were in Florida training and showing.

"I got an email from Lori yesterday," answered Hannah, happy to talk about her horse, Black Tie Required. He was a sixteen-hand seal-brown Thoroughbred. She had sent Black Tie to Florida with Bill and Lori and their daughter, Becca, who was showing him.

"Becca and Black Tie are doing well together."

"I heard you know what Uncle Matt is giving me and Jacob for our birthday," Jaden blurted, her emerald green eyes dancing with evident curiosity.

Her smile was infectious. Hannah felt the gnarled ache inside her ease.

"What makes you so sure that I know?" she asked, trying to keep her voice flat.

"Uncle Matt can't keep a secret," said Jaden candidly. "He mentioned to Jacob that he needed your help— something about delivery times."

"I've no idea!" Hannah pressed her lips together suppressing a smile.

"You're *not* a very good liar!" chided Jaden affectionately. "At least give me a hint."

"I'm not giving you a single clue—so—forget it!"

"Come on," pleaded Jaden, pressing her palms together.

Hannah glanced at Jaden. "Begging won't help."

Jaden stuck out her tongue.

Hannah laughed.

For the remainder of the drive, Jaden chattered constantly about horses. Hannah was grateful—it kept her mind blissfully distracted from thinking about Bethany and Jacob kissing.

CHAPTER 5

PAIGE JERKED IN HER SLEEP, a dream invading her mind.

They were under a tree planted by a stream. Robert had his back against the tree and she was leaning against him, resting her head on his shoulder. Robert was kissing her neck, his lips moving in a slow, steady trail. She turned to look up at him, but he turned his face from her. In the distance, she saw four chariots pulled by horses of varying colors coming in their direction. Robert stood up, extended his hand to her and pulled her up. The chariots arrived and she asked, "What does this mean?"

Robert smiled his glorious crooked smile, his beautiful green eyes flashed brightly. "These are the four spirits of the heavens, which go forth from presenting themselves before the Lord of all the earth," he said, picking up one of her hands. He pressed it to his mouth, his lips caressing the inside of her wrist. "Have faith, not doubt. Trust in His word—accept it, believe in it," he said, his gaze searing.

Robert's voice was intoxicating, his touch exhilarating. He slowly traced her lower lip with his thumb. "Trust what

I say," he whispered.

Suddenly, the tree by the stream grew swiftly; its height reaching all the way to the heavens. Robert turned and stepped into a chariot and his appearance suddenly altered, his body changing from burnished bronze to a dazzling white. The chariot spun off and he was gone.

Paige jerked awake. The dream was still vivid, the pleasure from Robert's kisses so real, her arms were covered in goose bumps. She rolled over and stared at the framed picture of Robert, Jaden and Jacob, on her bedside table, all on horseback, taken the weekend before he died. Today was April 3rd, the twin's seventeenth birthday, their seventh year without their father. She felt a wave of excruciating pain wash through her, intensifying the brokenness of her heart. She clutched at her pillow, and sobbed as the grief enveloped her.

Paige felt exhausted and depleted. She pushed herself up and out of the bed, and shuffled into the bathroom. She stared at her reflection in the mirror. A random pattern of red splotches covered her normally even-tone skin. Her brown eyes were puffy and her auburn hair was a tangled mess. She turned her face upward and whispered, "Lord Jesus, I'm a mess. Hear my cry—help me." She splashed water on her face and shuffled back to the bed. Crawling in, she pulled the covers up over her head, praying for the pain to end.

JADEN RUBBED HER mother's arm. Paige was in a deep sleep, and for a second she tried to ignore it.

"Mom, are you getting up?" Jaden asked sweetly.

Paige opened her eyes and saw her daughter standing next to her bed, staring down at her, frowning.

Paige blinked, and said, in a raw voice, "What time is it?"

"It's almost eight."

"Go ahead and feed," Paige whispered hoarsely.

Jaden nodded. "Ok. We'll take care of it," she said cheerily, patting her mother's head. She turned and walked to the bedroom door where Jacob stood waiting. They strolled together down the hall, and out the back door towards the jeep.

"I hate it when Mom's depression gets this bad." Jaden climbed into the passenger side, a scowl on her face. "Do you think she will ever get over Dad's death?" she said, fastening her seatbelt.

Jacob shook his head and started the Jeep.

"I don't know. She was deeply in love with him," he said, shifting into drive. They drove the short distance to the barn in silence. Approaching the barn, they saw Hannah's Porsche. Jaden turned to her brother, her expression perplexed.

"What's Hannah doing here at this hour on a Sunday?"

Jacob laughed. "Uncle Matt had our birthday presents delivered here." He parked the Jeep and Jaden sprang out, sprinting into the barn.

"Jacob—*hurry*!" she yelled from inside the barn.

Jacob strolled into the barn. Parked in the aisle was a Ducati 1198 motorcycle. He stared at the sleek red Italian motorcycle in astonishment.

Jaden, stood in front of a stall, a card in her hand, sniffling.

"What's wrong?" Jacob asked worriedly, meeting Hannah's gaze.

"Nothing's wrong," said Hannah, a reassuring smile on her face. "Matthew bought Jaden a horse that has evented at the two-star level."

Jacob walked over to his sister and put his arm around her shoulders.

50

"Look how beautiful she is," Jaden gushed, her eyes glistening with thankful tears.

"She's really big," said Jacob, his eyes sliding admiringly from the mare's magnificent head, to her strong powerful shoulder, to her highly muscled hindquarter.

"She stands 16.3," answered Hannah.

Jacob looked at his sister. "Are you just going to stand here and blubber?" he chided affectionately. He knew riding was a component of her soul.

Jaden laughed. Turning, she kissed her brother on the check, and then ducked under the stall guard, throwing her arms around the mare's neck.

Jacob's phone beeped. He reached into his jeans pocket, pulled it out and read the text message. "It's Uncle Matt," he said laughing. "He says, Happy Birthday."

Jacob turned to Hannah, cocked his head to the side and smiled. "Let's go for a ride."

Hannah stared into his eyes. Her heart somersaulted and thumped at a frantic tempo. "Sure," she said, trying to sound indifferent.

Jacob headed for the Ducati. "Coming?" he asked over his shoulder.

Hannah looked at him, her eyes wide in sudden understanding. "I thought you were talking about riding a horse!" she said, staring warily at the red motorcycle.

Jacob stopped and turned around. "I wasn't thinking. I'm sorry," he said apolitically.

Hannah shook her head. "What happened, happened a long time ago and I need to get over it," she said with a determined nod. "Let's go."

Jacob's lips curved into a wide, delighted smile.

Turning on her heel, Hannah disappeared into the tack room, and reappeared carrying two motorcycle helmets.

"One is from Matthew and one is from me," she said smiling shyly up at him. "I didn't know he had bought you one—Happy Birthday."

Jacob grinned and leaning in, gave her a brotherly kiss on the cheek. "Thanks," he said appreciatively.

The feel of his lips on her skin sparked a swirling sensation that swept through her entire body, flooding her with warmth. Feeling self-conscious, Hannah dropped her eyes and followed him to the Ducati.

On the motorcycle, Jacob inserted the key, and turned it clockwise. The digital instrument panel came brightly alive. Hannah threw her leg over the leather seat, hopped onto the back of the Ducati, and wrapped her arms around Jacob's waist, pressing her body against his. She could feel his hard muscles underneath his cotton shirt and the image of him shirtless flashed in her mind, igniting intense feelings that flamed through her.

CHAPTER 6

PAIGE FELT SANDPAPER RUB AGAINST her forehead. It took her a second to realize it was a cat's tongue. She opened her eyes. Gizmo was sitting on her pillow, staring at her, her long, thin tail, wagging reproachfully back and forth.

The phone rang. Paige reached around the cat to her nightstand, and picked up the phone. "Hello?"

"Dear, it's Sheila," said the familiar voice. "I'm in your house and I didn't want to startle you."

Paige rubbed her eyes, trying to make the sleep haze go away faster. Before she had the chance to respond, Sheila Butler walked into her bedroom, dressed in blue jeans and a crisp white shirt, a strand of pearls around her neck. Her round, friendly face was framed by frosted blonde hair, cut stylishly short. She was carrying a travel mug.

Paige's nostrils caught the scent of coffee. "How was the book tour?"

"Exhausting." Sheila handed Paige the mug. Both Sheila and William were successful authors. Sheila, a retired teacher, wrote cookbooks, and William, formerly with the FBI, wrote who-done-it mystery novels.

"Jacob came by for a visit," said Sheila. "He told me that you were having a difficult morning."

"I miss Robert so much," murmured Paige, her voice cracking.

"Today is your children's birthday. A day to celebrate," Sheila admonished, her voice soft and warm. "This is not a day to stay in bed feeling sorry for yourself."

Paige swallowed. "I never imagined that I would live out my life without him."

Sheila fixed her blue eyes on Paige, her gaze piercing. "You have to let go of your anger and stop wallowing in self-pity."

"If I hadn't asked Robert to run to the grocery store because I wanted strawberries, he would never have been on the road at that time and wouldn't have been shot and killed," Paige said in a low voice, staring at her lap. The tears in her eyes brimmed over and trickled slowly down her face.

Sheila sat down on the bed beside Paige.

"Robert saw a stranded motorist and he did what he thought was the right thing to do and he stopped," she said simply. "The choice to stop was Robert's. He could have driven by."

Paige blinked. Sheila's words ringing loudly in her head. She brushed the tears briskly away. "But *why* did it happen to Robert?" she whined.

Sheila reached out and placed her hand on Paige's hand. "Random, horrible things happen to millions of good people and I have no explanation for why. After my daughter died, I kept thinking to myself how unfair it was. I couldn't understand why it happened. I kept asking God, if you are good, why did you take my child?"

Arthur's younger sister, Catherine, died at the age of fifteen from cancer.

"I wanted to believe in God but I couldn't," she said,

sadness in her voice. "I was so angry and bitter and my heart was broken. I can remember days when I screamed at God asking him *why* Catherine died, but he never answered me. Years went by before I realized that I was only tormenting myself and I would never be able to figure it out—it was unanswerable."

Sheila studied Paige intensely. "I remember clearly the morning that I went into William's office looking for something and lying there on his desk was his Bible open at the chapter of Job. I sat down and read. I mean—look at Job. He lost his family. He lost all his money, his cattle and he suffered sickness—but the Bible says that he was the most righteous man on the Earth at the time."

"I thought to myself, how unfair, and yet, Job stuck it out with God. It was at that moment that I made two decisions," she said, her gaze unwavering. "The first decision I made was to trust God enough to not have to know why Catherine died, and the second decision was to stop wasting my life waiting for an explanation."

After a long pause, Sheila continued. "I trusted and believed and gradually I began to feel like I was coming out of the hell I had been in," she said. "I'm sharing this with you because I know what God can do when you let *Him* in. The hand of God has been working in my life and I believe it has in yours as well. Don't put a question mark where He puts a period."

Sheila got off the bed. "Now, I want you to get up and get dressed and come to my house," she said with a determined nod. "We're going to have a birthday brunch."

Paige nodded, her eyes filling with grateful tears. "Thank you, Sheila. You're my rock."

"Take a long, hot shower and come when you are ready." Sheila smiled lovingly, and gave Paige's arm a soft rub. She turned and walked from the room.

Paige felt Gizmo brush up against her arm. "Is there something you want?"

Gizmo's large yellow-green eyes stared back. She answered with three long meows. She flicked her tail, stepped to the edge of the bed, jumped down, and waddled out of the room.

SIXTY MINUTES LATER, Paige turned into the Butler's driveway. She pulled up to the detached garage and parked next to William Butler's black Range Rover. She looked curiously at the sleek red motorcycle parked in the driveway next to the twin's Jeep. She slid out of her truck and headed for the house.

The Butler's house was a two story brick home in the low country style with Tennessee fieldstone columns and a wood shingled roof. It had four bedrooms and over thirty-five hundred square feet and sat on five acres. Paige walked up the two brick steps, opened the side door and stepped inside. Her nostrils were instantly bombarded with the aroma of fresh coffee and freshly baked pastries.

The room, incorporating comfort with function, looked less like a kitchen and more like a lovely huge room. The area was open and warm, the ideal setting for living and entertaining.

"Hello dear," Sheila said over her shoulder. She had changed and was dressed casually chic in black pants and white shirt, topped with a brightly colored apron.

Jacob, Jaden and Hannah were sitting at the oversized kitchen island, all three laughing.

"Hi, Mom," Jacob and Jaden said in unison.

Paige fought back tears, ashamed of the self pity she'd indulged in. She walked over to her son and daughter, hugged them both and said lovingly, "Happy Birthday."

"Here, Paige," said William Butler, passing her a champagne flute filled with Mimosa. There was an outdoor look about William with his salt-and-pepper hair, and his round face, tan from hours spent in the sun playing golf. Deeply etched laugh lines surrounded his brown eyes.

"I made it just the way you like it," he said, winking at her.

Her lips turned up in a smile. "Thanks, William," Paige said, taking the glass from him. "Whose motorcycle is that out front?"

"Mine," said Jacob, grinning broadly at her. "It's my birthday present from Uncle Matt—isn't it awesome!"

Paige's jaw dropped in instant comprehension of why Matthew hadn't been forthcoming and why he was conveniently out of town. Jacob was addicted to speed and the thought of how fast the Ducati would go filled her with trepidation.

William, standing beside Paige, gave her a fatherly hug. "It will be alright," he said, his tone reassuring. "Jacob is very responsible and he isn't going to drive like a frenzied maniac. Are you son?"

Jacob shook his head. "No, sir."

Paige's eyes shifted slowly over to Jaden.

Jaden answered her mother's questioning look. "*A horse!*"

"*A horse?*" Paige repeated.

Jaden beamed. "Yep, an eleven-year-old bay mare by a stallion named Two Davids," she said. "She's gorgeous, Mom. I can't wait for you to see her."

"I can't wait," said Paige, gulping down the contents of her glass. She fumed silently at Matthew and decided it was best to temporarily bury her anxiety.

"Well—it's time to eat," Sheila announced with a wave of her hand. "We'll be eating out on the patio."

WALKING INTO THE BARN three hours later, Paige was thinking about what she planned to say to Matthew. She stopped in front of the stall containing Jaden's birthday present and her mouth dropped in astonishment. The mare was indeed magnificent, but it was her resemblance to the great Thoroughbred filly, Ruffian, that took her breath away.

Paige pulled her cell phone from her jeans pocket and sent Matthew a text message. Fifteen minutes later her phone rang. She answered it and heard his familiar deep voice. "You've obviously seen the horse."

Paige laughed. "You don't exactly play fair—you know I worshipped Ruffian as a child."

"When I saw the video of that mare," said Matthew chuckling. "I had to buy her for Jaden."

"Matthew, your gifts are very generous," said Paige, her voice full of emotion. "Thank you from the bottom of my heart."

"You're not upset with me?"

Paige sighed. "Well, I'm not thrilled about Jacob having a motorcycle," she said. "You know how much he loves speed."

"He's very responsible, Paige."

"But a motorcycle—*it's so dangerous*!"

Matthew snorted. "And running a horse at the upper levels of Eventing isn't?"

Paige thought about what he had just said. "Your right, Matthew—I hadn't looked at it that way."

"I love Jacob and Jaden as if they were my own. So indulge me—let me spoil them."

Paige laughed and their discussion turned to business matters.

CHAPTER 7

I T WAS THE FIRST WEDNESDAY morning in April, a bright spring day. Paige stepped into the barn and heard a chorus of nickers and a hee-haw.

Paige opened Gabriel's door and found him standing in the center of his stall, his large fluffy ears forward, happy to see her. She showed him a carrot and the little pink burro didn't hesitate. He walked to her and accepted the treat.

"How are you this morning?" she said, scratching his shoulder.

Paige had just finished feeding when she saw two men wearing camouflage walking towards her. She recognized the walk of the taller man.

"Good morning, Paige," said Matthew, engulfing her in a bear hug.

"I was wondering when I'd see you," Paige said. She turned towards the man standing beside Matthew. "Morning, Joe."

"Morning, Paige," said Joe Martin. The owner of Martin Feeds and Martin Construction was tall with a head of white hair and gray eyes framed by bushy eyebrows. Joe

Martin's farm touched Matthew's property at the southwest corner. Both men were avid outdoorsmen and between them had over seventeen hundred acres on which to hunt and play.

"Any luck this morning?" Paige asked, looking from one to the other.

"None," said Matthew. "We were on our way to A&P Market for some breakfast. Want to join us?"

Paige smiled. "Your timing is perfect. I just finished feeding."

"I want to see this new horse of Jaden's," announced Joe. "And this pink donkey I've heard Jacob talking about."

Matthew and Joe followed Paige to the stall containing the bay Thoroughbred mare. "Jaden named her Lyre," she said, sliding open the stall door.

"Why?" Matthew asked.

Ducking underneath the stall guard, Paige walked over to the horse's head, reached up and pulled aside the mare's forelock. "Jacob told his sister that he thought the u-shaped star looked like a lyre."

Matthew squinted, studying the star on the mare's forehead. "It does indeed," he said, sounding pleased.

They moved on to Gabriel's stall. Paige opened his door and the burro raised his head.

"He's cute," said Joe laughing heartily. He turned to Paige. "Jacob said he was wild when you adopted him."

Paige nodded. "He was. But, for the most part, he trusts us now. He is less aggressive around the dogs which I'm thrilled about."

"Donkeys make good guard animals," said Joe nodding affirmatively. "I have a big jack out with my herd of cows. He keeps the coyotes away from my newborn calves."

Gabriel had ceased eating. He looked alert. His head was high, his ears forward, and his body tense and rigid. Matthew, followed by Joe, took a step into his stall and when they did, Gabriel let out a loud snort and backed up several feet.

Matthew stopped suddenly, glancing back at Paige disapprovingly.

"What the hell's wrong with *him*?"

Paige looked bewildered and shrugged her shoulders. "I've never seen him do that, Matthew." She reached into her pocket, removed a carrot and gave it to Matthew.

"Try doing everything in slow motion," she advised in a low voice.

Matthew dropped to his knee slowly and carefully extended his arm with the carrot in his hand. Gabriel eyed the carrot and the two men warily, his large ears moving back and forth like two radars. Joe, standing slightly behind Matthew, raised his right arm in a rigid thrust to wave away a fly from Matthew's head. Gabriel snorted loudly and aggressively stomped his right foot. Then he turned and trotted out of his stall.

Paige followed Matthew and Joe out through the stall door and into the small back paddock. Gabriel was standing in the center, his head high, his ears forward, watching them as they approached. The burro stomped again and lurched ferociously forward several strides with his teeth bared.

Matthew and Joe stopped dead in their tracks.

"I've never seen him do this before," insisted Paige, coming up to stand beside Matthew and Joe. She stared at the normally docile pink burro.

"I can't imagine why he's acting like this."

Gabriel snorted again, and lowered his head, his long fluffy ears pinned back against his head, and stomped his left foot.

"He looks angry," insisted Matthew, glancing over at Paige.

Paige looked confoundedly at Gabriel. "I don't know, but something is definitely bothering him."

Joe waved a hand in the air and said in a dismissive

manner, "Let's go eat breakfast. I'm famished."

RETURNING FROM HER TRAIL RIDE on Bandana, Paige dismounted and led the bay Thoroughbred into the barn. Armani was standing quietly in cross ties. Jacob, wearing a light blue T-shirt, jeans and boots, came out of the tack room carrying his western saddle.

"Hey, Mom," he said, his husky voice sounded troubled.

"Bad day?"

"Yeah, something like that."

Paige looked at him concerned. "Anything to do with school?"

"No," Jacob said firmly. "It's personal."

Paige could tell by the expression on his face and the look in his eyes that he didn't want to discuss it. She watched as he easily swung the bulky saddle up onto the bay horse's back. Walking into the tack room, she grabbed a snaffle bridle and returned to Armani. She unclipped the cross ties, slipped the reins over his head, and took off his halter, replacing it with the bridle.

At the sound of a car door closing, Paige looked up to see Hannah, striding gracefully towards them, wearing a black tank top, black Pikeur breeches and tall, black boots, her dark hair cascading down her back.

"Hey stranger," Jacob said warmly, stepping around Armani and giving Hannah a hug."Where have you been hiding?"

"I've been studying a lot. That college language course I'm taking is harder than I thought," said Hannah, pulling back. "I see you're going for a trail ride."

Jacob nodded. "Come with me."

Hannah stared at him. His head was titled slightly to one side, and he was smiling. The shirt he was wearing clung to him nicely, complementing his arm muscles. She felt her heart quicken and opened her mouth to decline, when Jacob spun abruptly, proclaiming over his shoulder, "I'm going to get you a horse."

Hannah watched Jacob amble down the aisle. She heard the song "Collide" by Howie Day playing on the radio and she wondered if she was heading for a collision.

Paige chuckled. "Looks like you're going for a trail ride kiddo."

"Looks that way," Hannah muttered quietly, heading for the tack room.

Jacob helped her tack up Shiloh and together they strolled out of the barn. He didn't bother with the mounting block. Grabbing the horn of the western saddle, he swung himself up onto Armani's back, making it look easy.

"Show off," said Hannah, leading Shiloh to the mounting block.

Jacob grinned.

They walked through a small pasture, over a little creek and through a patch of woods that opened up at the lower end of an enormous meadow. Hannah and Shiloh, out in front, started trotting. Jacob cantered Armani up beside her, glanced over, a wicked grin on his face. Hannah asked the bay mare for more speed. They galloped together across the grassy meadow. Reaching the far end, they pulled their horses back to a walk.

"That was fun," Hannah said laughing. "Shiloh's faster than I thought."

The grassy path was wide and they were able to ride side by side.

"Are you excited about this weekend?" Jacob asked.

Hannah nodded.

"I can't wait to see Black Tie. I've missed my pony," she said playfully. She and Jaden were taking the horse trailer and Lyre, and they were going to Franklin, Tennessee, to spend the weekend with Bill and Lori Hoos at their farm, returning on Sunday with Black Tie Required.

They rode in silence, each occasionally glancing at the other.

Reaching the grassy edge of the lake, Hannah asked Shiloh to halt. She swung her right leg over Shiloh's withers, and she slid to the ground.

"The night after our motorcycle ride, I had one of those dreams again," she confessed.

"About the night your mom died?" asked Jacob, glancing worriedly at her.

"This dream was different from the others," admitted Hannah, leading Shiloh to the water's edge. "In this dream, I dreamed of a man crying tears of blood."

Jacob jumped nimbly to the ground. "Do you ever think about that day? About the car accident?" he asked, his voice gentle. He joined her at the water's edge.

Hannah, stared at the ground, and nodded slightly.

"Sometimes," she confessed, her voice laced with aggravation. "Time has only added more questions for me and it's maddening because I'll never have the answers."

"What do you remember?" Jacob prodded gently.

"My mom and I were on a curvy road. It was nighttime. Suddenly, two motorcycles appeared. They were driving beside us, really close," said Hannah, meeting his gaze. "I heard a loud bang. Our car started swerving wildly before running off the road and down a hill," she paused, shrugged and said, "My next memory is waking up in the hospital."

They both heard a beeping sound. Jacob reached into his jeans pocket and removed his iPhone. He looked at it.

"It's Bethany," he said apologetically. "We had a disagreement. She's pissed at me because I won't play football next year." Jacob had played football his freshman and sophomore years, but an injury to his hand had kept him from playing in the fall.

"I thought you had decided you were going to play?"

"I changed my mind—too time consuming. Besides, I need to work to help pay for out-of-state tuition. My grades aren't going to qualify me for any scholarships," joked Jacob, his lips curling into a crooked grin. Jacob was dyslexic but he was also academically lazy and his grades were barely passable.

Hannah smiled.

Armani and Shiloh finished drinking. Jacob and Hannah started walking, side by side, along the grassy edge of the lake. Jacob's phone beeped again. Removing it from his pocket, he looked at it and then hit the off button, returning it to his pocket.

"For some reason, my playing senior year means a lot to Bethany," he said with exasperation.

Hannah studied him, staring at the familiar structure of his handsome face. She thought about what First Corinthians said about love—that a friend loves at all times and Jacob was most assuredly her friend. She felt safe when they were together. He made her want to be a better person. It was suddenly, abundantly clear to her—she was absolutely, without a doubt, unconditionally in love with Jacob Winston. She wanted him to be happy—even if that meant his being with Bethany.

"It may seem silly to you but it obviously means something to Bethany," she said with gentle earnestness. "Be patient with her and she'll probably come around."

Jacob nodded his head and a long silence followed.

They walked together, side by side, along the water's edge.

"I'm flattered that your mom included me in the trip to Lexington for Kentucky Rolex," said Hannah, breaking the silence they'd been walking in. "It's going to be fun."

"My mom loves you. You're a part of our family," Jacob said, looking over and meeting her gaze. "I hope you know that."

Hannah nodded. Feeling self-conscious, she quickly

changed the subject. "What are you doing this weekend?"

"Uncle Matt invited me to go turkey hunting with him and Joe Martin," he said elatedly. "Besides, it's the weekend and the Ducati needs riding."

Jacob and Armani stopped. He was staring at Hannah. She recognized the playful smile spreading on his lips, the roguish glint in his eye.

"Race you home," he said, vaulting up onto Armani.

Hannah hollered in protest but he was already several strides in front. She mounted hurriedly and urged Shiloh into a canter, following Jacob and Armani down the path and into the woods.

CHAPTER 8

FRIDAY MORNING PASSED QUICKLY. WALKING into the school cafeteria at lunch looking for Jaden, Hannah saw her sitting at a table with Jacob—and Bethany Shevar. Her stomach did a nervous little flip at the thought of sitting at a table with Bethany. She had noticed a change in Bethany's demeanor and attitude towards her, especially whenever Jacob was around. She was walking slowly through the food line, distracted by her thoughts of Jacob and Bethany, when she heard a male voice beside her.

"Hannah—is that all you're going to eat?"

Hannah looked up to see the smiling blue eyes of Tanner Chapman.

"Hey, Tanner," she said, reaching for an apple. She dropped it next to the salad. "I'm not really that hungry."

They went through the line together and headed to Jacob's table. Hannah felt her stomach churning nervously the closer they got.

"Rough morning?" Jaden asked her when she sat down.

Hannah nodded. "I've had a test or a pop quiz in every class this morning."

Bethany, glued to Jacob's side, turned her head, her eyes on Hannah. "Did you finish the chemistry homework?"

"No," said Hannah, trying to keep her voice even. "Did you?"

"Yes," bragged Bethany, a note of arrogance in her voice.

"I'm going to be lucky if I get a B in that class," Hannah complained softly, looking down at her tray. "That class is hard."

"You're whining about getting a B?" teased Tanner, the corners of his mouth quirked upward on his attractive face. He shook his head, "I finished the homework, but I have no idea if I did it correctly."

"Hey," said a tall, well-built black teenager with a slight Tennessee drawl. Cory Price, quarterback of the football team and Jacob's best friend, dropped his tray on the table and slid into an empty chair next to Tanner.

Jacob glanced expectantly at Cory. "What did Coach say about your missing training weekend?"

Cory grinned. "Too many of us had conflicts that weekend so he's rescheduling it." He took a bite of his hamburger.

Jaden looked at Cory, her emerald green eyes wide, and asked, "So—you're able to go with us to Kentucky for Rolex?"

Cory nodded.

"Dillon Tull is going too." Jaden's gaze shifted questioningly to Tanner.

"I can't—got a family thing," said Tanner.

Bethany nuzzled against Jacob, laying a hand on his forearm. "Let's all go see a movie tonight," she purred, her long, elegant fingers caressing his arm. "I really want to see the movie, '*Beastly*'."

Jacob turned his head to look at her, a skeptical expression on his face.

"It stars Alex Pettyfer," Bethany said sweetly, looking

at him from underneath her lashes.

"Chic flick," Cory coughed.

Bethany shot him a sharp, scornful look. Cory smirked back at her.

Jaden shook her head. "Hannah and I can't go. We're leaving this afternoon for Franklin, Tennessee."

Hannah sipped her drink slowly, grateful for a conversation that didn't include her.

"What's in Franklin?" asked Tanner.

"Bill and Lori Hoos, our riding instructors," said Jaden. "We're going to their farm, Wil-lo Blue, for the weekend."

Bethany wrapped her other arm around Jacob, laying her head on his shoulder. "Are we going riding this weekend?" she asked, running her fingers through his hair.

Jacob looked at her, smiled and nodded.

"Hannah—how's that language class going?" Cory asked, looking across the table at her.

"I'm enjoying it."

"What language are you learning now?" questioned Bethany, a thin, unfriendly smile on her lips.

"Greek," replied Hannah.

"How many languages can you speak?" Tanner asked curiously.

"A lot more than I can," Cory admitted with a laugh.

Hannah flushed. "I'm fluent in Hebrew, German, French and Latin."

Tanner raised a dark eyebrow, an intrigued expression on his handsome face and asked, "What do you plan to do with all that?"

"*Michal's* going to be a spy when she grows up," teased Jacob, evident affection in his deep, husky voice.

Hannah rolled her eyes at him and felt herself redden further, her ears burned hot. She saw Bethany glaring at her, her blue eyes cold and hostile.

"I've got to finish my homework," Hannah announced,

standing up. She picked up her tray, looked around the table and said, "Later." As she turned to leave, from the corner of her eye, she saw Bethany pressed against Jacob, scowling at her.

"Bye, Han," Jaden yelled after her.

Jacob glanced at Bethany and said, "I'll see you later." He stood up, his tray in his hand, turned and followed Hannah towards the exit.

Bethany frowned. "Why did Jacob call Hannah . . . Michal?"

"Michal Hannah is her given name," answered Cory and Tanner in unison.

"Why doesn't she go by Michal?" Bethany asked, crossing her arms, her expression sizzling with displeasure.

"When Hannah came to live here, she was teased relentlessly about her name," answered Jaden. "So, she started using her middle name."

"I've never heard Jacob call her Michal?" spat Bethany.

"It goes back to when we were kids. We met Hannah when we were ten, her mother had just died. Her father exiled her to live here," Jaden said, meeting Bethany's gaze, her brilliant green eyes unwavering. "Jacob saw Hannah as an orphaned foal that needed protecting until it was strong enough to run free. So he appointed himself her protector and he stood up to any kid that picked on her."

Jaden smiled at Bethany.

"I remember Jacob being in the principal's office all the time for fighting. It didn't matter the size of the boy— he would take them on. Jacob had a lot of swollen lips and nose bleeds," she said, a note of pride in her voice. "Eventually, everyone got to know Hannah and the teasing stopped." She stood up, and reached for her tray, her eyes fixed on Bethany and said in a confident tone, "But to my brother, Hannah will always be, *Michal,* that vulnerable foal that he needs to protect and take care of."

Bethany bristled, her eyes blazing with acrimony.

Jaden turned and said over her shoulder, "See ya'll later."

———————— ···————————

JADEN, HER HAND OUT THE TRUCK WINDOW, waved. Paige watched until the truck and trailer pulled out of their barn drive, turned right and disappear from view. Returning to the barn, she started leading horses out to the back pasture.

Shiloh and Sophie were the last pair to be lead out. Upon release, the two mares took off at a gallop and disappeared over a hill. Timber, Armani and Maddie, at the water trough, wheeled and followed them, their tails high and flagged. Bandana and Gabriel followed unhurriedly at a walk.

Paige threw extra flakes of hay into Gatsby's stall, locked the tack room door and headed for home. Walking into the house, she found Jacob on the sofa watching ESPN.

"Hi, Mom," he said, not taking his eyes off the television.

"The keys to Hannah's Porsche are right here," Paige said, laying them down on the counter top. "Jacob?"

"What?"

"Promise me that you will drive at a reasonable speed and that you will drive smart," said Paige, her voice taut, her expression firm.

Jacob met her gaze. "I promise."

"What are your plans tonight?"

"I'm going out with Bethany," Jacob said, his gaze returning to the television. "We're going to see a movie."

"Well, I'm going to take a shower," Paige announced and disappeared down the hall. She returned an hour later wearing blue jeans and a tank top underneath a black jacket, her customary ponytail gone, her curly auburn hair flowing freely.

Jacob smiled. "You look nice Mom."

"Thanks," Paige said, kissing the top of his blonde head. "I'm meeting Nancy for dinner." She tapped him on the shoulder. "Jeep keys please."

Jacob dug into his jeans pocket for keys and dropped them into her outstretched hand.

Walking towards the door, Paige said over her shoulder, "Please don't be out late."

ENTERING THE FLATIRON GRILLE Paige spotted Nancy sitting at a table in the bar area.

"Been here long?" she asked, sliding onto a tall chair.

"Nope," Nancy said. "I just sat down."

"I'm glad you suggested this place," said Paige, looking around. "It's chic and comfortable."

A young pretty waitress appeared, took their order and wandered off.

"The food here is fantastic," Nancy promised, looking across the table at Paige. "I didn't think you'd mind but Rebecca is coming."

"No, of course I don't mind," Paige said, her eyes scanning the menu. "It will be good to see her."

Rebecca Martin Newland arrived, slid onto the chair next to her older sister, leaned over and gave her a hug.

Nancy pulled back to look at her, a confused expression on her face. "Your hair wasn't this long when I saw you two days ago," she said, her fingers holding blonde curls.

"They're extensions," Rebecca said proudly, turning her head back and forth swiftly. Long, silky curls swirled around her shoulders. "My friend Winnie who owns Pink Aspen Salon made them for me."

"They look awesome."

"Thanks." Rebecca smiled lovingly at her sister.

The waitress returned with their drinks, took Rebecca's order and disappeared.

Rebecca turned to Paige, smiled and said, "Long time no see."

"I agree," Paige said. "You look blissfully happy."

Rebecca's lips parted in a broad smile, her eyes crinkling.

"I really am," she said candidly. "For the first time in my life, I understand what it feels like to have joy."

"I haven't seen you since you remarried," Paige said and raised her glass. "A much belated congratulations."

Rebecca nodded her head in appreciation. "Thank you."

"What happened to the whole 'I'll never marry again' thing?'"

"Kurt's the right man for me," beamed Rebecca. After a disastrous first marriage to Dr. Andrew Martin, surgeon and son of Joe Martin, Rebecca had been steadfast that she would never again marry. "Joe told me what Matthew gave the twins for their birthday."

Paige stared at her surprised.

"Even though Andrew and I are no longer married, Joe still considers me his daughter-in-law," bragged Rebecca. "We're very close."

"Are things any better with your ex-husband?" Paige asked cautiously.

"I'm afraid not," replied Rebecca, frowning.

Paige looked at her amazed. "Even after all these years?"

"It's been eleven years since they were divorced," Nancy interjected, a hint of indignation in her deep, raspy voice. "Yet, to this day, Andrew continues to tell lies about Rebecca." She stood up and said, "I see Jeff Watson. If you'll excuse me—I need to talk to him." She drifted across the restaurant.

Paige looked at Rebecca, an incredulous expression on

her face. "Why does your ex-husband act like that?" she asked, a note of disgust in her voice.

"Andrew's insecure. He requires everyone's admiration and an overwhelming need for people to like him," Rebecca said simply. "When our marriage fell apart, I believe the reason he demonized me publicly was so people wouldn't look too closely at him and his two failed marriages."

"I didn't know he was married before," said Paige, surprise in her voice.

"The marriage only lasted six months," Rebecca replied. "Andrew prefers that no one know."

"Marriages fail and people get remarried. That kind of thing happens," retorted Paige. "Why all the drama—why just not be honest about it?"

Rebecca shook her head. "Andrew's filled with anger and resentment," she said, her elbow resting on the table, her chin in her hand. "His bitter feelings control him and prompt the hurtful things he does and says."

Rebecca's gaze was steady and unrelenting. "It takes heart and courage to look inward and truly, honestly examine oneself. Trust me—this is something I know," she said with a sarcastic laugh. "I assure you that I didn't want to accept blame and fault for our marriage not working."

Rebecca sighed. "But over the past couple of years, I've worked on humility and what it involves," she said with heart-felt earnestness.

"Andrew needs to get over it and move on," insisted Paige.

"Isn't that a bit hypocritical coming from you?"

Paige prickled, her brown eyes narrowed. *"Excuse me?"*

"Offending you was not my intention," Rebecca implored, her tone genuine. "What I meant was—you've been holding unforgiveness in your heart for seven years."

"That's different," Paige snapped angrily, glaring at Rebecca. "Ron Chatum killed my husband and robbed my children of their father."

The furious expression on Paige's face dissolved and her shoulders relaxed.

"Forgiving someone who has harmed you, caused you pain or betrayed you is challenging," Rebecca said. "Ron Chatum took the love of your life from you. I get that—and you're heartbroken, you're angry and you're hurting."

Paige sighed deeply and looked away from Rebecca's gaze.

"Paige," Rebecca said in a soft voice. "Holding onto unforgiveness in your heart will mess you up spiritually and you'll never know peace or joy. Do yourself a favor and forgive."

"I can't help the way I feel," admitted Paige, looking wretchedly down at her hands in her lap.

"You *can* choose not to feel that way," said Rebecca. "You do realize that your forgiving Ron Chatum helps you—and not him?"

Paige looked uncertainly at her. "What do you mean?"

"Unforgiveness is like a heavy weight you carry around with you every day," said Rebecca. "Do you want to walk around for another seven years feeling like you have for the last seven?"

"No," Paige mumbled, her voice barely audible. "It seems so unfair."

"I agree. It does seem that way." Rebecca shifted, reaching into her purse for a pen. Resting her elbows on the table, the pen in her hand hovering over a cocktail napkin, she fixed her blue eyes on Paige.

"Forgiveness is *required* of Christians," she said in a firm voice, and she began to write. "Read Matthew chapter eighteen, verse thirty-five; Luke chapter eleven, verse four; Ephesians chapter four, verse thirty-two and Colossians chapter three, verse thirteen." She pushed the napkin across the table to Paige.

"Paige, do you believe in God?"

Paige's eyes flicked down and she stared unseeingly at

the napkin on the table. In the years following Robert's murder, her anger had blossomed into rage and resentment, closing her heart to God.

"After Robert died, my faith in God was shattered," she said finally, her voice cracking.

"Bad things happen to good people, Paige. You'll never have the answer to why," Rebecca said simply. "But, you have the power to change your life beginning today. Read the Word. The radical transformation from the opinionated, prideful, highly judgmental person I used to be, to the person I am now, is a result of reading His Word." She smiled warmly.

"I see the twins at church. You should come with them sometime!"

Paige nodded and said slightly stiffly, "I'll think about it."

"Nancy told me that you have added to your petting zoo," teased Rebecca lightheartedly to change the subject.

Paige grinned. "Since the last time I saw you, we've added three new quadrupeds. A cat Jaden named Gizmo, a dog Jacob named Roscoe, and a donkey, I named Gabriel."

Rebecca looked at Paige skeptically. "Is Gabriel really pink?"

"Yes, he's listed as a pink burro on his BLM papers," said Paige. "The way I see it—if the United States Government says he's pink—I can say he's pink."

Rebecca's lips turned up in a smile. "What are you planning on doing with him?"

"What do you mean?"

"Are you going to use Gabriel for anything, like to ride or pull a cart."

Paige laughed, shaking her head, "Oh, no—Gabriel's strictly yard art!"

CHAPTER 9

Robert appeared. He was walking towards her leading a donkey covered in bright, shiny armor.

"Get rid of all bitterness, rage, and anger, Paige," he said, stopping beside her. "Don't look to another source to think right. The Word is alive. Its truth will not pass away. Be steadfast in your belief of the Word, allowing it to dwell in you richly. Joy and peace come through believing." Removing two pieces of armor draped over the donkey's withers, Robert said:

Put on the full armor of God so that you can take your stand against the devil's schemes.

Robert put a belt around her waist and cinched it, then he added a breastplate.

She turned towards him confused and pleaded, "I don't understand?"

Taking her hand in his, he said:

Stand firm then, with the belt of truth buckled around your waist, with the breastplate of righteousness in place and with your feet fitted with the readiness that comes from the gospel of peace.

They walked together down a narrow path, and into a grassy meadow. A magnificent white war horse with a long flowing mane galloped up to them and halted. Attached to the saddle on the horse's back were a glittering helmet and a jeweled sword. Robert put the helmet on her head, then removed the sword, handing it to her. He stared at her intently and said in commanding voice:

And take the helmet of salvation and the sword of the Spirit, which is the word of God.

Robert vaulted up onto the white horse, looked at her, and said in a tender voice:

For the word of God is living and powerful, and sharper than any two-edged sword, piercing even to the division of soul and spirit, and of joints and marrow, and is a discerner of the thoughts and intents of the heart.

And forgive us our sins, for we ourselves also forgive everyone who is indebted to us who has offended us or done us wrong. And bring us not into temptation but rescue us from evil.

Suddenly, there was a great rushing wind. The war horse snorted, his nostrils quivering and he pawed anxiously at the ground. Robert smiled a stunning smile, turned his white horse and galloped off. The donkey, a cross marked on his back and shoulders, trotted after him.

———————•••———————

PAIGE OPEND HER EYES, her room was filled with Sunday morning light. She heard the low purring of a cat and turning her head, she saw Gizmo staring at her, her long, thin tail waving back and forth like a blade of grass in a light breeze.

"You're a strange cat," she whispered. She sat up, wiping the sleep from her eyes. Glancing over at the digital clock on the nightstand, her gaze fell on the book Robert had given her the day the twins were born. Leaning over, she picked it up. The leather was soft and smooth to the touch. She opened the book and started to read.

———————•••———————

PAIGE WAS PREPARING BREAKFAST when she felt Gizmo bump against her leg.

"You want to go out?"

Gizmo barked a meow.

Paige followed the waddling calico cat towards the back door, and found it open. Matthew and Jacob, both dressed head-to-toe in camouflage, were coming through the door.

Matthew stepped aside. "Excuse me Your Royal Highness," he said, sweeping his arm in a mock curtsy to Gizmo.

Gizmo, her head high, her tail up, meowed several times and sauntered past Matthew and out the door.

"We try to get out of her way," Jacob offered, following Matthew in.

"Attitude is in abundance this morning in the Winston animals," Matthew said gruffly. "That donkey of yours sure has his share!"

Paige raised an inquiring eye in their direction. Jacob was the one who answered.

"Gabriel charged Uncle Matt and Joe this morning."

"*He charged*?"

"He practically attacked us," Mathew insisted.

"What were you doing hunting in that pasture," admonished Paige, crossing her arms, scowling at him. "Did you forget that I told you the horses would be out in that pasture through the weekend? Between you and Joe Martin, you have seventeen hundred acres to hunt on and—"

"I honestly forgot," Matthew said brusquely.

"Please, help yourself," Paige said pointing to the stove. She looked at Jacob and asked, "Did Gabriel act out towards you?"

"No." Jacob was standing at the stove filling his plate with eggs, biscuits and bacon. "It was if Gabriel didn't want me anywhere near Uncle Matt or Joe."

Turning, Jacob walked to the table and sat down. Duke and Roscoe followed him, both lying down behind his chair.

"For a little guy, he can be persuasive," said Jacob adamantly.

"What exactly did he do?" Paige asked.

"The first time he charged Matthew and Joe, I was about twenty-five yards away from them," Jacob said. "I started walking in their direction and Gabriel cut me off—like he was trying to herd me away from them. When he realized he couldn't, he charged—"

"With his teeth bared and his ears pinned flat back," added Matthew, looking unhappy.

Paige filled up her plate with food and joined them at the table. "Clearly, Gabriel does not care for you or Joe," she said looking at Matthew.

"Maybe it's that awful after shave you use, Uncle Matt," Jacob teased.

Matthew pretended to be annoyed.

Paige laughed. "Was Joe upset about Gabriel?"

"Not at all," said Matthew, grinning. "He found the little burro entertaining."

Paige reached across the table and patted Matthew's hand. "I guess we could start calling Gabriel number four," she joked.

Matthew chuckled. He was a successful business man but having been married and divorced three times, personal happiness had eluded him and he had on occasion referred to his ex-wives as belonging to the same species as Gabriel.

Jacob put down his fork and reached into his pocket for his beeping mobile phone. He looked at it, and then laid it on the table.

"That blasted thing has been beeping for over an hour," grumbled Matthew. "I don't know why you don't turn it off."

"Is it Bethany?" Paige asked.

Jacob nodded.

"I know you've heard me say this but I think that girl is trouble, Jacob," barked Matthew. "She calls you constantly, practically stalking you with texts and phone calls."

Paige looked at Jacob. He was staring straight ahead, lips pursed and his jaw clenched. She knew he had already heard an earful from Matthew. She quickly changed the subject to Matthew's kitchen renovation.

Jacob stood up and slapped his Uncle on the shoulder. "Thanks for taking me hunting this morning," he said. "I appreciate your including me."

"Anytime son," Matthew said stifling a laugh. "Next time, we'll go somewhere far away from that crazy donkey of your mother's."

"Going to read?" Paige asked Jacob.

Jacob nodded and turning, he walked down the hall with Roscoe on his heels. "Matthew, you worry needlessly about him," Paige admonished affectionately.

"I suppose I do," agree Matthew with a sarcastic huff. "But no high school girlfriend of mine looked like a Victoria Secret model."

"Jacob looks at people inside-out, regardless of how alluring the outside package is. Stop worrying." Paige looked across the table.

"I had dinner Friday night with Nancy and her sister, Rebecca."

Matthew nodded.

"Did you ever meet Joe Martin's wife, Adrianna?" Paige asked.

Matthew shook his head. "No."

"Where was she from?"

"Argentina," said Matthew. "Adrianna Vargas was the only child of a business tycoon from Argentina who was worth something like fifty-two million dollars when he died in 1961."

"Wow! That's a lot of money," cried Paige. "When did Joe and Andrew move here?" She sipped her coffee.

"I think it was sometime in the late seventies."

"How old is Joe?" prodded Paige.

Matthew frowned in contemplation. "I'm not sure—late eighties or early nineties."

"Where was Joe born? Does he have any family?"

"I don't know where he was born and he's never talked about his family," said Matthew, irritation in his voice. "Why all these questions about Joe?"

"Rebecca didn't know how old Joe was or where he was born. I was curious if you did," Paige said simply. She stood up. "I want to tell you about the First Advantage Network."

"Let's go to the office then," suggested Matthew and he pushed back from the table.

CHAPTER 10

I T WAS THE SATURDAY BEFORE Easter and the sun was beginning its descent in the western sky. Paige pulled into the Butler's driveway behind a silver Ford truck and her son's Jeep, parked and got out.

Cory Price and Tanner Chapman climbed out of the cab of the Ford. Jacob jumped out of his Jeep, wearing a blue T-shirt and black shorts, his hair windswept, his eyes hidden behind dark glasses. He started walking brusquely towards the door.

"Where's Bethany?" inquired Paige, falling in behind him.

"Not coming," he said over his shoulder, irritation in his voice, following Cory and Tanner into the Butler's house.

Sheila Butler was working on a new book and had asked for taste testers. Her reading glasses were perched on the bridge of her small nose and she was staring intently at a piece of paper in her hand. She looked at Paige and said in exasperation, "My penmanship is really appalling. I can't make out what I wrote."

Paige grinned.

"Where are Hannah and Jaden?" Jacob asked, looking

around.

"They're upstairs in the media room watching 'Secretariat," Sheila said. She looked at Jacob confused. "Where's Bethany? I thought she was coming?"

Jacob shook his head.

"Well—*she's not*," he said firmly, removing his sunglasses.

Sheila arched her eyebrow and remained silent; her gaze shifted over to Cory and Tanner.

"I hope you boys brought your appetite," she teased.

Tanner grinned. "Yes—ma'am."

Tilting his head slightly to the side, Cory smiled broadly. "When have I ever *not* had an appetite for your cooking, Ms. Sheila?"

Sheila beamed.

"We're going upstairs," Jacob announced. Turning, he strolled from the room with Cory and Tanner behind him.

Sheila shot an incredulous look at Paige and said, "Hannah told me about Gabriel attacking Joe Martin last Wednesday."

"Thankfully, Joe wasn't hurt," said Paige, heaving a deep sigh of relief. She walked to the oversized kitchen island, and sat down.

"Why did Gabriel act out like that?"

"I've *no* idea," said Paige with a mild shrug. "Joe came to the barn looking for Matthew. Gabriel was roaming free in the barn aisle. Joe stopped at Lyre's stall to talk to Jaden and Hannah. Next thing I know, Joe's on the ground and Gabriel is ripping the man's shirt off with his teeth."

"That is odd behavior," stated Sheila.

"*Yeah!*" cried Paige. After a short pause, she said, "When I first saw Joe's arm, I thought Gabriel had bitten through his skin, but it turned out to be a strange looking tattoo. It kinda of shocked me that Joe Martin would have a tattoo!"

"We're all guilty of being young once," laughed Sheila,

peering at Paige over her reading glasses.

"You're right about that," agreed Paige.

The kitchen door opened and a mane of curly brown hair appeared.

"Smells good in here, Ms. Sheila," announced Nancy Laplace, coming in and embracing her.

"Thank you dear."

"How was Australia?" asked Nancy. She walked over and sat down on a stool beside Paige.

"We had a wonderful trip, but it's good to be home," replied Sheila. "I received numerous compliments on the pair of earrings you made me."

"Thanks." Nancy nodded appreciatively. Once in the banking industry, she now designed jewelry using unusual mediums.

"Would you like some of my special tea?" asked Sheila.

"I'd love some, thank you," said Nancy. "How's Arthur?"

Sheila's blue eyes narrowed and she said firmly, "My son is on my *putz* list!"

"Why? What's he done?" asked Nancy.

Sheila handed her a glass. "He's seen Hannah only four times in the last eighteen months."

"There must be something going on that we don't know about," quipped Paige.

"Yeah—Arthur's met someone he's serious about," Nancy said pointedly. She sipped her drink.

"No, it's probably work related," protested Paige. "Arthur's still madly in love with Henda . . . there's no way it's another woman."

Nancy stared disbelievingly at Paige, her eyes wide. "Arthur's a living, breathing, handsome forty-nine year old man whose wife has been dead for seven years. Maybe he's tired of being alone."

"I think Nancy is right," Sheila admitted. "For Hannah's eighteenth birthday in October, I've asked Shawn Wyatt to make a video for her. I want to include her mother's family. I asked Arthur to bring all the pictures with him when he comes to Jackson next month. Instead, he mailed the lot of them." She pointed to a box.

"That arrived today. I have a feeling that means he's not coming," she said, her voice heavy with disappointment.

"May I see them?" asked Paige eagerly.

Sheila nodded.

Paige slid off the stool, walked across the kitchen, picked up the box, and returned to where she was sitting. She laid the box down. The flaps opened easily. Reaching in, she removed a handful of pictures, and placed them down on the kitchen island.

Nancy picked up a picture of four people in bathing suits on a speed boat. She flashed it at Paige and asked, "Is that Hannah's mother?"

Paige glanced at the photograph of herself, Robert, Arthur and a sultry young woman with long dark hair. "Yes."

"Henda was gorgeous," said Nancy.

"She was, indeed," agreed Paige.

"Henda was more than beautiful," Sheila said frankly. "She was kind, witty and incredibly smart. She could speak half a dozen languages."

"Where did they meet?" asked Nancy intrigued.

"They met in Paris and a party," replied Sheila.

Paige picked up a photograph and gasped, her left hand flying to her heart.

"I lost my pictures of this trip," she said, staring at the picture of herself, Robert, Arthur and Henda, all four in formal fox hunting attire, all laughing. It had been taken on a trip to Ireland.

"Take it," insisted Sheila, smiling warmly.

"Thanks," Paige whispered gratefully, her eyes meeting Sheila's.

Paige shuffled through the pictures: Hannah, as a young girl, sitting on a chestnut pony with four white socks; Hannah smiling proudly, holding up a blue ribbon; Hannah with her parents skiing; at the beach; and standing in front of the Eiffel Tower.

"Sheila, where was this taken?"

Sheila peered down her nose at the photo Paige held out and said, "That was taken at the Chateau de Vignon in Grenoble, France."

Paige stared intently at the picture of Hannah standing with her parents and a large group of people in front of a magnificent Baroque structure that looked like a castle. "Who are all those people?"

"That's the Bonet's—Henda's family," answered Sheila.

"Do you know which one is Miriam?" asked Paige.

Sheila's eyes flicked over the photograph.

"That's Miriam," she said, tapping the picture with a manicured nail.

"Wow! Miriam was blonde and blue-eyed," Paige said in astonishment.

"Henda and Miriam were physical opposites. Miriam was a taller version of their mother, Zara," said Sheila. "Henda had the dark hair and eyes of their father, Isaac."

"Who is Miriam?" asked Nancy.

"Miriam Reynolds was Henda's older sister," answered Paige. "Miriam, her husband, Kevin, and their two children, Caleb and Lily, died in an explosion."

"That's horrible!" exclaimed Nancy.

Paige nodded in agreement. She looked at Sheila and asked, "Are Zara and Isaac still alive?"

"Zara died in 1987. I've no idea whether Isaac is alive or dead," confessed Sheila with a shrug. "Arthur refuses to discuss anything about Henda's family."

"Weird," mused Paige.

"I agree," said Sheila.

Nancy reached into the box for more pictures.

"These look old," she said, withdrawing a handful of black and white photographs. She laid them down.

Paige picked up a photograph of an exquisite young woman dressed in formal fox hunting attire, riding sidesaddle on a white horse. She was flanked on one side by two young girls, both on horses. Her mouth dropped open, her eyes wide in stunned amazement.

"Look," she cried, showing Nancy and Sheila the picture.

"That looks like Hannah!" exclaimed Nancy.

Paige read the writing on the back of the photograph.

Angelina, Gabrielle and Zara, 1938

"Who are Angelina and Gabrielle?" she asked, looking at Sheila.

"Zara's older sisters," answered Sheila.

"Wow—the resemblance between Hannah and Angelina is uncanny," Paige said in earnest, staring at the picture.

"How cute!" Nancy raved, handing Paige a picture of three smiling girls in a cart, pulled by a donkey with long, fluffy ears.

Paige laughed and turned the picture over.

Caroline, Chloe and Lydia Bonet, 1940

Jaden, wearing old jean shorts and a T-shirt, her long golden hair cascading down her back, walked into the room.

"When are we eating?" she asked, picking up a picture. She looked at her mother and snorted, "You and Dad look so young!"

"We were," Paige said smiling at her.

"Is that Hannah's mom in the picture with you?" asked Jaden, her green eyes studying the picture intently.

"Yeap," said Paige.

"Jaden, please round everyone up—it's time to eat," instructed Sheila.

SHEILA WAS CLEANING up the kitchen when Jacob

sauntered back into the room and slid onto a stool at the oversized island. He looked around.

"Where's Mom, Nancy and William?"

"Nancy left. Your mom and William are out on the patio having a discussion about Ron Chatum."

Jacob's eyes widened. "Really?" he said.

"Your mom has decided she wants to meet with him."

"When did all this come about?"

Sheila smiled warmly at him. "Let her tell you." Changing the subject, she asked, "So, what did you like best?"

"The crab strudels were my favorite." Jacob leaned forward, his arms on the island. "Do you think Arthur will come home in May?"

Sheila's expression turned sad. "I don't know. I hope so. I really do. I love my son but lately he hasn't been acting like the father I know him to be."

"What do you think is going on?"

"I have a suspicion he has met someone."

Jacob nodded.

"That's what Hannah thinks," he said with a slight nod. "She's afraid that he is going to cancel on her again."

"I know she is," agreed Sheila.

Jacob stared unseeingly at the mahogany-topped kitchen island. After an extended pause, he said. "Tonight, when I went to Bethany's, she told me that her cousin was getting married next weekend and she is expecting me to escort her to the wedding."

Jacob ran a hand through his blonde hair and leaned back.

"She said that if I really cared about her I would skip going to Rolex next weekend and take her to the wedding," he said, clearly aggravated. "This was the first I've heard about her cousin's wedding and she's known about Rolex for weeks."

Sheila didn't say anything.

Jacob continued. "She's always scheming, trying to

talk me into doing what she wants me to do or what she thinks I should do," he said. "And when I don't do what she wants, she gets mad at me and pouts."

"Bethany's a *joy-sucker*," said Jaden, sliding onto the stool next to her brother.

Jacob and Sheila looked at her.

"A joy-sucker?" questioned Sheila with a soft chuckle. "Is this a *Jadenism*?"

Jaden nodded. "Yeah—a joy-sucker is someone that has no joy and so they try to suck it out of those who do. Just like what Bethany's doing to you, Bro!" she said, looking at her brother, her expression hopeful. "Does this mean you're no longer dating Bethany?"

Jacob frowned at his sister. "I didn't know that you disliked her so much."

"I don't dislike her as a person," Jaden insisted. "I just don't think the two of you are a good fit."

Jacob stood up.

"I bet Bethany's already bombarded you with text messages, hasn't she?" said Jaden, staring at her brother. She knew by the look on Jacob's face that she was right. "How many has she sent?"

"Does it matter?" Jacob asked.

"No, but I'm curious," admitted Jaden, grinning.

Jacob shook his head and asked, "Where are Tanner, Cory and Hannah?"

"Upstairs watching *Happy Gilmore*," said Jaden.

Jaden watched her brother leave. Turning back to Sheila, she said through a sigh, "The sooner he breaks up with Bethany the better."

Sheila frowned. "Jaden, you know your brother can handle himself," she said, sliding a crock bowl of chocolate mousse in front of Jaden.

Jaden eyed the mousse hungrily.

"I know Jacob can handle himself. That's not it," she said, taking the spoon Sheila handed her. "Bethany's got a reputation as a mean girl—the kind who, if hurt, will retaliate like a venomous snake."

Jaden ate several spoonfuls of the mousse.

"I see how Hannah looks at Jacob when she thinks no one is watching. I know she's in love with him," she said and laughed. "I know Mom's seen it and I know you've seen it too."

Jaden got off the chair. "How much longer until Bethany sees it—if she hasn't already?"

Not waiting for a response, Jaden picked up the bowl and walked in the direction of the patio doors. Calling over her shoulder, she said, "This is really awesome, Ms. Sheila, thanks."

CHAPTER 11

———————◆•◦•◆———————

T
HE LAST SATURDAY IN APRIL dawned cloudy but without rain. Jaden awoke bright-eyed, excited to be in Lexington, Kentucky for the 2011 Rolex Three Day. Hannah, in the double bed beside her, was still sleeping. She quietly got up, gathered her clothes and stepped into the hotel bathroom. When she emerged from the bathroom thirty minutes later, dressed in blue jeans and T-shirt, Hannah was pouring coffee.

"Morning," Jaden said, staring at the breakfast cart standing in the middle of their room. "When did you order room service?"

Hannah yawned. "Last night, you were already asleep."

Jaden, standing beside the cart, started removing dish covers, revealing a generous amount of food: Eggs Benedict and scrambled eggs, French toast, bacon and biscuits, a large platter of fresh fruit and bagels. She looked at Hannah and said sarcastically, "I don't think you ordered enough food."

"I ordered what I thought would be enough for *all* of us," Hannah said plainly.

Jaden picked up a plate and filled it with bacon and

eggs, a biscuit and some fruit. "How long will it take you to get ready?"

Hannah shrugged. "Not long."

"I want to be on that cross country course before the first horse goes," said Jaden, sinking down into the chair next to Hannah.

"Do you think the guys are up?"

Jaden glanced around at the bedside clock. "I know Jacob is up. He'll be reading."

"I tried calling their room but the line was busy," said Hannah, sipping her coffee.

"Jacob's probably got it off the hook," Jaden said. "Did you try texting?"

Hannah nodded. "I did," she said, alighting from the chair. "I'm going to shower."

"I'll go check on them," announced Jaden, putting her plate down. She jumped to her feet and marched for the door.

Jacob's room was on the other side of the Griffin Gate Marriott and when Jaden arrived, she found the door was ajar. She rapped quickly, pushed the door open.

"Hi," she said, walking into the room.

The television was on ESPN.

Dillon Tull, his thick dark brown hair in slight disarray was slouched comfortably in a club chair,

"Morning," he said, a broad smile on his handsome face.

"Morning," added Jacob, without looking up from the book he was reading. Cory Price, stretched out on the bed, asked, "Is Hannah up and dressed too?"

"She was getting ready when I left," answered Jaden.

"Let's go eat. I'm starving," said Cory and in one fluid movement, he was up and on his feet. Jaden's emerald eyes widened, her mouth dropped at the change in Cory's body since the previous summer. He was taller, his shoulders broader. His dark ebony skin was smooth, his muscles

93

chiseled and well-defined.

"Jaden, are you going with us?" Cory asked, pulling a T-shirt over his head.

Jaden felt her brother's eyes and glancing at him, saw him smirking at her. "Mmm . . . no . . . thanks," she stammered. "Hannah ordered room service."

"Enough for us?" Dillon asked.

"There's plenty for everyone—come to our room," Jaden said turning on her heel. "Do you remember the room number?" she asked, not waiting for an answer, pulling the door closed behind her.

———————————

TRAFFIC INTO THE KENTUCKY HORSE PARK was heavy but organized. After finding a place to park, they walked the distance to the entrance, stood in line, presented their tickets and they were at jump number eighteen before any horse and rider had yet come through.

Jacob pointed to the jump complex before them.

"This combination is The Head of The Lake," he said to Cory and Dillon who both stood staring, wide eyed, at the multipart combination of obstacles.

"I never imagined the scale of these jumps," exclaimed Dillon.

"It was purposely designed to be daunting," said Jaden. "In the sport of Three Day Eventing, the Cross Country phase, what we're seeing today . . ."

"Tests the bravery of the horse and rider, as well as their physical fitness," interrupted Cory, reading from the program.

Jaden smiled at him. "Yes."

The audible excitement of the large crowed was heard—a horse and rider were approaching. The pair jumped over the first obstacle, a high brush, and dropped down six feet into water. The horse splashed through the lake to the second jump, a huge, solid obstacle in the shape of a frog, jumped over it, galloped a left bending line, clearing two jumps, both in the shape of ducks. As the horse and rider galloped out of the lake and away, there was a roar and a thundering applause from the crowd for a fine ride.

Cory turned to Jaden, a look of admiration on his face. "When you ride Rolex Three Day, I want to groom for you!"

"Cool, isn't it," agreed Jaden, practically bouncing, a euphoric smile on her pretty face. "I've got goose bumps," she said, glancing down at her arms.

They watched five other pairs come through the Head of the Lake complex before heading on to jump twenty-one, the Stepped Table.

At jump twenty-two, the Normandy Bank, they watched a horse and rider approach, jump up the bank and over a large log rail, take four strides to a narrow corner brush, jump it cleanly and gallop on.

Jacob and Hannah were walking slowly, falling behind the others.

"Jaden loves this," Jacob said affectionately, indicating with a slight nod towards his sister. She was busy explaining to Cory and Dillon why accuracy to the corner brush jump was critical.

Jacob shot a curious look at Hannah. "Do you want to ride Rolex?"

"Maybe," replied Hannah with a dismissive shrug. "Cory and Dillon seem to be enjoying this."

"I think they are." Jacob laughed and said through a smile, "I caught Jaden checking Cory out this morning."

"I can see that," admitted Hannah with a nod. "They're great friends, Cory has the qualities Jaden likes and—"

"He *rides*," said Jacob. "My sister would never be interested in someone who wasn't into horses!"

"That's for sure!"

Jacob and Hannah watched another horse and rider

clear the Normandy Bank and gallop on towards jump twenty-three. Hannah could tell by his facial expression and the set of his jaw that he was preoccupied about something. They walked along in comfortable silence, each occasionally glancing at the other.

Finally, Jacob said, his voice low, "I broke it off with Bethany."

Hannah felt elation flood through her, and immediately felt guilty for feeling happy about the news. "When?" she asked, keeping her eyes on the ground, afraid he would see the relief she felt.

"Thursday—after school." Jacob looked down, and then glanced up at Hannah. "Bethany went ballistic when I told her I wasn't into her. She kept insisting that she was in love with me. She said I had hurt her and she threatened to get even with me."

"Oh, Jacob, I'm sorry," said Hannah softly, hoping her voice sounded even.

Jacob shrugged and turned to watch a horse and rider navigate the longer alternative route of jump twenty-six, the Offset Brushes.

"How about lunch?" suggested Cory, coming up to stand beside Jacob and Hannah.

"I'm up for lunch," agreed Jacob happily.

———·•·———

ARRIVING AT THE FOOD COURT forty minutes later, Dillon and Cory were overjoyed by the huge selection of food vendors. The five of them strolled casually through the food court examining the wide variety of choices.

Jaden pointed in the direction of a low, grassy hill. "We always eat over there," she said. "I know what I'm getting—see you on the hill."

Hannah and Jacob wanted the same thing and wandered

off together, leaving Dillon and Cory where they stood undecided.

Dropping down on the grass ten minutes later Dillon asked, "Where's Cory?"

Jaden looked around and shrugged. "Don't know. You were the one with him."

"He mumbled something and then walked off in that direction," Dillon said, pointing at an enormous building.

"I'll text him." Hannah reached into the beige backpack sitting on the ground beside her, and pulled out her iPhone and typed.

Where r you?
12:30PM, Apr 30

Her cell phone beeped. She read the text out loud.

Alltech arena watching reining
12:32PM, Apr 30

Jacob's head snapped around.

"I forgot about the Reining Freestyle being today," he said, evident excitement in his voice. "With a twenty-five thousand dollar purse, there will be competitors from all over."

"Text him and tell him I'm on my way," Jacob said to Hannah, jumping to his feet. Carrying his lunch with him, he hurried off in the direction of the arena.

Hannah typed.

On r way
12:34PM, Apr 30

Hannah pulled off her sweatshirt, rolled it up and stuffed it down into the backpack.

"Want me to carry the backpack?" asked Jaden.

Hannah shook her head and rose to her feet. "You carried it all morning. I've got it," she said, slinging the pack over her left shoulder. She followed Jaden and Dillon down the hill.

Passing through the trade fair, Hannah spotted the familiar colors of a vendor she favored.

"I'll catch up with ya'll later," she yelled, heading for the Bit-of-Britain tent.

WALKING OUT OF THE SMALL CHANGING CUBICLE an hour later, wearing a pair of black Pikeur breeches, Hannah was startled by Jacob's voice.

"Those look good on you, Michal," said Jacob appraisingly.

Turning around, Hannah saw him leaning against a post, his arms crossed, smiling his drop-dead crooked smile. She felt her heart swell with joy and her cheeks turn pink.

"Thanks," she said shyly trying not to sound pleased. "What are you doing here?"

"Looking for you," Jacob said, taking a step towards her.

Hannah felt her heart hammering, her pulse was racing. "*Me*?"

"You have the backpack," said Jacob, indicating the balled up hoodie that he had under his arm. "Where is it?"

Hannah looked away hurriedly to hide her disappointment. "It's in there," she said, pointing towards the curtained cubicle behind her. "Where is everybody?"

"Somewhere out on the course," answered Jacob.

Hannah returned to the cubicle and changed out of the breeches and back into her jeans. Pushing the curtain aside, she strolled out with the breeches draped over her arm, carrying the beige backpack.

"How did you know where to find me?"

"It wasn't that hard," Jacob said, following her to the check-out table.

Reaching into the front pocket of her jeans, Hannah took out a credit card, and gave it and the breeches to the check-out girl. She looked at Jacob, smiled and asked, "Am I that predictable?"

Jacob shook his head. "Not at all, but I do know your taste when it comes to anything horse related."

"Thank you for shopping with us. Please come back," said the pretty twenty-something girl, smiling invitingly at Jacob as she handed the plastic bag to Hannah.

Jacob, completely unaware of the girl staring at him, his eyes on Hannah, reached out and took the backpack from her.

"Next vendor?"

Hannah smiled crookedly at him and said, "I thought you hated shopping?"

"I do." Jacob grinned, taking the plastic bag from her. He jammed it down into the backpack, and slung it over his shoulder.

Together they strolled out of Bit-of-Britain and into the sunshine, the blue sky above crystal clear.

"Let's walk the first half of the course," suggested Hannah.

"Okay," agreed Jacob.

They walked along casually in comfortable silence, watching all the activity around them.

"You could ride at this level," said Hannah, with a wave of her hand, breaking the silence.

"I don't have the desire to put the hard work in, especially on Dressage," said Jacob. "Anyway, I'm planning on going to Montana State."

"Why?"

"Because it's in Bozeman," Jacob said simply.

"You really love it out there don't you?"

"I do," replied Jacob, his lips curling into a smile. "Explaining Montana to someone who has never been there is difficult—it has to be experienced. To me, Montana is God's cathedral on this enormous scale."

In one spiraling moment, a heavy sadness hit Hannah— after graduation next year, their futures would be going in different directions

Jacob stopped walking and was staring intently at her. "What's wrong?"

Hannah's head snapped up. She forced a smile and said quietly, "Nothing."

Jacob resumed walking. "When I asked you if you wanted to ride Kentucky Rolex, you said maybe. What did you mean?"

"I love this sport but riding at the four-star level takes hard work and a lot of time," replied Hannah, pausing, "And there are things I want to do."

Jacob glanced over. "Such as?"

"I want to find my mom's family."

"What family? I thought everyone was dead," said Jacob, regarding her closely.

"My Aunt Miriam and my grandmother are dead. I'm assuming my grandfather, Isaac, is dead," said Hannah, sadness in her voice. "Grundy and I were close and if he were alive, I'd have heard from him." She smiled.

"I'm referring to my mom's seventeen cousins," she said simply. "My grandmother, Zara, had four sisters."

Jacob's eyes widened. "That's a big family."

"When I was little, we had these family gatherings at my grandmother's childhood home in Grenoble, France. My great Aunts would tell stories about life during World War II. My grandmother and her two older sisters, Angelina and Gabrielle, were with the French Resistance," Hannah said, a soft wistful smile on her lips. "I wish I'd known my grandmother."

"I bet she was pretty like you."

"Thank you," Hannah said shyly, the color rising in her cheeks. "Actually, my Grandfather always told me that I resembled my grandmother's oldest sister, Angelina Bonet. My grandmother, Zara, was a blue-eyed blonde."

They walked in silence. When Jacob finally did speak, his voice was gentle. "I've been thinking about that dream you had—of the man who cried tears of blood." He stopped walking, his eyes meeting hers.

"Maybe riding the motorcycle activated something in your sub-conscious," he said, lifting his hand to her face. "Maybe your brain is remembering something about the person who removed you from the car before it burned."

"It's so frustrating not being able to remember!"

"Maybe you're not supposed to remember," said Jacob, his fingers tenderly stroked her cheek. "All that matters is that *someone* saved you."

Jacob's touch ignited a euphoric assault on every nerve in her body. Hannah looked quickly away, afraid her eyes would betray her burning desire for his touch. Glancing around, she was startled to see they were standing at jump number thirteen, The Land Rover Hollow.

"Here comes a horse," a man in the crowd yelled.

Jacob and Hannah turned to watch the approaching horse and rider. The pair jumped the large log leading into the hollow easily. As the horse approached the second jump in the combination, a narrow four-foot-nine brush, it stepped sideways, missing the jump all together, but not losing a stride.

"Was that a run out?" Hannah asked, looking at Jacob.

Jacob was about to say something when they heard a familiar deep voice, calling their names. Turning, they saw Dillon, followed by Jaden and Cory, striding towards them.

"We've been wondering where you two were," said Dillon, stopping in front of them.

"There about a dozen riders left," Jaden said. "I think we should head back to jump eighteen. Then we're not far from where we parked."

Jacob nodded. "Sounds like a plan."

Together they walked in the direction of the Head of the Lake water complex to watch the last of the riders.

CHAPTER 12

O N THE FIRST MONDAY IN May, after a night of
thunderstorms, Paige returned to the house from
feeding the horses and was surprised to see Jaden,
up and dressed, sitting on the sofa next to her brother.

"You're up early," she said to her daughter.

Jaden looked up. "I've got a quiz today."

Paige was pouring a cup of coffee when her phone
rang. Answering it, she heard the anxious voice of Sheila
Butler. "Is Hannah there?"

"She's not here, Sheila," Paige said. "Why, what's
wrong?"

"Arthur called this morning to say he wouldn't be coming
for a visit," Sheila said rapidly. "Hannah was so angry that
she threw her phone across the room and stormed out of
the house."

"Sheila, let me talk to the twins and I'll call you back
shortly," Paige said disconnecting. Turning to the two
worried faces staring at her she said, "Arthur cancelled—
Hannah has run off."

"That ...," began Jaden.

"Don't say it, Jaden," Paige admonished softly.

Jaden crossed her arms, her green eyes blazing and muttered under her breath, "Well, he is,"

"Do you think Hannah went to the barn?" Paige asked.

Jaden nodded decisively. "I would bet on it."

"I agree," added Jacob.

"Should we go look for her?" Jaden asked, stuffing her books into her backpack.

Paige sipped her coffee and thought a moment. "Jacob, do you have anything major going on at school today?"

"No."

Paige looked at Jaden and said firmly, "You have a quiz today so you are going." Turning to Jacob she said, "You and I will go the barn and look for Hannah. I'll take you to school after we find her."

Jaden frowned, her eyes radiating with displeasure.

"Alright," she grumbled. Rising from the sofa she caught the keys Jacob tossed her, slung her backpack over her shoulder, and headed for the door.

ARRIVING AT THE BARN fifteen minutes later, Paige and Jacob were both relieved to see Hannah's car. Jacob was out of the truck before Paige had come to a complete stop. Paige jumped out of the truck, lowered the tail gate for Duke and Roscoe and followed her dogs into the barn.

Jacob was standing at the tack room door. "Black Tie's stall is empty and Hannah's cross country saddle is gone." He pulled his iPhone from his pocket and announced, "I'll call Sheila and let her know."

Paige felt something soft and velvety brush against her arm and turning, she saw Gabriel.

"Hi, buddy. I must have forgotten to clip your stall guard this morning," she said, scratching one of his favorite spots on his shoulder. His long, fluffy ears relaxed.

"Talking to the donkey?" asked Jacob, returning his phone to his pocket.

"I am. He's a good listener," replied Paige, kissing the burro on his head. She turned to Jacob and said, "Time to get you to school."

Jacob shook his head. "I prefer to wait for Hannah's return," he said firmly.

"Let's start stalls then," suggested Paige.

"Do you want me to turn Gabriel out in the pasture?"

"No, he's fine."

Gabriel stood in the aisle and watched them and receiving no further scratches or carrots, he turned and walked away.

Paige and Jacob were working on the last stall when they heard the sound of horse's hooves on cement. A riderless Black Tie was coming up the barn aisle. The bay thoroughbred appeared unharmed and stood quietly as Paige examined him.

"I'll get two horses tacked up," Jacob said anxiously, his voice ringing with unease.

"Okay." Paige began removing Black Tie's tack.

Fifteen minutes later Jacob led Timber out of the barn and grabbing the horn of the western saddle, swung himself up and onto the big gray horse.

Paige followed him out. "What's your plan," she asked, leading Bandana to the mounting block.

"You go north and I'll go southwest towards Joe's place." Jacob picked up the reins, called Roscoe and turning Timber, trotted off.

AFTER TWO HOURS of riding the hilly, wooded trails, in search of Hannah, Paige returned Bandana to the barn. The seventeen-year-old gelding was tired and she needed a fresh horse. There was no sign of Hannah and her alarm was escalating. She cinched the girth and gave Sophie a light pat on the neck. She glanced up and saw Sheila Butler striding purposefully up the barn aisle—worry etched clearly on her face.

"I've got the poster Jacob asked me to bring." She waved a large rolled piece of paper in her hand. "Jacob called me and told me where to find it."

Paige pulled a halter over Sophie's bridle.

"Good thinking—I'd forgotten about that poster," she said leading the Paint mare to her stall. Matthew had an aerial photograph of his farm blown up into a sixteen-by-twenty inch poster. The aerial picture included Joe Martin's farm. "I brought coffee," Sheila said, holding up a thermos.

"Thanks."

"Jacob said you've searched everywhere on this farm."

Paige nodded. "Jacob wants to look over at Joe Martin's."

"Where is Jacob?" questioned Sheila, looking around for him.

"He's on his way back. Timber threw a shoe."

Seconds later, they heard hooves on cement. Paige looked down the aisle, and saw Jacob, his brow creased, unmistakable distress in his eyes, leading the big gray horse.

"Who do you want me to put your western saddle on?" she asked, stepping forward. She took the reins from him.

"Armani." Jacob stepped into the tack room.

"Thanks," he murmured, taking the poster from Sheila. He unrolled it on the countertop, and stared with intensity at the poster. Leaning forward, he plucked a pen from a container and started methodically marking points on the map.

"I've got Sophie and Armani ready to go," said Paige, coming into the tack room. She gave his arm a concerned squeeze.

"Jaden's on the way with Cory and Sheila's going to take the gator. Show us where you want to look next." She looked down at the poster.

"I think we should start here at Joe's and then slowly move in this direction." Jacob moved his finger across the poster from one spot to the other.

"Sheila, take this path to this old dirt road," he said in a direct manner, using the pen as a pointer. "We will rendezvous at this spot in an hour."

"At the old barn by the three meadows?" asked Paige.

Jacob straightened. "Yes," he said, nodding his head decisively. Glancing at Sheila he asked, "Got your cell phone?"

Sheila patted her backside. "In my jeans."

"Let's roll," said Jacob, striding purposely out of the tack room.

Paige and Sheila followed him out.

Leading Armani and Sophie out of the barn, they saw Jaden, accompanied by Cory Price.

"Anything new?" cried Jaden anxiously.

"Afraid not," said Paige softly. "We'll find her."

Not willing to wait, Jacob vaulted up into the saddle. "I'm going to find Hannah," he said determinedly. Wheeling the bay horse around, he cantered off, Roscoe lumbering after him.

Paige lead Sophie to the mounting block and said to Jaden, "I turned Bandana and Timber back out," Glancing around at Sheila, she said, "Please show them on the poster the area that Jacob wants searched."

AN HOUR LATER Paige arrived first at the rendezvous spot. She was walking Sophie in large circles on a long rein when she heard a piercing whistle. Looking up, she saw Jacob and Armani cantering across a grassy meadow. He waved, motioning for her to follow him. Paige gathered up the reins, and pressed Sophie into a canter.

Jacob was already a good distance ahead of her when he topped a hill and disappeared from sight. Cresting the hill, Paige was shocked to see Gabriel. The little pink burro was grazing several feet away from where Jacob had just dismounted. Drawing closer, Paige could see Jacob, on his knees, leaning forward staring downward.

"Is Hannah down there?" she yelled nervously.

Jacob didn't look around.

"*Yes!*" he shouted, fear ringing in his deep voice.

CHAPTER 13

H ANNAH, 7-FEET DOWN, WAS SITTING on the ground, covered in layers of rust-colored mud, her knees pulled in close to her body, her arms wrapped around her legs. She looked up see Jacob on his knees leaning over the opening, his face plastered with panic.

"Are you hurt?" he questioned, his eyes wide with alarm.

"No," answered Hannah, her voice barely audible. A choking sense of relief exploded in her heart and she felt tears pool in her eyes.

"Mom—call Sheila and tell her where she can find the winch strap and clean towels," ordered Jacob not taking his eyes off of Hannah. He jumped into the funnel-shaped, tractor-size sinkhole, nimbly landing on his feet, his boots disappearing beneath thick squishy mud. He knelt down beside Hannah, his eyes hurriedly scanning over her body.

"I was crazy with worry when I couldn't find you," he confessed, his hands moving across her shoulders and down her arms, his fingers gently probing, examining her.

"I tried climbing out, Jacob, but the walls are soft and I kept slipping backwards," Hannah wailed, tears trickling down her mud-smeared cheeks. "This hole is like a cold, muddy grave!"

"Shush . . . I'm going to get you out," whispered Jacob tenderly wiping her tears with his fingers.

"When I saw Gabriel looking down at me," sniffed Hannah, meeting his gaze.

"I knew you'd eventually find me."

"I never saw Gabriel leave the barn," murmured Jacob, helping Hannah to her feet. He pushed a dangling strand of her dirt-caked hair behind her ears.

Hannah glanced at him, frowning. "How did you know to—"

"Roscoe did that funny hoppy thing he does when he picks up a scent, he took off and I followed him here." Jacob snaked his arm around Hannah, crushing her to him. "Ready to get out of here mud-bunny?" he said smiling a lopsided smile.

SHEILA THREW HER arms around Hannah, holding her tightly.

"It's a blessing that you're alright," she whispered, stroking Hannah's mud caked head.

Sheila released Hannah, her gaze shifted to Jacob. "Thank you, Jacob, for finding her."

"I didn't find her," Jacob admitted, nodding towards the burro. "Gabriel did."

Sheila glared at Jacob in frowning disbelief, and then she looked at Hannah questioningly.

"Gram, can we go please." Hannah tugged at her grandmother's elbow and said in a rush, "I'm cold. I have a headache and I want to go home."

Jacob picked Hannah's helmet up, and followed her to the gator, dropping it into the back. He grabbed a towel and stepped to Hannah.

"See you back at the barn," he murmured, wrapping the towel around her shoulders, his eyes glowing with tenderness.

"See you."Hannah swallowed, thankful for the dirt covering her face and turned quickly away from his intense gaze, dropping into the passenger seat.

Sheila climbed into the driver's seat, and started the gator and the gator lurched forward.

"Gabriel must have followed you," Sheila stated simply.

"Not possible. When I left the barn, he was in his stall," insisted Hannah. She looked around and saw Jacob vault up onto Armani. He waved, turned and trotted after Paige heading in the direction of the woods.

"Is it possible that Gabriel picked up your scent?"

"He's a donkey, Gram, not a blood-hound!"

"Maybe an Angel steered him," suggested Sheila, casting a sideways glance at Hannah.

"I seriously doubt an Angel guided Gabriel to the sinkhole," murmured Hannah sarcastically with a disbelieving shake of her head.

"Well then, explain how Gabriel found you when you were miles from the barn in a sinkhole 7-feet beneath the earth?"

"I don't know" said Hannah decisively. She pulled her feet up, and shrunk down into the seat.

"Gram, I'm sorry I stormed out like that and caused you to worry," she said apologetically. "I was furious about Dad!"

Sheila reached over and gave her arm a light pat but didn't say anything.

After a long silence, Hannah said without looking at her grandmother, "Did Dad tell you that he is getting re-married? And the wedding is in a couple of weeks?"

"Yes, he did," said Sheila, taking Hannah's hand. "He called back after you left the house."

"I don't want to go to this wedding by myself," Hannah blurted, her voice highly agitated. "Meeting this—"

"You won't be alone," said her grandmother reassuringly. She gave Hannah's hand a firm squeeze. "Your grandfather and I will be with you."

Hannah smiled at her gratefully. "I'm glad you and Grandpa are going. This is going to be hard for me."

"I know it is and you're going to handle it with grace," said Sheila, giving Hannah's hand another loving squeeze.

"I didn't give Dad the chance to tell me anything. What's the name of the woman he's marrying?"

"Her name is Diana Wakefield Grant."

"Please tell me she's not young!"

"She's forty-eight," said Sheila.

Hannah sighed in relief. "Good—she's old."

"Forty-eight is not old!" protested Sheila

"It's old to me!"

Sheila smiled at her and then laughed. "At seventeen, I suppose it is."

"When is the wedding?"

"The second weekend in June."

"In London?"

Sheila shook her head. "The wedding's going to be in Italy. It sounds like it will be lovely. Diana—"

"You've spoken with her?"

Sheila nodded. "I did," she said warmly "She seemed charming and genuinely concerned about your feelings."

Hannah, her expression shifting from annoyance to dismay, stared at her grandmother. "Does she have children?"

"She has three children. Tristan, the oldest, is twenty-two," Sheila said. "The second son, Edmund, is sixteen and Maria is thirteen."

Hannah looked away quickly. The news stung, wounding her and she felt her eyes filling with hot tears.

"If he wants a new family, then he should have one,"

she screamed angrily. "I refuse to go to his wedding." She briskly wiped away a tear.

Sheila hit the brakes and the gator jerked to a stop. She turned towards Hannah, her expression stern, her blue eyes glaring.

"Your father has acted badly, yes, and he has hurt you. You are very angry at him. I get that," she said firmly. "But you're not going to wallow in self-pity and act badly yourself. You're going to this wedding. *Do you understand me!*"

Hannah, shocked by her grandmother's reaction, nodded in acceptance.

Sheila's expression softened immediately. "It's important you learn, *now*, not to be ruled by your feelings—turn this into something fun."

"What do you mean?"

Sheila put her foot on the gas pedal and the gator lurched forward. "Invite Jaden to come with us."

"That's a fantastic idea, Gram!" Hannah cried happily, her large expressive brown eyes sparkling with enthusiasm.

"I'll see to it that your father picks up the expenses," assured Sheila, chuckling with satisfaction.

"Gram, when I was in the sinkhole, I was praying," confessed Hannah, her voice low. "I felt this strange presence and I opened my eyes, looked up and saw Gabriel. He was staring at me—as if he was telling me he would watch over me, guarding me until I was found."

Sheila smiled. "God works in unconventional ways."

"Donkey's must be special," said Hannah. "In the Bible, a donkey is the only animal Jesus rode."

CHAPTER 14

THOUGHTS OF THE IMPENDING TRIP to Italy kept Jaden from sleeping soundly and in the morning she growled at Jacob when he shook her awake. By the time she stumbled downstairs, it was too late for breakfast.

"Where's Mom?"

"She and William left early this morning for the prison," said Jacob, walking towards the door. "Your backpack is in the Jeep—let's go!"

"What's your rush?" muttered Jaden, following him out the door.

"I don't want to be late," Jacob said brusquely. He opened the Jeep door and jumped in.

Jaden, in the passenger seat, fastened her seat belt. She turned on the radio and hearing the song, "Good Life" by One Republic, cranked up the volume.

After the song ended, Jacob threw a curious, sideways glance at his sister and asked, "What are you so keyed up about?"

"Arthur's getting married in June in Italy and I'm going with Hannah, Sheila and William to the wedding,"

Jaden blurted out breathlessly, her eyes sparkling with excitement.

Seeming to forget the road for a moment, Jacob asked, "When did all this happen?"

"Last night," Jaden gushed. "I've already started my packing list and—"

"*Jaden*" said Jacob, impatience in his voice. "I was referring to Arthur. When did he get engaged? Who is he marrying? What's her name?"

"Oh—I don't know that."

Jacob shook his head in frustration. After a long silence, he added, "I'm glad you're going. This is going to be hard for Hannah."

"It is," said Jaden, nodding in agreement. She studied her brother. She knew by the intensity in his eyes and the tightness of his jaw that he was troubled.

"What's bothering you this morning?"

Jacob frowned. "I found out that Bethany's saying nasty things about Hannah."

"Such as?"

"Don't go ballistic," insisted Jacob, his deep voice serious.

"I won't go ballistic," argued Jaden.

Jacob shot her a quick, knowing look.

"I won't go ballistic," Jaden repeated with a smile.

"Bethany called Hannah a gutter-slut and—"

"WHAT!" Jaden yelled. "*Wait until I—*"

"Let me handle it, Jaden," demanded Jacob in a commanding tone.

Jaden's eyes blazed with anger. "When do you plan to confront Bethany?"

"Sometime today."

"How did you find out about this?"

"Cory told me yesterday," replied Jacob. "I made some calls last night for confirmation."

Jaden turned to her brother anxiously. "Does Hannah

know?"

"I don't know. I haven't talked to her." Jacob glanced over at Jaden, his expression stern and said, "Give me your word that you'll stay out of this and let me handle it."

Jaden grabbed Jacob's pinkie finger and intertwined it with hers. "I pinkie-swear that I'll stay out of it," she said in a firm, level voice.

JADEN WALKED OUT of the cafeteria lunch line and looked around. Spotting Dillon, Tanner, and Cory she headed in their direction.

"Why are you way over here?" she asked sitting down across from them.

Tanner pointed. "For the view."

Jaden looked in the direction he indicated. Bethany was sitting at a table filled with her posse of friends.

Jacob slid into a chair between his sister and Tanner. "Where's Hannah?"

"She's in the library finishing an assignment that was due yesterday," answered Cory.

"Does she know what Bethany's been saying?" asked Dillon.

Cory nodded. "She knows. She overheard some people whispering about it this morning."

Jaden turned to her brother, her eyes flashing fiercely. "When are you going to go talk to that *witch*?"

"After I have something to eat," answered Jacob, mild irritation in his deep voice.

Jaden sat back in her chair, crossed her arms, clenching her jaw against all the things she wanted to say. She watched her brother eat unhurriedly. Finished, Jacob pushed his chair back unceremoniously, stood up and walked calmly in the direction of the table where Bethany sat with her friends. A hushed silence seemed to follow as he passed tables.

Bethany had her back to Jacob and was visibly distressed to find him standing beside her. Her body stiffened noticeably and her face reddened. Jacob was speaking when she stood abruptly and stomped gruffly off towards the door. Jacob, an unreadable expression on his face, strolled casually after her out of the cafeteria.

ARRIVING HOME AFTER school, Hannah opened the kitchen door and smelled the sweet scent of freshly baked bread and pastries. Her grandmother was moving busily around the kitchen. Sheila smiled lovingly and said, "I've made Pain au chocalot and Angel wings."

"Pain au chocalot," Hannah said, dropping her backpack to the floor.

"Jack Cotic from Humboldt Chrysler, Dodge, Jeep called this morning. He said your truck is in," said Sheila, placing the sweet roll down before Hannah.

Hannah tore the layered dough pastry apart, plucking a piece into her mouth, chewing slowly. She had no appetite.

"How was school today?" asked Sheila.

"Fine," muttered Hannah, her voice faint.

"What's wrong? I can tell that something is bothering you," said Sheila, concern in her voice.

"I don't want to talk about it right now, Gram." Hannah met her gaze, her eyes imploring. "Maybe later."

Sheila nodded.

Hannah picked up her backpack, announcing over her shoulder, "I'm going to change clothes."

HANNAH WALKED OUT THE kitchen door towards her car. At the sound of an approaching vehicle, she looked up and saw a Jeep coming towards her. It stopped and Jaden jumped out of the driver's side. Eyeing Hannah, she said teasingly, "You're not dressed for the barn."

"I'm on my way to Humboldt to pick up my new truck."

Jacob emerged from the passenger side. He was dressed in faded, worn jeans and a dark gray shirt that clung to his frame, his eyes concealed behind dark Ray-Bans.

"Can I come?" he asked, striding purposefully towards her, smiling a shockingly tempting smile.

Hannah felt her heart leap wildly. Jacob stopped before her. She dangled the keys to her Porsche in front of him, hoping he wouldn't notice her hand shaking. "Want to drive?"

Jacob grinned sideways and took the keys from her.

Jaden turned on her heel, and climbed back into the Jeep. "You two have fun," she yelled before pulling out of the driveway.

Jacob started the Porsche and glanced over at Hannah. "I looked for you after school."

"I didn't go back to my locker."

Jacob shifted the Porsche into reverse. "What are you getting?"

"I ordered a thirty-five hundred Longhorn Mega cab," replied Hannah.

"Sweet." Jacob pulled out of the driveway and onto the street.

Recognizing a Carrie Underwood song, Hannah turned up the volume. They rode together in silence.

After several miles, Jacob said, "I talked to Bethany today."

Hannah scowled. "What did you say to her?"

"A lot of things—*trust me!*" Jacob said sincerely.

Hannah could tell by his facial expression and the look in his eyes that he wasn't going to explain further.

"Michal, don't let Bethany get to you. You are so much better than that," Jacob said, giving her a quick look.

"I'm trying not to, Jacob," answered Hannah, in a faltering voice. "I really am, but what she said about me was spiteful and hurtful."

Jacob clicked on the turn signal and pulled into A&P Market's parking lot. He put the car in park, removed his sunglasses, turned and looked at Hannah, and said in a gentle voice, "Don't let it get to you."

Hannah glared at him.

"Bethany smeared my reputation, Jacob," she yelled furiously, her face reddening as hot unwelcome tears pooled in her brown eyes. "She called me a gutter-slut and told everyone that I slept with you at Rolex!"

"I know you're angry and you're hurting. You've had a rough week—learning you're dad is getting married and now these vicious rumors" said Jacob softly. "But don't let this define you."

Hannah felt her emotions brim over and tears streamed down her cheeks.

Jacob twisted in his car seat, reached over and put his arms around Hannah pulling her close.

Hannah pushed back from Jacob.

"What if people believe her?" she cried heatedly.

Jacob, his expression soft and tender, gently brushed away her tears with his fingers.

"Anyone who knows you, knows that what Bethany said isn't true," he said softly. "People are going to think whatever they want—you can't change that."

"Why would Bethany do this?" said Hannah, her voice raw. "I thought she and I were friends."

Jacob shrugged. "Trying to answer why another person does something is impossible," he said simply. "Add it to your 'I don't Understand' file."

"I know you're right, Jacob," mumbled Hannah through clenched teeth.

Raising his left hand, Jacob tenderly caressed her cheek. "Feel better now?" he asked sweetly.

"I suppose," said Hannah half-heartedly.

Jacob shifted the Porsche into drive and pulled onto the highway.

"Let's talk about your trip to Italy," suggested Jacob, his lips parting in an infectious crooked smile. "Jaden is really excited about going with you to your Dad's wedding."

Hannah's heart melted and she grinned sheepishly.

"My Uncle Kent and his wife Geeta were married on the Amalfi Coast," said Jacob. "The pictures from their wedding were amazing. Where in Italy is the wedding?"

"Dad has made reservations for everyone at the Amalfi Hotel Marina Riviera in a village called Positano," said Hannah. "From what I saw online, the views are spectacular. Positano sits in the hills above the coast."

"Is that where the wedding will be?"

Hannah shook her head. "No. The ceremony is going to be on a yacht."

"*A yacht!*" Jacob, his eyes wide, asked, "Is this a new acquisition of your dad's?"

Hannah laughed. "No. Believe it or not, the yacht belongs to my soon-to-be step-brother, Lord Tristan Wakefield."

"*Lord* Tristan Wakefield? How old is this—*Lord*?"

"He's twenty-two."

Jacob looked at her questioningly. "How does a twenty-two-year old afford a yacht?"

"His father died three years ago and he inherited the Wakefield Corporation, as in—Wakefield Hotels and Casinos," explained Hannah. "He's immensely wealthy."

"Does my sister know about the yacht?"

Hannah smirked. "No, and I don't want her to know. I want it to be a surprise."

Jacob and Hannah laughed together.

"You'll have to send me pictures," declared Jacob.

"Most definitely."

"So, is Tristan the only child?"

"No, there are two younger ones. Edmund is sixteen and Maria is thirteen."

"And the name of your soon-to-be step-mother is?" prodded Jacob.

"Diana Wakefield Grant," mumbled Hannah, her voice glum.

"Jaden said she was a widow."

"She is." Hannah looked away, staring out the window at the passing landscape. "She's been married twice. Her last husband died several years ago."

"What about her first husband, Lord Wakefield?"

"They divorced almost two decades ago."

Jacob glanced sideways at her. "What's really bothering you?"

Hannah frowned and her shoulders stiffened. "What do you mean?"

"Are you bothered by the fact that she's been married twice before?"

Hannah crossed her arms. "No," she retorted grumpily. "What's your point?"

"I think you feel like your dad's getting another family and you're being replaced," said Jacob, his voice soft. "Maybe you're not looking at it from the right prospective." Reaching out for her hand, he interlocked his fingers with hers.

"Try to be happy for your father that he has found love again," he said.

His strong hand was warm. Hannah stared down at her fingers intertwined with his. He lifted her hand to his lips, brushing her knuckles with feather-like kisses. Hannah felt her heart slamming forcefully against her chest, her blood scorching through her veins. When her eyes met his, Jacob smiled lovingly and she felt her hurt and anger dissolve.

CHAPTER 15

O
N THE FIRST THURSDAY IN June, Paige was busy in the kitchen preparing a late dinner when Jaden strolled in wearing an old pair of boxers topped by a faded, tattered orange Tennessee T-shirt. Her long golden blonde hair was arranged haphazardly on top of her head and an avocado green mud mask was on her face.

Paige frowned at her. "You're planning on washing that off before we eat." It wasn't a question.

"Of course," retorted Jaden saucily. "When's dinner?"

"Your brother just called. He'll be here any minute. Would you please set the table?"

Jaden set three place settings, and walked to the refrigerator. She swung the door open, staring inside at the contents.

"Where's the cottage cheese?"

"It's in there somewhere," insisted Paige, without looking around.

Jaden was searching the refrigerator shelves when she heard the clang of the back door and her brother's voice.

"Hi, I'm home and I've brought a guest."

Jaden removed a carton of cottage cheese. She turned, expecting to see Cory, Tanner or Dillon, but instead found the guest standing beside her brother to be a tall, dark, stunningly handsome stranger.

"Mom, Jaden—this is Jonathan King," Jacob said, gesturing casually with his hand. "He works with me at Martin Feeds."

Jonathan King was several inches taller than Jacob, and his shoulders far broader. He eluded cool, casual magnetism with his dark brown hair swept across his forehead, grazing his dark, straight eyebrows. His chiseled face was nearly perfect in its symmetry, his cheekbones high and prominent, his jaw sculpted.

"I don't want to be an imposition, Mrs. Winston," he said cordially in a deep, husky voice, extending a tan muscular arm.

Paige shook his large outstretched hand. "Not at all, I've made plenty. And please call me Paige."

Jonathan's gaze shifted to Jaden. "Hi," he said, his sensuous lips parting in a dazzling smile.

He was the handsomest man Jaden had ever seen. Butterflies exploded deep in her stomach sending a tingling shiver through her legs and arms, the carton of cottage cheese slipped from her grasp, splattering at her feet on the floor.

"Way to go, Jaden," teased Jacob.

Jaden felt a warm flush creeping across her cheeks under the mud mask.

Jacob walked over and grabbed a role of paper towels sitting on the counter behind Jaden. He looked at her and said with a wink, "I've got this."

Jaden grinned thankfully at him, squared her shoulders and stepped to where Jonathan stood. She looked him in the eye, extended her hand and said in a rush, "Hi—I'm Jaden."

"Nice to meet you," said Jonathan, his expression

unreadable, but there was hint of humor in his eyes.

Jaden pointed to her face nervously and stuttered, "I'm going to—go—wash this off." Turning on her heel, she walked hurriedly from the room.

"Where are you from Jonathan?" asked Paige.

"Phoenix. I'm a senior at Arizona State."

"Phoenix is wonderful. I've got an aunt and two cousins who live there," said Paige warmly. "What brought you to Jackson?"

"My uncle and aunt moved here ten months ago," Jonathan said. He was standing with his hands jammed into the pockets of his jeans.

"I'm visiting them for the summer."

"Where do your parents live?" asked Paige, smiling.

"My parents are deceased," Jonathan said casually. Seeing the concerned look on Paige's face, he quickly added, "My parents died when I was a baby. I have no memory of them."

Paige nodded slightly. "Where do your aunt and uncle live?"

"They bought a small farm not far from here," Jonathan said.

"Is this the first time you've been to Jackson?" Paige asked.

Jonathan nodded. "Yes, ma'am, it is."

Paige looked up when Jaden walked in. She was wearing a black top and black yoga pants, her long blonde hair falling loosely around her shoulders, her flawless skin free of the mask. Paige asked Jacob to turn off the television, come to the dinner table and after everyone was seated, asked him to give the blessing.

"Dig in, please," she instructed and passed a salad bowl to Jaden.

Paige looked across the table at Jonathan and asked, "Do you play any sports?"

Jonathan nodded. "I like pretty much any outdoors

activity. But I love rock climbing the most, especially free-solo climbing."

"What's that?" inquired Jaden.

Jonathan's gaze shifted to her. "It's when you use nothing more than your hands and feet to climb."

"No equipment at *all*?" asked Jaden in astonishment.

"None."

"Sounds risky," Jaden mused lightly. "Why do it?"

"I like the physical challenge," bragged Jonathan with a grin, his eyes glowing with confidence.

Jaden felt her heart start racing frantically and looked quickly away from his disarming gaze.

"How long have you been climbing?" Jacob asked.

"Ever since I was a kid," Jonathan said shrugging. He looked at Jacob and asked, "Ever climb?"

Jacob shook his head. "Never."

"If it involves risk or speed then Jacob's all about it" interjected Jaden.

"I would never free climb, Jaden," objected Jacob, looking at his sister appreciatively. He rotated his right hand. "I wouldn't want to injure this hand."

"Good to know you draw the line somewhere," teased Paige.

Jacob grinned at his mother.

Jonathan threw a questioning, sideways glance at Jacob. "What happened to your hand?"

"I broke my wrist last summer," Jacob said indifferently.

"Yeah, that's putting it mildly," snorted Jaden, rolling her eyes. "You spent over four months in a cast because you broke your scaphoid."

"How did you break your scaphoid?" asked Jonathan.

"I came off a horse."

"Jacob was trying a new stunt that didn't work out," said Jaden, affection in her voice.

"Jonathan—do you ride?" asked Paige.

Jonathan shook his head. "I've not had the opportunity

to be around horses. I've lived in big cities all my life."

Paige turned to Jaden and shifted the conversation. "I think we should take Gabriel with us to the Champagne Run horse show."

"Gabriel's the donkey?" Jonathan asked smiling.

Paige looked at him surprised. "You've heard of Gabriel?"

Jonathan nodded. "Jacob mentioned him and Mr. Martin has talked about him."

"Joe's talked about Gabriel? What did he say?" Paige prodded anxiously

"He said Gabriel has a lot of attitude."

Paige arched an eyebrow.

"I'm surprised Joe hasn't said more," she said with an incredulous laugh. "Especially since Gabriel—"

"Tore his shirt off," blurted Jaden.

Jonathan eyes widened. "He attacked Joe? Why?" he asked curiously.

"Gabriel doesn't like Joe," asserted Jacob with a matter-of-fact shrug. He threw a sideways glance at his sister and asked affectionately, "Have you finished packing yet?"

"I'm done!" said Jaden with a satisfied smile.

Jonathan's gaze shifted to Jaden. "Going somewhere?"

"Italy!" exclaimed Jaden, her green eyes shimmering with excitement. "My best friend's dad is getting married on the Amalfi Coast. I'm flying over tomorrow."

———

AFTER DINNER, Paige was at her desk in her office flipping through a pile of mail when Jaden strolled in. Jaden shut the door and collapsed sideways into a leather chair with a huff. "If I punch Jacob, will you ground me?"

Paige leaned back in her chair, her expression amused. "Why would you want to punch your brother?"

"Because the *tool* didn't give us a heads up he was

bringing home a stranger," retorted Jaden. "*Seriously Mom*, have you been paying attention? Did you see what I was wearing?"

Paige stifled a smile.

"Jonathan flummoxes me," grumbled Jaden, crossing her arms.

"He did seem to have an odd effect on you," agreed Paige, grinning warmly at her. "I've never seen you so flustered over a guy."

Jaden stared at a picture of her father on the desk. "Did Dad flummox you?"

Paige looked lovingly at Robert's picture. "Yes . . . I suppose he did," she said softly. She looked back at Jaden and asked, "What happened to your rule of not being interested in anyone who doesn't know anything about horses?"

"I'm not interested in Jonathan," Jaden protested hastily. Feeling the color rising in her cheeks, she turned her eyes away. "When is the tool leaving for Montana?"

Paige smiled. "Your *brother* flies out of Memphis next Tuesday."

"Are you going to be okay by yourself?" asked Jaden, her green eyes worried.

"I'll be fine," Paige said confidently. She chuckled. "Besides—I'm not alone. I have Duke, Roscoe, Gizmo, and Izzie to keep me company."

CHAPTER 16

ITWAS JUNE TWENTY-FIRST, THE first day of summer. Jacob was returning home after two weeks in Montana. Paige was anxious to get to the airport— she was grateful that the traffic on Interstate 240 was light and flowing swiftly. Hearing the song, *"Every Breath You Take,"* by Sting playing on the radio, she cranked up the volume. The song took her back to another place and time—being a teenager in love with Robert. She blinked. She didn't feel the stabbing pain that usually accompanied thoughts of her deceased husband. She smiled, a feeling of contentment washed through her, filling her with peacefulness.

Paige spotted Jacob, dressed in jeans and shirt, standing at the curbside, a large duffel bag at his feet. Pulling to the curbside, Jacob tossed his duffel bag into the truck bed, opened the door and jumped in.

"Hi," he said smiling at his mother.

Paige leaned over and gave him a welcoming hug.

"I'm so glad you're home," she said, her eyes shining with happiness. She released him and said, "With both you and Jaden gone, the weeks passed at a snail's pace."

"Did Jaden have a good time in Italy?"

"She hasn't stopped talking about it," smirked Paige. "Hannah's step-brother, Tristan Wakefield, took everyone on a ten-day cruise through the Mediterranean on his yacht." She pulled into traffic.

"Hannah sent me pictures."

"Tell me about your trip?" Paige urged.

"Uncle Matt hooked me up with a friend of his, Ted Sloan. Ted put me into some of the best fishing ever," said Jacob, a joyful expression on his face.

"Did you do any fishing in Yellowstone?"

Jacob smiled. "Yes, we fished a couple of places in Yellowstone, including Slough Creek," he said. "We fished for Golden Trout in a mountain lake. We floated the Boulder River and another day, the Yellowstone River."

Paige glanced at Jacob. "Are you scheduled to work at Martin Feeds?"

"Not until next week."

"Good," said Paige, relief in her voice. "I need you around the farm. We have seven new horses."

"Seven!" exclaimed Jacob.

"They won't be staying. They'll be leaving when they're strong enough."

"What happened?"

"I got a call from the sheriff last week," said Paige. "One of his deputies stumbled upon a field in south Madison County with over fifty horses, all in really bad shape. They'd been without food and water for a long time. The horses that could be saved were fostered out. I volunteered to take seven."

After an extended silence, Jacob turned to his mother and said, "Did Ron Chatum make parole?"

Paige nodded, her eyes on the road. "He did," she said calmly.

Jacob stared at his mother in surprise.

"You don't look upset?"

"I'm not," said Paige, meeting his gaze. "I no longer feel malice towards him." Her eyes returned to the road.

"I did myself a favor. The last time I met with Ron Chatum, I looked him in the eye and told him that I forgave him," she said, casting a sideways glance at Jacob. "Rebecca Martin was right. By letting go and forgiving—the bitterness and the hatred I'd been holding onto for years just dissolved." She smiled happily. "I feel—*lighter*."

They rode in silence for several miles.

"By the way" said Paige, breaking the quiet. "Tomorrow— Joe Martin is bringing over his new horse, Thor. The horse will be your new project."

"Why me?"

"Because Thor's a stallion," replied Paige. "He's big— and full of himself." She looked over at Jacob. He was grinning. On her son's face she saw the stunning smile of his father, and a feeling of absolute joy filled her heart.

CHAPTER 17

THE SECOND DAY OF SUMMER started bright and hot. Hannah, dressed in a light blue shirt, beige riding breeches and brown field boots, was sitting at the kitchen island drinking a glass of orange juice and eating a bagel smeared in cream cheese. Her grandmother was cleaning up the kitchen.

"Do you need to borrow my car today?" Sheila asked over her shoulder.

Hannah shook her head. "Jaden's picking me up."

"When are you getting your truck back?"

"Tomorrow," said Hannah. Sliding from the chair, she carried her plate to the sink, rinsed it off and put it into the dishwasher.

"Thanks for breakfast, Gram," she said, giving her grandmother a kiss on the cheek. "Jaden should be here any minute."

Hannah headed for the stairs and her bedroom. The sunny color scheme of her room was cheerful. Her large poster bed, a mirrored dresser and nightstand from Neiman Marcus, gave the room an air of sophistication, glitz and glamour. She strolled into her room and threw herself across her bed, closed her eyes and thought about Jacob. She hadn't seen him in weeks. She was anxious to get to the barn. She heard Taylor Swift singing on her radio, "*The way you move is like a full on rainstorm and I'm a house of cards. You're the kind of reckless that should send me runnin'...*"

Scrambling off her bed, Hannah snatched up a hair brush, and cranked up the volume on her radio.

"*Drop everything now, meet me in the pouring rain, kiss me on the sidewalk, take away the pain,*" she sang, strutting across her bedroom, her long dark hair billowing out behind her.

"*Cause I see sparks fly whenever you smile, get me with those green eyes, baby, as the lights go down.*" Hannah stopped at her dresser, she pointed to a picture of Jacob playing polo.

"*Give me something that'll haunt me when you're not around, cause I see sparks fly whenever you smile,*" she crooned and she twirled. From the corner of her eye, she saw a dark shirt—Jacob was leaning against her doorframe with his arms crossed, smiling.

"Don't stop on my account. I was enjoying the show," insisted Jacob, endearing humor in his deep voice. He shifted his feet. His dark shirt clung to his broad shoulders and chest, the color accentuating his eyes. His muscular forearms were golden-brown.

"How long . . . have you . . . been standing there?" Hannah stuttered, her voice shrill, her cheeks burning in mortified embarrassment. She whipped around, turning away from his amused gaze. She fumbled with the radio dial.

"Welcome home," she said, trying to sound unfazed. She walked swiftly past him, heading for the stairs. "Where's Jaden?"

"Anna and Brooklyn, two of her students, had family issues arise so she moved their riding lesson up an hour," said Jacob. "I volunteered to come get you."

"Thanks." Hannah felt her heart take off. She avoided his eyes, afraid he'd see how thrilled she was.

Jacob shuffled beside her. "Did you like the Amalfi coast?"

Hannah nodded.

"The village of Positano was lovely," she said, focusing on the stairs.

"The Amalfi Marina Riviera hotel was in a centuries old building perched high on a cliff, slopping down to the sea."

"Nice," Jacob laughed. "Jaden really enjoyed the cruise through the Mediterranean and going to Capri." He glanced at Hannah as they walked through the kitchen towards the back door. "She raved about your step-brother's yacht. She said that it had a gym, game room, and a helicopter pad."

"Did you get the pictures I sent you?"

Jacob nodded. "Tell me about your new step-mother."

"Diana is pretty—she looks younger than her age," Hannah said affectionately, her pink lips turning up in pleased smile. "She's warm and genuine. Dad and she seem really happy."

"What about your new siblings?"

"Tristan Wakefield was not what I expected," admitted Hannah.

"How so?"

"Dad told me that Tristan was a playboy." Hannah hesitated at the door. "I was expecting him to be arrogant because he was so young and wealthy—but he wasn't." She opened the back door and walked out into the bright June day.

Jacob followed her out the door.

"What's he like?"

"He's charming, unassuming and fun. He dotes on his little sister, Maria," said Hannah. "Maria's adorable. She has an angelic face and eyes like blue marbles."

Jacob pulled the keys from his jeans pocket and slid behind the wheel of his Jeep.

"Jaden really liked Maria," he said, putting the key in the ignition. "I got the impression she liked Edmund too. She didn't say anything about Tristan."

Hannah frowned, her head tilting to the side. *"Really?* Nothing?"

"Not-a-thing."

"I'm surprised. Tristan and Jaden were together a lot," said Hannah, pulling the seat belt across her chest.

"Does Tristan ride?"

"Oh yeah!" exclaimed Hannah. "When he was a teenager, he showed jumpers and evented. Now he plays polo . . . and he owns a stable of racehorses."

Jacob shrugged. "There's no telling with my sister."

Hannah smiled, nodding in agreement.

Jacob reached over and picked up her hand. Raising her hand to his lips, he tenderly kissed her hand.

"I've missed you," he murmured, his lips gliding softly over her knuckles

Hannah felt her insides clench, the touch of his lips igniting an electric sensation that raged through her body like wildfire. She chewed on her lip, groaning internally, trying to suppress the urge to launch herself at him.

They rode in silence, each occasionally looking at the other and when the barn came into view, Hannah laughed. "Your project has arrived."

Jacob parked the Jeep. They got out and walked side-by-side into the barn towards a group of five people clustered around a large palomino horse, the color of butterscotch, with four white stockings.

Jacob stopped beside Joe Martin. "Hi."

"Hello, son," said Joe, his gray eyes beaming, he slapped Jacob lightly on the shoulder.

"I appreciate your help with my horse ."

Jacob nodded, his eyes sliding admiringly over the

horse's confirmation.

A tall young boy with short, cropped brown hair and blue eyes walked up. "Hi, Jacob."

"Hi, JG," Jacob said smiling at him. Glancing at the two young girls with him, he said, "Hi, Caroline—Hi, Hailey."

Both girls blushed and Jacob turned his attention back to the horse. "He's a fine-looking animal, Joe."

"Thank you," replied Joe in his honey-tongued voice, handing the lead rope to Jaden.

Jaden led the stallion down the aisle and into a stall.

CHAPTER 18

⬥•◆•⬥

I T WAS THE LAST SATURDAY in June, and Hannah was in the tack room zipping up her boots when she heard a deep, husky unfamiliar voice, "Why are there so many horse trailers here?"

Looking up, she saw a tall, broad-shouldered stranger wearing a dark Arizona State T-shirt and jeans. A maroon baseball cap was pulled low on his forehead, partially hiding his eyes. She smiled and said, "Jaden's having a Gymkhana for her summer riding students."

He nodded, extending his hand. "I'm Jonathan King. What's a Gymkhana?"

"Hi, I'm Hannah," she said, shaking his hand. "A Gymkhana is competition games on horseback."

Jonathan crossed his tan muscular arms. "Is Jacob around?"

"He'll be back in a minute," said Hannah, walking to the opposite wall. Reaching up, she grabbed her bridle, picked up her saddle, crooking it under her arm and headed for the tack room door.

"Mind if I tag along," Jonathan asked.

Hannah looked back over her shoulder. "Not at all."

Jonathan followed her to where a bay horse stood in cross ties. "Is this your horse?"

"This is Black Tie Required," beamed Hannah. She threw on a white saddle pad then her cross country saddle and cinched the girth.

"What kind of horse is he?"

"He's a Thoroughbred." Hannah removed the halter and slipped on a snaffle bridle. She glanced at Jonathan and said, "How do you know Jacob?"

"I work with him at Martin Feeds," replied Jonathan.

Hannah stared at him intently.

"Have we ever have met before? You look so familiar," she said assuredly. "I can't shake the feeling that I should know you."

"Maybe I have one of those faces," said Jonathan smiling.

Hannah smiled back. "I guess so."

At the sound of the gator, they looked around to see Jacob coming in their direction, a large Rottweiler sitting in the passenger seat.

Jacob stopped the gator and looked at the dog and said, "Out Roscoe."

The dog looked at him with his round seal-looking brown eyes but didn't budge.

"Out Roscoe," commanded Jacob. The dog jumped grudgingly out, landing on the ground at Jonathan's feet.

Jonathan hopped into the gator next to Jacob.

Passing by Hannah at a crawl, Jacob asked, "The ring is full. Where are you going to ride?"

Hannah buckled the chin strap of her helmet. "I'm going for a trial ride."

"Don't fall in any holes," teased Jacob affectionately, winking at her.

Hannah smiled. "You boys have fun fixing fences."

JADEN, WEARING A TANK TOP, riding breeches and half chaps, was leading Lyre, tacked up in snaffle bridle and Dressage saddle, down the aisle when she glanced up. Swaggering confidently in her direction was Jonathan King, his eyes hidden behind dark glasses. His cocky strut took her breath away, butterflies fluttered wildly in her stomach.

"Pretty horse, yours?" he asked, falling in beside her.

Jaden nodded and said hurriedly, "Her name is Lyre."

"Why did you name her Lyre?"

Jaden halted Lyre. Stretching up, she moved the mare's forelock out of the way.

"Her star resembles—"

"A lyre—the ancient musical instrument that King David played," said Jonathan with an approving nod. "Very cool."

Jaden stared at him in surprise.

Jonathan reached out to touch Lyre.

"Hold out your hand so she can get the smell of you," advised Jaden.

Lyre smelled Jonathan, her whiskers brushing against his hand causing him to smile.

"Where's my brother?" Jaden asked, trying to sound casual.

"He forgot his work gloves and went back to get them."

They walked out into the sunshine.

Jaden stopped abruptly.

"Here, hold her for a minute," she said, placing the reins in his hand. Not waiting for his response, she spun and started running, yelling over her shoulder, "I forgot my gloves."

A minute later, Jaden walked out of the barn holding her gloves. Jonathan and Lyre were nowhere in sight. She called out, "Jonathan?" Hearing his voice, she walked around the corner. Lyre was grazing happily, Jonathan standing beside her.

"She wanted some grass and dragged me over here," he said apologetically.

"No worries," insisted Jaden, suppressing a smile. Taking the reins from him, she said, "Lyre had your number the moment I put those reins in your hands. She knew she could get away with bad behavior." She squeezed her fingers around the reins, flicked her wrist gently, clucked and started walking forward, Lyre at her side.

"Your horse is very determined and strong," said Jonathan with a low laugh, a note of admiration in his deep, husky voice. He fell in closely beside her, his arm brushing against hers.

"She is, indeed" agreed Jaden, focusing on the ground, trying to stifle the rush of nervousness she felt by his nearness.

"Jacob told me you compete in Three-Day Eventing, but he didn't explain what it was."

"Back when the cavalry used horses and not tanks, several types of riding had to be mastered in order to pass a cavalry test. That's the sports roots," Jaden said confidently. Talking about horses was familiar ground and she felt her muscles relax. She glanced at him.

"Eventing is an equestrian triathlon that combines three different disciplines, Dressage, Cross Country and Stadium Jumping, into a competition set over a one day or two day or there day period."

"Sounds interesting."

They walked casually in the direction of the ring.

"I heard Joe Martin hired you on as a farm hand," Jaden said finally.

Jonathan nodded.

"He must like you because he doesn't normally hire anyone without farming experience," Jaden said, surprise in her voice.

"I'm looking forward to it. I've no doubt that I'm going to learn a lot," said Jonathan. "How long have you known

Joe Martin?"

"Most of my life. He and my Uncle Matt are good friends."

"Have you always lived on a farm?"

"Yes, mostly," said Jaden. "We moved out here when I was six."

Jonathan smiled and asked casually, "Are you planning to go to college?"

"I know I want to ride professionally. I haven't decided about college yet," Jaden said with certainty.

Jonathan glanced over and asked, "What about riding in the Olympics?"

"What a dream that would be!" raved Jaden, meeting his gaze. "What about you? What are your plans after graduation?"

Jonathan shrugged indifferently. "I was thinking about becoming a spy," he teased, his sensual mouth curling upward in a wry smile. "Actually, I have no plans beyond college."

Looking up at him, Jaden wondered what it would be like to be kissed by him. She looked quickly away, thankful they had reached the ring. She lifted the reins over Lyre's head, pulled down both stirrups, and snapped the chin strap on her helmet. She slipped her gloves on, glanced over her shoulder at him and said, "Mind giving me a leg up?"

CHAPTER 19

THE GLOWING COLORS OF TWILIGHT danced across the antique pine floor, bathing the spacious office in soft ambient light. The room exuded masculinity, from its custom furniture, leather paneled walls dotted with bullet casings next to the rich mahogany floor-to-ceiling shelves crammed with books and bronze sculptures of the American West. Joe Martin, sitting at his desk working, looked up when his housekeeper, Mrs. Haynes, walked into the room. She was carrying a large, square-shaped parcel covered in gilded gold paper.

"I've put your dinner in the warmer," she said, placing the square parcel on the massive, ornate desk in front of him. "Early birthday present?"

"Joke from an old friend," Joe said sarcastically.

"Hannah Butler returned Thor's halter. I had Jonathan King take it down to the barn."

"Thank you." Joe opened a desk drawer and removed envelope.

"Here," he said, handing it to her. "For your granddaughter's birthday."

Mrs. Haynes surprised eyes widened, her hand flew to her heart.

"That's so thoughtful of you, Mr. Martin," she gushed happily.

Joe cleared his throat and said, "Was anyone in my office today?"

"Not that I'm aware of," said Mrs. Haynes. "Is there anything else you need me to do?"

"No, goodnight," Joe said in a dismissive tone.

"Goodnight and thank you," said Mrs. Haynes, turning to leave.

Joe stared at the package. It was the first day of July. He'd forgotten about the date's significance. It had been overshadowed by his discovering that someone had been in his office, in his secret room. He reached for the parcel. His long fingers slowly pried open the paper.

Joe eyed the oddly shaped crystal bottle of Remy Marin Louis XIII Grand Champagne Cognac and thought about the man who sent it. He reached for the phone and dialed the number emblazoned in his brain. After several rings, he heard the clear voice of his old friend.

"You have obviously received my gift," said Vitor Lessard. "How is my godson doing?"

"Andrew's medical practice continues to grow," said Joe impatiently, and he said in rush, "I've reason to suspect that someone has been in my *private* room."

"Why do you hang on to those antique trinkets? Those items are evidence that link you to your past!" Vitor scolded.

"That's why they are in that secret room!" said Joe sternly.

"You're positive that someone was in there?" asked Vitor, a hint of alarm in his voice.

"I'm positive that several items had been moved," Joe insisted. "No one but me should be able to access it!"

"Do you have anyone new working around the farm?"

"Yes," admitted Joe. "I hired a college student from Arizona named Jonathan King. I had him checked out, and I didn't find anything suspicious."

"Why, after sixty-six years, would someone be sniffing around you? What event precipitated this?"

"I don't know!" snapped Joe.

"Did you ever have your arm tattoo removed?" said Vitor angrily. "Maybe someone recognized your tattoo!"

After an extended pause, Joe said brusquely. "There's no point in our bickering. We're both old men with pasts that must remain buried, hidden forever."

"Agreed," said Vitor.

"What was the name of the family that owned the Chateau de Vignon?"

"Bonet—*why?*" asked Vitor suspiciously.

"Do you have any pictures of them?"

"Why?" repeated Vitor, his voice laced with irritation.

"There's a girl, a neighbor of mine, who reminds me of one of them."

"Which Bonet does she resemble?"

"If I could remember—I wouldn't need the pictures," barked Joe.

"What's the girl's name?"

"Her name is Hannah Butler."

"Hannah Butler," repeated Vitor excitedly. He laughed and said, "Send me a picture of her and get me some of her hair too!"

"Why?"

"If she's who I think she is, I was lied to seven years ago and—"

"And this excites you?" said Joe in a hard, mocking voice.

"It means one of Zara Bonet's grandchildren—"

"I thought Zara's three grandchildren were all dead!"

"I was told they were!" protested Vitor calmly. He laughed sardonically and said, "Don't you understand?"

"Understand what?"

"If this girl is Zara Bonet's granddaughter—it means the Legatee is alive!" said Vitor elatedly.

"*Holy shit!*"

143

CHAPTER 20

NTERING THE BUTLER'S HOUSE LATE in the afternoon on July Fourth, Paige was overwhelmed with the aroma of freshly baked cake.

"Smells good," gushed Paige, inhaling deeply.

"William and Nancy are outside. I'll be out in a minute," said Sheila, busily applying icing on a cake.

"Is there anything I can do to help?"

"Not a thing, dear," replied Sheila over her shoulder.

"Ok." Paige walked to the French doors, stepped onto the flagstone patio, heading to where Nancy and William sat.

"Hi," said Nancy spotting her.

Paige sat down on the teak sofa.

"We were wondering when you'd get here," said William in his fatherly tone, a smile spreading across his tan face.

"I've was on the phone with the Sheriff," said Paige.

Nancy frowned.

"Remember my telling you how a sheriff's deputy found stolen horses in a field in South Madison? And that I took several in," said Paige.

Nancy nodded.

"They've located the owner of the last horse I have." Paige's gaze flicked to her daughter, Jaden sitting on Cory's shoulders in the pool, playing a game of chicken with Jacob and Hannah.

"That's good news," William exclaimed.

Paige nodded, smiling broadly. "The horse's name is Inki. His owner, Danielle, is an Eventer and she lives here in Jackson."

"Jaden's going to be thrilled," said William genially.

"Yes, she is," Paige agreed.

"Did the authorities ever locate the person responsible for stealing the horses?" Nancy asked curiously.

"They did," said Paige. "They found him sitting in a San Antonio, Texas jail where he'd been arrested for a DUI."

"He was part of a drug cartel running horses down to the border to be used for smuggling drugs into the USA," volunteered William.

"Nasty business . . . what those drug cartel's do to those horses!" exclaimed Sheila, laying down a wicker tray, loaded with glasses, a plastic ice bucket and two tavern pitchers.

"This one has *my* special tea," she said, tapping the glass pitcher with her manicured finger.

Everyone poured a drink. William raised his glass.

"Since this is July Fourth, I would like to make a toast to our brave military personnel," he said boldly. "To our men and women in uniform—thank you for protecting our freedom, and God bless all of you."

Sheila raised her glass. "Ronald Reagan said, '*If we ever forget that we're one nation under God, then we will be one nation gone under'.*"

"Live simply, love generously, care deeply, speak kindly, leave the rest to God," said Paige. "Reagan said that too!"

Cory, with Jaden on his shoulders, moved swiftly counter clockwise into deeper water, unbalancing Hannah on Jacob's shoulders. Hannah tumbled over, pulling Jaden

145

down with her.

Jaden emerged from the water, her nose bleeding.

"Jacob has a boney elbow," she sputtered, pinching her nose.

Walking to the pool's edge, Sheila beckoned, waving her hand at Jaden. "Come on. I've got something for that," she said in a motherly tone.

Jaden walked up the pool steps, grabbed a towel and followed Sheila into the house and into the kitchen.

"Have a seat," Sheila ordered softly.

Jaden collapsed in the chair Sheila indicated.

Sheila opened a drawer and removed a small tin box.

Jaden giggled. "I can't believe you still have these."

"Your brother doesn't get the bloody noses he used to," said Sheila with a chuckle. Opening the lid, she pulled out a tampon already cut in half, and inserted into Jaden's nostril.

Glancing down, Jaden picked up the leather photo album lying on the counter top. "What's this?"

"Photos of Henda's family," said Sheila, walking to the kitchen island. "I'm trying to organize them."

Jaden opened the book. "Mom told me what you're doing for Hannah's birthday," she said, giving Sheila a quick glance. "I think that's really cool. Hannah's going to *love* it."

Sheila beamed.

"Who are these two people in the picture with Hannah?" Jaden held up a picture of a young Hannah standing in-between a tall, scrawny boy with long, shaggy, dark hair and a skinny girl with long, pale blonde hair.

Sheila glanced up. "That's Caleb and Lily Reynolds, Hannah's cousins."

"Aren't they the ones who died in the explosion?"

Sheila nodded.

Jaden stared at the picture. "What breathtaking blue eyes!"

The back door opened and they heard Tanner Chapman's familiar voice.

"Hi," he said, striding into the kitchen.

Jaden glanced up; standing beside Tanner was Jonathan King. Nervous butterflies erupted in her.

Tanner stared wide-eyed at Jaden. "*Is that* what I think it is in your nose?"

Jaden's face blushed crimson. "Jacob hit me in the nose—it was bleeding—a lot," she stammered. Mortified she yanked the cotton plug from her nose and jumped hastily to her feet. The album in her lap fell with a thud, several pictures ejected from the album and scattered across the hard wood floor.

Jonathan bent over and gathered up the pictures. He straightened, stepped forward, and handed the pictures to Jaden. He was smiling, his eyes shining in evident amusement.

"Thanks," breathed Jaden taking the photos from him and placing them face up on the counter top. She threw an appreciative, sideways glance at Jonathan and saw him staring down at the pictures. His smile had disappeared and she caught a glimpse of pain in his eyes.

"You two boys go outside," Sheila said, pointing to the French doors. "We'll be eating shortly."

"That's code for 'get out of my way'," joked Tanner, walking towards the door. Jonathan followed Tanner out, pulling the door closed behind him.

Jaden stomped her foot.

"The iniquity of it," she cried, stomping over to the kitchen island. She collapsed down on a stool. "I'm so embarrassed," she groaned, glancing out towards the pool at Jonathan.

"Your nose stopped bleeding," said Sheila softly. She walked over, wrapped an arm around Jaden's shoulders, and gave her a squeeze. "You'll live through this and a lot more—now back outside," she said smiling warmly, steering her to the door. "We'll be eating in a little while."

Sneaking quick glances over to where Jonathan sat, Jaden walked hurriedly over to a teak lounge chair, sitting down beside Cory with a huff.

"How's the nose?" questioned Cory.

Meeting his gaze, Jaden said sharply, "I don't know what's hurting more, my nose or my pride."

Cory frowned. "Sorry, you'll have to explain."

Jaden told him about her tampon-stuffed nose. Cory laughed uncontrollably.

"It's not funny, Cory!" Jaden scowled. "It was embarrassing!"

"How is that not funny? It's hilarious," replied Cory, laughing even harder.

"It's just not!"

"When have you ever cared what someone might think of you?" Cory asked seriously.

Jaden laid her head back, closed her eyes and didn't say anything.

Cory whistled playfully and said in a low voice, "Oh, now I get it—you like Jonathan!"

"I'm not interested in him at all," said Jaden coolly.

"Does he ride?"

Jaden, her eyes closed, ignored Cory. After a long pause, she said in a resigned voice, "*No.*"

Cory laughed again.

"I thought you said you'd *never, ever* be interested in anyone who didn't ride?"

"I'm not interested in him!" argued Jaden.

"*Jaden Elizabeth*," Cory said. "Look me in the eyes and tell me that."

Jaden opened her eyes and meeting his gaze, burst into laughter.

"Ok," she whispered. "I admit I think he's beautimous."

Cory looked at her straight-faced. "Actually, I'm kind of stunned," he said, his voice flat.

"What do you mean?"

A playful smile spread slowly across Cory's handsome face. "He doesn't nay or eat hay and he has only two legs."

Jaden stuck out her tongue. "Stick to football, not comedy."

Cory grinned broadly.

"Please say you'll come with us to the Champagne Run horse show in two weeks," begged Jaden, pressing her palms together. "I could use a good groom!"

Cory shook his head.

"I'd love to, Jaden, but I have a conflict that weekend," he said and gestured towards Jacob, sitting with Hannah on the pool steps. "You've got Jacob."

Jaden rolled her emerald green eyes at him. "If he wasn't so wrapped up in Hannah he might be worth something," she said lightheartedly.

"Maybe Jonathan can go as your groom."

Jaden looked across the pool to where Jonathan sat talking with her mother and William. It irritated her that he had such a nerve-jolting affect on her. If he went with them to the horse show, she feared she would be utterly distracted by his presence. She shook her head.

"He knows nothing about horses."

"You could train him."

Jaden flushed. She opened her mouth to protest but Cory interrupted her. "Jaden, we've known each other since we were five and I can tell you really like this guy."

Jaden's eyes flicked back to Jonathan. The depth of her desire for him disturbed her. She sighed. "He's a senior at Arizona State. After this summer, I'll never see him again."

"You don't know that," retorted Cory.

"Yeah—*whatever.*"

After a long silence, Cory asked, "Is Dillon coming today?"

"No, he's out of town. Are you staying for fireworks tonight?"

Cory shook his head. "Can't—got plans."

"With who?" prompted Jaden.

"I'm *not* saying. You'll go ballistic on me."

"I won't!" Jaden insisted strongly.

Cory flexed his muscular, well-shaped arm, and extended his pinkie finger.

"Pinkie-swear like when we were kids," he said.

Jaden looked him in the eyes and interlocked her pinkie with his. "I promise I won't go ballistic," she said, her voice level and firm.

"Bethany Shevar."

Jaden stiffened and she felt Cory's finger tighten around hers. She glared disapprovingly at Cory. "I'm still *angry* at Bethany for the lies she told about Hannah."

"Hannah told me she's forgiven Bethany—why are you still angry at her?" said Cory, his eyes serious. "Bethany's changed a lot, Jaden."

"Since when?" Jaden snapped.

"I can't say exactly," admitted Cory. "She came to me a few days after Jacob confronted her in the cafeteria. She told me she wanted a life upgrade. She asked me for help learning how to be a *Word Walker* and—"

"A what?" laughed Jaden softly, her voice ringing with affection.

"That's what I call a person who uses the Word of God to guide their life."

"I like that," mused Jaden, nodding her head.

"Anyway," continued Cory. "We were spending a lot of time together and I realized I really liked her."

Jaden remained quiet. After a long silence, she looked over at Cory.

"Reading the Word does change you," she said frankly.

CHAPTER 21

———————◆•◆•◆———————

IT WAS THIRTY MINUTES AFTER nine on Thursday morning, July fourteenth, when Jacob, Jaden and Hannah arrived at the barn. Getting out of the Jeep, Jaden and Hannah walked together into the barn while Jacob transferred their luggage to the horse trailer dressing room.

Jaden and Hannah, both wearing t-strap cotton tops, jean shorts and cowboy boots, were standing in the tack room reading a note Paige had left them when Jonathan King walked in wearing blue jeans and a Arizona State T-shirt.

"Morning," he said.

Hannah looked up and smiled warmly. "Morning, Jonathan."

"Hi," said Jaden, her eyes on the piece of paper, her traitorous stomach jumping nervously. "We're dividing up the task list Mom left us."

"Where is your mom?" Jonathan asked.

"She needed to take care of some things in Jackson before we leave town," said Jaden.

Jonathan nodded. "Who takes care of the horses when

151

you are away at a horse show?"

"Joe Martin has a couple of workhands that Mom pays," replied Jaden, giving him a quick glance.

Jacob, wearing jeans and an old, gray sleeveless T-shirt, his blonde hair in disarray, strolled in, "What needs to be done?"

Jaden handed him the list. "I really don't want task *four*."

Jacob glanced at the paper and his eyes flicked to Hannah. "Will you help me with four?"

"What's it worth to you?" teased Hannah, winking at him.

Jacob grinned sideways at her, his eyes glowing with obvious adoration.

Jonathan glanced at the list in Jacob's hand.

"Is Gabriel that hard to bathe?" he asked surprised.

"You've *no* idea," answered Jaden, rolling her green eyes.

Black Tie and Lyre had been bathed and only Gabriel remained. Jacob led a reluctant Gabriel out to the grass. Turning the hose nozzle dial to on, Hannah trickled water across Gabriel's front hoof. He pulled his hoof up, his large, fluffy ears, flattening. She switched the water to his other hoof and he instantly switched feet.

Jacob laughed. "Gabriel looks grumpy."

Hannah grinned. "I know." She switched the water to his other hoof and he instantly switched feet again. She slowly raised the water up his leg. Gabriel jumped forward trying to escape.

"I've got him," Jacob said, grabbing Gabriel's lead rope.

Hannah raised the nozzle to Gabriel's shoulder. The donkey's large, fluffy ears flicked forward. She grinned mischievously and flicked her wrist, spraying Jacob, soaking his T-shirt and hair.

Jacob brushed his hand through his wet hair, reached out, and yanked the hose away from Hannah.

"I'll handle the water," he said, his eyes shining with laughter. Lifting the hose high, he sprayed Hannah, drenching her hair and clothes.

Hannah squealed and jolted backwards.

"Okay, okay," she blurted, her hands thrown up. "We're even."

"Are we?" asked Jacob, grinning crookedly.

"Truce—let's finish Gabriel," said Hannah.

Jacob nodded.

Hannah was rinsing the last of the soap off when Gabriel bucked suddenly, springing forward like a deer, breaking free. Hannah hollered with laughter, accidently spraying Jacob again.

Jacob grabbed Hannah, pulling her close. Leaning in, he announced, his husky voice playful, "You need to be punished." He scooped her up in his arms.

"Jacob, put me down," Hannah ordered, trying to sound angry.

Jacob shook his head, his eyes full of wicked mischief, and he stepped toward a large water puddle.

Hannah recognized the glint in his eyes. *"Don't you dare, Jacob Robert Winston,"* she shouted. *"Don't even think about it!"*

Jacob grinned and carefully, dropped Hannah into the wet mud puddle. The liquid squished beneath her. Grabbing a handful of mud, she chunked it at Jacob.

Jacob jumped aside, easily dodging it.

Hannah picked up another handful of mud and hurled it at him, again missing him.

"Would it help if I stood still," laughed Jacob, smiling. He opened his arms out wide.

Hannah laughed.

"Will you at least help me up?" she pleaded, her lovely brown eyes inviting.

Jacob extended his arm out. Hannah grasped his outstretched hand and he lifted her to her feet. She grinned saucily at him, and then smeared a handful of mud across his face. Before Jacob had the chance to wipe the mud from his eyes, Hannah leaned in and brushed her lips against his.

Jacob stumbled. Hannah pushed him over and he landed in the puddle, instantly submerged in brown liquid. Propping himself up an elbow, Jacob wiped the mud from his eyes.

"Are you going to give me a hand up?" he asked, a lopsided grin on his handsome face.

Hannah shook her head, turned and sprinted for the barn. Running through the barn, she heard the song, "*All Summer Long*" by Kid Rock playing and she grinned. Rounding the back corner, she saw Jonathan, standing with his arms crossed, watching her—Jacob was nowhere to be seen.

"Have you seen Jacob?" Hannah asked, drawing near.

Jonathan shook his head. Suddenly, unexpectedly, his arm shot out, his reflexes cat-like. "I've got her, Jacob," he shouted.

Looking around, Hannah saw Jacob running towards them. He was shirtless, his taut, chiseled stomach muscles flexing with each stride, mud dribbling down his tan muscular chest. "Thanks," he said when he got to them. He swept Hannah up in his arms.

"You're going down with me," Hannah promised.

Jacob, his eyes shimmering with amusement, shook his head and said, "Just you."

At the puddle's edge, Hannah kicked hard, freeing a leg, tripping Jacob. He fell sideways, pulling her down in his arms, landing on his side. They broke out into laughter.

Jacob rolled, pinning Hannah beneath him in the brown, squishy liquid.

"Jacob—get off me," Hannah ordered, trying to sound indignant, her eyes laughing.

"No," Jacob murmured leaning down, his face close to

hers. "Kiss me", he whispered hoarsely, his eyes scorching with desire.

Hannah felt the electricity between them ignite. Her heart was thundering, her pulse raced, longing sensations singing in her veins. Neither Jacob nor Hannah noticed the music had stopped playing.

"*Jacob*, you let her up NOW!" they heard Paige yell.

RECOGNIZING THE KEITH URBAN song playing on the radio, Paige turned up the volume. She looked over at Jacob, sitting in the passenger seat, listening to his iPod, staring off into the dark Kentucky night. Glancing at the clock on the truck dashboard and seeing the time, she took a deep breath. It was late, 10 p.m. She refused to feel agitated for being six hours behind schedule.

Looking in the rear view mirror, she saw Hannah, asleep against the truck door. Jaden, in the middle, was staring at Jonathan, asleep against the other door. She watched her daughter staring at Jonathan and she wondered if his coming along was a mistake.

Paige slowed down and turned into the Lexington Horse Park and drove towards the barns. The changing speed and turn woke Hannah, who sat up, her lovely brown eyes heavy with sleep.

"Good nap?" asked Paige, catching Hannah's eyes in the mirror.

Hannah nodded.

"When are Bill and Lori getting here?" asked Jaden.

"They will be here some time tomorrow morning," answered Paige, pulling up in front of barn twelve. She turned the truck off. Jacob and Hannah jumped out. Getting out of the truck, she threw a quick glance at Jaden and said, "Wake Jonathan up."

Placing her left hand on Jonathan's muscular shoulder, Jaden shook him lightly. Jonathan jerked instantly awake, his face rigid, irate and his right hand reflexively grabbed Jaden's arm in a steel, vise-like grip. Seeing Jaden, his face quickly softened and he looked surprised.

"Sorry," he murmured in a low voice, he released Jaden's arm.

"No worries," Jaden said gently. "We're at the Kentucky Horse Park."

BY EARLY AFTERNOON on Friday, the barn area was buzzing with frenzied activity. Hannah, riding Black Tie, returned from her dressage lesson with Lori Hoos, to find Jonathan sitting in a chair reading Sports Illustrated.

Hannah asked Black Tie to halt. She brought her right leg across his withers, sliding to the ground. "Where is everyone?"

"I don't know," Jonathan said, getting to his feet.

Hannah unclipped the chin strap of her helmet, removed it, and shook her hair out.

"Anything I can do to help?" asked Jonathan.

"Would you mind holding Black Tie while I untack him?"

"Sure."

Hannah ran the stirrups up, unhooked the girth, pulled off the saddle and saddle pad and carried everything into the tack stall. She returned carrying a leather halter and lead rope.

"Are you completely bored?" she asked.

Jonathan's dark brows knotted in a frown and he shook his head.

"Not at all. Why would you say that?"

"Cause this isn't for everybody," answered Hannah, gesturing to the barn area. "Especially for college guys from big cities."

Jonathan's lips parted in a devilish smile. "I had *no* idea there were so many pretty girls that rode horses."

Hannah laughed and removed Black Tie's bridle.

"Anything else I can help you with?"

Hannah looked at him, and smiled appreciatively.

"I'll be back shortly. I'm going to bathe my pony."

HANNAH TOSSED BLACK TIE AND LYRE another flake of hay and checked their water. She looked in on Gabriel. The burro was contentedly munching on hay.

"Gabriel," she said softly, holding out a carrot.

Gabriel's fluffy ears pricked forward, he stretched out his muzzle, his lips gently plucking the carrot from her palm.

Hearing the song "Barefoot Blue Jean Night" by Jake Owen on the radio, Hannah turned up the volume and she sat down to clean tack. Busy working on a bridle, she looked up and saw Jonathan approaching, flanked by two college-age girls. He dropped into a chair beside Hannah.

The brunette glanced back over her shoulder, throwing Jonathan a carnal look. "See you tonight, Jonathan," she said suggestively.

Hannah smirked. "I see you've made friends."

Jonathan nodded, watching them walk away.

"Have you seen, Jacob?" asked Hannah.

"Not for a while," replied Jonathan, picking up a sponge. He wet it, then dipped it into the soap and began cleaning a girth. After an extended pause, he asked, "Your accent isn't American. Where you were born?"

"I was born in Jerusalem," Hannah said. "When I was three, I moved to London and after my Mom died, I came to live here."

"Ten is young to lose a parent," said Jonathan, his deep voice tender.

Hannah looked away from his intense gaze. "Where were you born?"

"Berkeley, California."

"My grandfather, Isaac, was born in Berkeley, California," said Hannah, smiling.

"Do you like living in the States?" asked Jonathan. "Do you miss England?"

Looking up, Hannah saw his head was down, his eyes on what he was doing.

"I miss England at times, but I love it here," she said. "Ever been to England?"

Jonathan looked up and smiled. "A couple of times." He finished cleaning the girth, laid it down and reached for another one. "When did you start riding?"

"When I was toddler—it's in my blood," said Hannah. "My mother rode. So did her mother and father. "

"Do you want to ride professionally like Jaden does?"

Hannah shook her head. "No—I don't feel the *twingle* Jaden does."

"Twingle?" repeated Jonathan looking amused.

"It's a *Jadenism*," Hannah said laughingly. "It's what Jaden calls that special feeling you get deep down in your gut when you get excited about something."

"You two seem really close." Jonathan finished cleaning the girth, laid it down and reached for another one.

"Like sisters." Hannah put the clean bridle aside.

"How do you like working for Joe Martin?" she asked, reaching for another bridle.

Jonathan smirked. "I'm learning a lot."

"Joe travels often," said Hannah. "I've heard his house is filled with treasures."

Jonathan nodded.

"You've no idea," he said in a low voice, a hint of sarcasm in his tone.

They worked in silence.

Hannah stopped suddenly. "*How* did you know that my mother died when I was ten?"

Jonathan froze momentarily. "Mmm . . . Jacob told me," he said, his expression shifting abruptly into an unreadable mask.

"What is it you want to do after graduation?" he asked.

Hannah shrugged and said through a laugh, "I've no clue."

"You probably possess skills you're unaware of," said Jonathan in a tone of affection. "You have plenty of time to figure it out."

Hannah's eyes widened. "What time is it?" she asked worriedly.

Jonathan looked down at his watch. "Almost four."

Hannah sprang to her feet. "I've got to go—the cross country walk with Bill is at four."

BY LATE AFTERNOON, the cross country course walk with Bill had been completed. The horses and Gabriel were fed and watered and a time and place for dinner was agreed upon. Arriving at the restaurant there was a 45-minute wait for their group of twenty-seven. Eventually tables were pushed together and everyone was seated. Jacob and Hannah were sitting at one end of the table, their heads together, lost in a private conversation. Paige was settled at the other end between Becca Hoos and Morgan Shaw.

Paige peered over her menu, looking at Morgan. "I saw the picture you posted on Facebook of Carmac with his muzzle on Bill's sleeping head—I loved it," she said with a laugh. "Carmac looks fantastic. I can't wait to see him go tomorrow."

"Thanks," said Morgan, a proud smile stretching across

her pretty face. Carmac, a seventeen-hand chestnut thoroughbred and grandson of the great AP Indy, was her horse.

Paige glanced at Jaden sitting beside Lori Hoos, completely absorbed in a conversation. Jaden hadn't looked twice at the college girls flirting openly with Jonathan. Paige realized she had been worrying needlessly about her daughter's focus. Jaden loved competing and not even a handsome co-ed was going to distract her from her goal.

Paige returned to reading her menu. Having decided on a grilled chicken salad, she put the menu down and turned to Becca Hoos.

"Jaden's been telling me all about your horse, Celtic Rhythm." She leaned close to Becca and whispered, "Don't tell Jaden, but dapple gray is my absolute favorite color."

Becca grinned.

"You look happy, Paige," Morgan said, laying her menu down. "Happier than I've seen you in a long time."

"I am," Paige said sincerely and turned to the waitress with her order.

CHAPTER 22

SATURDAY MORNING CAME EARLY AND by six, Jaden, Jacob and Hannah were at the Lexington Horse Park barn twelve. Jacob was leaning against the stall door watching Hannah braid Black Tie's mane. Jaden, in the next stall braiding Lyre's mane, looked up to see Jonathan walking towards them; a steaming Styrofoam cup of coffee was in his large hand.

"There's Jonathan," she announced. He was dressed in the same clothes from the previous night, his dark hair wet and disheveled.

"I brought you a clean shirt. It's in the tack stall," Jacob said when Jonathan stopped beside him outside Black Tie's stall.

Jonathan nodded in appreciation and took a sip of his coffee.

"Rough night? Brunette or the blonde?" teased Hannah.

"Both," replied Jonathan with a cool, smug smile.

"We've been here *two* nights, and you've already slept with three girls," Jaden said coolly.

"You make it sound like that's a bad thing," Jonathan said, sounding amused. "I'm sure Jacob appreciated having the room to himself."

"Have you ever had a serious relationship?" asked Jaden hastily.

Jonathan took a sip of his coffee. "Define serious."

"You know what I mean," chided Jaden.

"If you mean—have I ever had a serious sexual relationship—the answer is yes," Jonathan said, his full lips curving into a cocky smile.

"Have you ever been in love?" prodded Jaden, trying to sound nonchalant.

"No, I've never been in love," answered Jonathan, his gaze shifting to the burro's stall. He eyed the blushed-colored donkey.

"I've noticed that Gabriel is the only donkey at this horse show," he said.

"I kid you not," answered Jacob. "My Mom would have that donkey living in our house if Jaden and I said okay."

"That's the *truth*," agreed Jaden with a laugh.

Paige appeared carrying two bags of Chick-fil-A.

"Breakfast!" she announced, putting the bag down. "I've got the starting times for today's Dressage and Cross Country and it's going to be tight."

"Who goes first?" asked Jacob.

"Hannah and Black Tie go first. Jaden and Lyre follow four riders later," answered Paige. "Jonathan, it would be great if you could help Jaden since Jacob and I will be at the Dressage ring with Hannah."

"Sure." Jonathan nodded. Turning his eyes on Jaden he said with a smile, "Just tell me what you want me to do."

Jaden looked quickly away from his attentive gaze, forcing herself to focus on the ground.

"Thank you, Jonathan," said Paige. "When they go this close together, it can get hectic."

"When do I need to be up at the Dressage ring?" asked Hannah.

Paige looked down at her watch.

"Be up at the ring in forty-five minutes," she said. "Lori will already be there."

THE DRESSAGE RING was set up within an enormous fenced area. Around the outside edge were letters, starting from the point of entry and moving clockwise, each letter specifying what movements were to be performed.

Hannah and Black Tie were the next to go. Jacob was crouched down hurriedly applying hoof polish. Finished, he straightened and smiled up at Hannah. "Have fun."

"The wind has picked up," said Hannah, her eyes on the enormous ring before her.

"Use his spookiness to your advantage," suggested Lori Hoos coming to stand beside Jacob.

Hannah nodded. It was her turn. As she entered the ring at a working trot, a gust of wind caught a plastic bag. Black Tie reacted to the crackling sound, his ears pricked forward, and his trot exerted more energy.

Black Tie halted squarely and balanced. Hannah saluted and proceeded at a working trot to the right. As they reached the letter M, the wind picked up again, the bag swirling in the air. She felt Black Tie react to the rustling bag, and she added impulsion to his extended trot across the diagonal.

After the extended trot, Hannah was able to bring Black Tie back to a working trot. She turned up the center line, performing an adequate leg yield to the right to the letter M, transitioning at M, a bit late, into a working canter. She did a half circle at a medium canter, opening up his stride, allowing him to show his powerful gait, returning back to a working canter at the letter B.

At the letter M, she rode a half circle of ten meters to

the left, returning back to the track at the letter B where she transitioned, somewhat awkwardly, into a counter canter. At the letter E, she returned to a working trot, turning right down the center line at C, and performing a satisfactory leg yield to the left all the way to the letter F.

Hannah repeated all the same movements and by the time she reached the letter A, transitioning into a medium walk, she could tell that Black Tie was ready for his walk break. His free walk across the diagonal was relaxed and loose, with an enormous swing in his gate. At letter C, she picked up a working trot again, turning right at B, then right again at the letter X where she halted and saluted.

Walking from the ring, Hannah patted Black Tie on the neck and headed straight towards the spot where Jacob stood waiting. Kicking her feet out of the stirrups, she swung her right leg over and slid down into his waiting arms.

"That was awesome," Jacob said lovingly, lowering her slowly to the ground. He tenderly brushed a stray hair away from her eyes.

"I'm proud of you."

Hannah smiled fondly. "Thanks."

"I'll take Black Tie back to the barn. You stay here and watch Jaden," said Jacob, taking the reins from her.

RETURNING TO THE BARN, Hannah discovered that Jacob had unbraided Black Tie's mane.

"How did Jaden and Lyre do?" he asked, stepping out of Black Tie's stall.

"They did great," said Hannah exuberantly, flinging her black coat across the aluminum portable saddle stand. She collapsed into a director's chair, pulled her helmet off, and shock out her hair. She turned her face towards the sun, and closed her eyes. The feel of the hot sun on her skin disappeared. Opening her eyes, she saw Jacob standing over her.

Jacob bent down and placed his hands on the chair arms, his face inches away from hers. He smiled invitingly and said, his voice low and gravely, "Anything else you'd like me to *do*?"

Hannah cocked her head to the side and beamed coquettishly. "Nothing springs to mind."

Gabriel hee-hawed and activity in the barn area seemed to stop as people looked around searching for the source of the funny noise.

"That's not something you normally hear at horse shows," said a young woman riding past on a big chestnut horse.

Gabriel hee-hawed again.

Jacob and Hannah looked around and saw Jaden and Lyre approaching.

"How was Lyre?" asked Jacob, taking the reins from his sister.

"She was behind my leg on the first diagonal and we had some balance and straightness issues with the counter canter," Jaden said, removing her black coat and throwing it over the back of a chair. She removed her helmet, dropping it next to Hannah's helmet. "But overall—I'm pleased."

Hannah handed her a bottle of water.

"You had an awesome ride, Han," Jaden said sincerely, plopping down into the director's chair beside her. "That was the best test I've ever seen you ride."

"Thanks," said Hannah. "Lori told me to use his spookiness to my advantage."

"Well, you did a good job," Jaden said, taking a drink.

Jacob emerged from Lyre's stall. "Where's Mom?"

"She stayed with Lori to watch Carmac and Celtic Rhythm go." Jaden looked around and asked, "Where's Jonathan?"

"We haven't seen him," said Hannah.

Jaden snorted. "After two nights of nocturnal activities, he's probably somewhere sleeping," She put on a baseball cap and pulled the cap low over eyes.

"Thanks for taking care of my horse, Jacob," she said, standing. "I'm going back to the Dressage ring. See you later."

———————————— ••• ————————————

TWO HOURS LATER, Hannah was in the tack stall struggling with the clasp on her necklace when she heard Jacob's voice, "Need some help?"

"Actually yes," said Hannah, glancing up at him. Holding out the necklace, she dropped it into his open palm.

Hannah watched him but his eyes were on what he was doing. He reached behind her neck, his fingers brushing against her skin, clasping the lobster closure and then gently tucked it under her T-shirt. His eyes found hers and he smiled lovingly.

"Nervous?"

Hannah shook her head and slipped on her protective riding vest.

Jacob diligently checked her vest, his eyes meeting her gaze. Raising his right hand, he tenderly caressed her cheek, running his fingers gently down her face.

"All I think about is you," he whispered, unbridled longing in his voice. He slowly traced her lower lip with his thumb. "I've *wanted* to kiss you for a really long time."

Hannah shivered, hunger for his touch assaulting every nerve ending. Her legs felt like jelly.

Jacob took her face between his hands, his fingers curling around her jaw and throat, his eyes fixated on hers. He leaned in, his mouth claiming hers hungrily, passionately.

Hannah felt intense heat filling her, coursing through

her veins. Her hands moved to his head, her fingers twisting in his soft hair, clutching at him pulling him closer.

"*You two pick now to start kissing? You've had all summer*—AND YOU PICK NOW!" Jaden roared. She was standing in the doorway, hands on her hips, her green eyes glowing with annoyance.

"*Bill's waiting on you, Han,*" she cried. "*You should be on your horse!*"

"Black Tie's ready to go," said Jacob, his eyes never leaving Hannah's. "Just need to get him from his stall."

Jaden snorted, spun on her heel and stomped off.

Jacob's mouth found Hannah's again.

"Jacob," breathed Hannah. "I've got . . . to go."

Jacob grinned, straightened, and taking her hand in his, headed for the tack stall door. Hannah followed him to where Jaden stood holding Black Tie.

"I've already tightened the girth," insisted Jaden, giving her brother a fierce look. She handed him the reins.

Hannah picked up her helmet, put it on, snatched up her crop and turned to follow Jacob and her horse.

"Good luck, Han," Jaden hollered.

Hannah glanced back. "Thanks—you too!"

They walked away from the barn area and stopped by a tree. Jacob pulled down the left stirrup, then the right one. He vaulted her up into the saddle and adjusted her foot in the stirrup, his hand lingering on her leg.

Hannah grinned.

Jacob looked up and smiled. "What are you laughing about?"

"I'll tell you after Cross Country," Hannah laughed.

Jacob nodded. "I'll meet you at the start box."

Hannah stared into his eyes. "I'm crazy in love with *you,*" she said and not waiting for his response, asked Black Tie to trot forward. Arriving at the warm up area, she knew by the expression on Bill's face that he was displeased.

"You're late," he said firmly.

"I'm sorry," replied Hannah, pressing her lips together to suppress a joyful smile. Bill pointed to one of the warm-up fences and said, "Go—you don't have much time."

Hannah and Black Tie jumped the vertical twice. She heard the announcer call her number.

"Thanks, Bill," she called over her shoulder. She trotted Black Tie towards the start box.

Jacob was standing at the start box, his hands jammed into the front of his jeans. He smiled.

"Have fun," he yelled.

Hannah smiled back and walked Black Tie into the start box. She experienced the familiar adrenaline rush building. Her heart was racing in excited joyous anticipation.

"Ten seconds," shouted the horse show attendant. "Three . . . two . . . one—have a good ride!"

They were off.

Black Tie settled quickly into a gallop, his muscles stretching, and lengthening, covering ground at a fast speed. The thrilling sensation of galloping a horse at such speed enveloped her—it was like flying without wings. The first five jumps were all straightforward and they jumped them without any issues. Approaching jump six, a combination, Hannah remembered what Bill had said about pace—that it was key on the approach.

Black Tie jumped through the two elements without difficulty and they galloped on towards jump seven, a large but straightforward obstacle. They jumped seven and then eight cleanly. Knowing the combination coming up demanded confident, skilled riding, Hannah glanced down at her stop watch, checking their time. The longer route would use up a lot of time. She decided to take the shorter, more difficult route.

Black Tie was a stride away from the fence when Hannah, out of the corner of her eye, saw something furry coming at them. Black Tie saw it too, just as his front legs left the ground—and everything went black.

CHAPTER 23

WHEN HANNAH OPENED HER EYES, she saw her grandmother sitting in a chair beside her bed. She had no idea where she was or how she had come to be there. Her mouth was dry and her body ached. She felt battered.

"Where am I?" Hannah croaked.

"Saint Joseph Hospital in Lexington, Kentucky," said Sheila in a warm voice, an expression of love on her face. She stood up, bent down and hugged Hannah gently.

"The hospital," exclaimed Hannah. Her memory was hazy. Closing her eyes, she saw Jacob's smiling face. She remembered their kissing and her riding away feeling like she was floating. She remembered bursting out of the start box and flying around the course. Her eyes flew open.

"Did I have a fall?" she asked her grandmother.

"Yes."

Hannah panic stricken, blurted, "Black Tie, is he ok?"

"Other than some scratches, he's unscathed," said Sheila, her tone soft and reassuring. "You're the one who got banged up."

Hannah stared down at her body under the white sheet,

her eyes flicking to her grandmother. "How banged up am I?"

"You sustained a cracked collar bone and a broken ankle," said Sheila simply.

Hannah flicked the sheet aside and stared at the plaster cast on her left ankle.

"God had his hand on you yesterday," Sheila said with conviction. "There's no other way to explain how you weren't hurt more seriously."

"Yesterday? What day is it?"

"Sunday evening," replied Sheila. "Grandpa and I arrived late last night."

"Where's Grandpa?"

"He drove Jacob to the hotel."

Hannah's expression brightened, her lovely brown eyes flashing with joy.

"Jacob refused to leave the hospital last night. He went to shower and will be back shortly," said Sheila. "I've never seen him so distressed. That boy is in love with you."

Hannah beamed and was about to say something when the door creaked opened and Jacob strolled in. He was dressed in jeans and a white T-shirt that hugged his shoulders and chest. He ran his fingers through his still damp hair.

"Hey stranger," he said, somewhat shyly, the color rising in his cheeks. "How are you feeling?"

"Stiff and groggy," croaked Hannah.

Sheila leaned over and kissed Hannah on the forehead.

"I'm going to go get myself a cup of coffee," she announced. She turned to Jacob.

"Can I get you anything?"

Jacob shook his head. "No thanks," he said, his eyes flicking up to her face, then darting quickly back to Hannah.

"I'll be back in a while," Sheila said as she marched towards the door.

Jacob pulled a chair close to the bed. The expression on his face was one Hannah had never seen before. Picking up her hand, he held it against his face.

"I've never felt fear like I did when I saw you and Black Tie crashing to the ground. I was so scared," he whispered, his eyes boring into hers. "I couldn't get to you fast enough . . . it was like I was running in place." Turning her hand palm up, he pressed his lips to the inside of her wrist, his lips flicking slowly across her skin.

"I kept repeating, 'Please don't take her, please don't take her,' and when I got to you . . . you weren't moving," Jacob said, his voice faltering. "I thought you were dead and all I could think was that you didn't know how much *I love you*." He swallowed, his gaze intense, his eyes radiating with love. "I can't imagine what it'd be like living each day without you." He kissed her hand again.

Their eyes held and the silence deepened. Finally, Jacob asked, "Do you remember your fall?"

"I remember approaching the fence and seeing something furry running out," replied Hannah. "Then everything went blank."

"That fury something was a dog that got away from its owner."

Hannah looked distraught. "Did the dog get hurt?"

"Neither animal got hurt. You were the only one," Jacob said. "Black Tie spotted the dog on takeoff and he slowed, catching his forearm on the jump, causing his body to rotate, sending you flying through the air."

"Will you tell me the truth?" pleaded Hannah.

Jacob nodded.

"Is Black Tie really ok?"

Jacob laughed and rolled his eyes.

"Yes, your horse is fine," he growled playfully. "He had a couple of scratches on him—that's all. Actually, it's amazing neither of you were hurt worse."

Hannah smiled in relief. "Gram said that he was fine,

but I wasn't sure if she was protecting me from the truth."

"I spoke with Mom—they got back to Jackson about two hours ago. She said Black Tie was happy to be home and he finished his dinner," said Jacob reassuringly.

"What about Jaden? Did she see the crash?"

Jacob nodded. "She saw it."

"Did it have any effect on her ride?"

"It unnerved her," admitted Jacob. "But no it didn't. Bill took her aside and talked to her and she went out and did everything he told her to do."

"If I'd seen her crash, I know I couldn't have done that," Hannah said admiringly.

"Your crash really freaked Jonathan out. He'll probably never go to another horse show." Jacob was lightly tracing his fingers up and down her arm. His touch sending tingles through her body.

"Jacob—that tickles, stop it," stammered Hannah.

"Stop what," asked Jacob, his eyes locked on hers. Lifting her hand to his mouth, he tenderly kissed the back of her hand, then flipped her hand over and nibbled delicately on the inside of her wrist, his tongue swirling in tiny circles.

Hannah groaned, trying to jerk her arm away. "That— what you're doing—it's driving me crazy."

Jacob stood up and leaning down, kissed her tenderly. His mouth moved to her neck, his lips brushing against her skin.

"You have my heart, *Michal*," he whispered in her ear.

A middle-aged nurse entered the room, announcing spiritedly, "It's time to get some vitals."

Jacob straightened, and turned to the nurse, an impish grin on his face.

"Get her blood pressure first," he said, heading for the door.

The nurse smiled down at Hannah. "That boy seems mighty crazy about you," she said. "He refused to leave your side."

Hannah smiled blissfully and asked, "How long will I be in the hospital?"

The nurse plucked a thermometer into her open mouth.

"Dr. Franzen is talking with your grandparents now," she said. "I imagine you will be with us for a couple more days."

CHAPTER 24

O N THE LAST SATURDAY IN July, two weeks after Hannah's fall at the Champagne Run horse show at the Lexington Horse Park, Jacob carried her out of the Butler's house and he carefully deposited her in the passenger seat of the Jeep. Roscoe and Duke, in the back, greeted her arrival enthusiastically with slobbering licks.

"Hi, boys," she said, petting them. Spotting her grandmother's picnic basket, she looked at Jacob surprised. "What are you up to?"

"Sheila put something together for us before they left for Atlanta this morning," confessed Jacob grinning sideways at her. He turned the key in the ignition and shifted into drive.

Hannah glanced up at the sky and looked at Jacob skeptically.

"A picnic? Today?" she teased.

The day had started muggy and sticky hot. Thick, heavy clouds now blanketed the sky and severe thunderstorms were predicted for the west Tennessee area.

"It's not supposed to turn nasty until later today." Jacob drove out of the driveway and onto the road. "Mom called this morning. She's enjoying her girl's trip in Virginia."

Hannah laughed. "Is she still coming back on Tuesday?"

"She said she was."

After driving two miles, Jacob turned off onto a dirt road on Joe Martin's farm and drove until the road ended at a lake. He parked. Roscoe and Duke jumped down, bounding happily towards the water, and splashed loudly into the lake. Jacob jumped out of the jeep and swaggered to the passenger side. He put one arm around Hannah's back, the other slid under her legs, and he lifted her effortlessly from the jeep.

Hannah wrapped her arms around his neck.

"I didn't know you were such a romantic," she said, running her fingers through his soft hair.

Jacob smiled. "I'm not a romantic—this was Roscoe's idea."

"I'm not a complete cripple you know. I can walk," laughed Hannah.

Jacob lowered her slowly, gently to her feet.

"You never told me what the doctor said yesterday," he said, his gaze flicking down to her left ankle.

"He told me that my bones are healing nicely, but when school starts next week, I'll still be wearing the walking cast," said Hannah, slight irritation in her voice.

Jacob reached into the jeep, lifting out the picnic basket and a blanket. They turned and headed side by side towards a soft grassy area by the water's edge. Jacob laid the picnic basket on the ground and helped Hannah spread the blanket out. Hannah lowered herself onto the blanket and Jacob collapsed down on his back beside her. Grabbing Hannah, he pulled her onto his chest.

"Where did the summer go," he groaned, tucking an arm under his head.

"I don't know," said Hannah, reaching for his hand, hungry for his touch. She interlocked her fingers with his.

"Next summer, I want to go with you to Montana," she

said decisively, meeting his gaze.

Jacob laughed.

"I've been thinking too," he said, his thumb making small circles on the back of her hand. "I want to go with you to England."

"Really?"

Jacob nodded.

"What about your annual trip to Montana?" Hannah asked surprised.

"Montana isn't going anywhere."

With the tip of her finger, Hannah lightly traced his lips.

"I want to learn to fly fish," she said and grimaced playfully. "But I don't want to take the fish off the hook?"

"Most certainly—that's all part of the experience," murmured Jacob, gnawing playfully on her finger.

Hannah's lips parted in a sultry smile. "What would tickets to the Olympics be worth to you?"

"Depends on the events the tickets are for."

Hannah rolled her brown eyes nonchalantly. "Just . . . basketball, diving, swimming, judo, gymnastics—"

"No equestrian," Jacob smirked, a note of humor in his deep voice. "Not interested!"

Hannah laughed.

"Think your dad and Diana would mind if we stayed with them?" asked Jacob.

"Not at all. Did I tell you that they bought a new house?"

Jacob shook his head. He rolled Hannah gently over on her back. Lowering his head, he pressed his lips into the hollow of her throat, his lips delicately caressing her skin in a steady trail of kisses across her neck and up to her ear.

Hannah shuddered, her breath catching, his kisses sending a rampage of warm sensations surging through her. Her mind and body felt as if she were melting into him.

It started raining great sheets of gushing rain.

Jacob rolled onto his back laughing.

Hannah, laughing, scrambled to her feet. "I'm getting soaked!"

Jacob sprang up, pulling off his drenched T-shirt, his muscles glistening with wetness.

"What are you doing?"

Jacob opened his arms out wide.

"Remember when we were kids, the game we played in the rain?" He laughed and started running.

"The airplane game," said Hannah laughing with him.

Jacob ran in a figure eight pattern, stopping in front of Hannah. He shook his head vigorously, the water dripping from his drenched hair, adding to the streams of rain running down his tan muscular chest. He smiled crookedly, his eyes bright and earnest, extended his hand and said, "Come dance with me." He stepped forward, wrapped an arm around Hannah's waist, and pulled her close.

They started moving slowly, swaying in place.

Hannah ran her hands up and down his bare back, her hands sliding across his wet, warm skin, his muscles hard beneath her fingers.

Jacob kissed her temple, then the tip of her nose, his lips gliding slowly down to the corner of her mouth. He gently nibbled on her lower lip.

"I've loved you all along," he murmured through his kisses. His hands moved caressingly up her back, his fingers twisting in her hair holding her head as his tongue hungrily explored her soft mouth.

Hannah felt herself whirling and clutched at him, pulling him closer, clinging to him as their wet bodies swayed against each other in the rain.

At the sudden jolting crack of lightning, followed by a low rumbling of thunder, Roscoe and Duke came running. The sheets of rain turned into a waterfall. Jacob and Hannah scrambled around, gathering everything up. By the time they drove into the Butler's driveway, the wind was strong, bending and thrashing tall trees and the sky had darkened to a dark gray black.

Jacob pulled to the side door. "I'll bring everything inside," he said hurriedly.

Hannah climbed out, hobbled up two brick steps and opened the door. Duke and Roscoe trotted in behind her. She picked up the remote control sitting on the kitchen island, aimed it at a small flat screen television sitting on the counter top and pushed the on button. She turned to WBBJ.

Gary Pickins was standing in front of the weather map, indicating with his hand.

"A third layer of hot dry air acting like a cap, allowing warm air underneath to warm further, has caused more instability," he said. "Conditions will continue to deteriorate the next couple of hours."

"Are we under a tornado watch?" Jacob asked coming into the house.Hannah shook her head, handing him a cotton towel. "Severe thunderstorm warning."

Jacob wiped his face and arms, put the towel down and walked to the kitchen desk where a medium size box sat. Reaching into the box, he removed a weather radio, plugged it in and turned it on.

"You need to go help Jaden with the horses," Hannah said coming up beside him, slipping her hands under his wet shirt, clutching at him, pulling him closer.

"Go, I'll be fine," she whispered, brushing her lips against the corner of his mouth.

"I'll leave Roscoe with you," Jacob offered, smiling.

Hannah glanced down at the Rottweiler sprawled on his back in a goofy position on the hardwood floor.

"I know you love your dog," she said candidly. "But Gram left a clean house, and Roscoe farts, smells awful and—"

"He does smell bad," laughed Jacob.

Arm and arm, they walked towards the back door. Jacob opened the door.

"I'll be back as soon as I can," he said and turning, he ran out into the rain towards his Jeep, Roscoe and Duke cantering after him.

Hannah leaned against the door frame, watching until the Jeep disappeared from view. She closed and locked the door.

CHAPTER 25

———————•·•———————

THE POWER WAS OUT. JADEN was on the sofa reading by candlelight when she heard the back door clang open and her brother's highly distressed voice yelling, "Hannah's gone!"

"What do you mean she's gone?" exclaimed Jaden, looking skeptically at him. His white Tennessee T-shirt was dotted with large, wet spots. "Was her truck in the garage?"

"Yes. The back door was ajar and candles were burning but no Hannah anywhere." Jacob stretched out his arm, Hannah's iPhone in his hand.

"I found this on the floor in the great room."

Jaden took it from him and scrolled through the text messages.

Barn chores almost finished.
7:35PM, Jul 30

K.
Miss u!
7:39PM, Jul 30

Miss u 2
7:55PM, Jul 30

Going home 2 take shower. Will come over after.
8:34PM, Jul 30

OMG! I think tree fell on house. Heard breaking glass!!
8:59PM, Jul 30

Be there soon.
9:11PM, Jul 30

Jacob paced anxiously, back and forth, running his hands through his wet hair, his expression shifting from confusion to tortured worry.

"Where could she be?" he said, his voice agitated. "Check her voice mail."

Jaden clicked on Hannah's messaging app. "There's nothing there."

"Give me the phone," Jacob instructed, grabbing the phone from Jaden. "Hannah told me earlier she was recording a video for You Tube." His fingers danced over the screen searching for Hannah's video icon. Finding it, he hit the key.

Seconds later they saw Hannah, in her bedroom, holding a hair brush, "Jacob," she purred coquettishly. "My rendition of—WHAT ARE YOU DOING IN MY HOUSE? WHAT DO YOU WANT? LET GO OF ME—" Hannah's phone had fallen to the carpeted floor and they saw the bottom of large, leather boots. They heard Hannah's muffled scream, thumps and other unrecognizable sounds, and the deep voice of a man with a heavy accent said, "I gave her enough to keep her asleep for a couple of hours."

"We're cutting it awfully close," growled a voice Jacob and Jaden both recognized.

181

"The weather is an unforeseen complication," said the man with the heavy accent.

"I don't give a DAMN about the weather! That helicopter better be here at the appointed time," snapped Joe Martin, palpable fury in his voice.

"Bring her, now!" ordered Joe.

Jaden looked at Jacob horrified.

"Oh my God! Why would Joe Martin do this?" she screamed, springing to her feet. "This doesn't make sense! I don't understand! We've got to call the police!"

Jacob yanked his phone from his pocket and started dialing.

"I've got no service," he said, throwing his sister a sideways glance. "Where's your phone?"

Jaden pointed to the counter.

Jacob leaped deftly across the sofa and grabbed her phone off the counter.

"You've got no service either," he said, irritation in his voice. He handed it to Jaden, turned on his iPhone's flashlight and headed for the utility room.

"Jacob!" Jaden cried, following him. "What are we going to do?"

Jacob didn't respond. Inside the utility room, he stepped to a cabinet, opened the door, and rummaged hurriedly through it.

Jaden stomped her foot and shouted frantically, "What are you looking for?"

"Those stubby flashlights that Uncle Matt gave us," said Jacob hurriedly.

Jaden walked swiftly to a closet, flung the door open, grabbed a camouflage backpack off the floor and marched back to Jacob. She handed it to him. "I think they're in here."

Jacob stuck his hand into the backpack and said, surprise in his voice, "Jaden, look what I just found."

Jaden aimed her iPhone's flashlight at what he was

holding. It was his old hunting slingshot, the one their father had given him. He stuffed it back into the backpack. Unzipping a pocket, he found the stubby flashlights.

"Go put jeans on," he ordered.

Jaden returned minutes later dressed in blue jeans, a rain slicker over a T-shirt and sat down nervously beside Jacob on the bench.

"Do you have a plan?"

Jacob nodded. He leveled his gaze at her and said in firm voice, "You're going to drop me off at the barn and then go to the police. Armani and I will cut across the pastures to Joe's."

Together they walked out into the sprinkling rain.

"Jacob—LOOK!" screamed Jaden, pointing at a large oak tree lying on its side across the driveway.

"We'll take the Ducati," announced Jacob, disappearing inside the house. He reappeared seconds later carrying two helmets.

"I hope you remember the driving lesson I gave you." He put his helmet on.

"I do!" assured Jaden, pulling on her helmet.

Jacob indicated to Jaden to sit in front of him and he gave her the key. She put her hands on the handle bars. Using her left thumb, she clicked on the high beams, released the clutch and the Ducati lurched forward. The motorcycle wobbled several times but didn't fall over and after maneuvering the motorcycle around the tree, Jaden was on solid pavement. In less than five minutes, they were at the barn. Jacob jumped off and ran, flashlight in hand, into the dark barn.

Jaden turned the Ducati around, bent low, shifted, and sped out of the driveway. She turned right onto the county road and had only gone a block when she hit the brakes and the motorcycle skidded to a stop. She stared at the road in front of her—the one that would take her to the authorities in Jackson thirty miles away. Her eyes flicked to the road on the left—the one that would take her to a phone in less than five minutes.

Jaden glanced at her watch, time was ticking away. She couldn't afford to choose wrong. Removing her helmet, she closed her eyes, and turned her face upward. "*Lord,* I put my trust in you and I ask you to guide me down the right road."

She took a deep breath, exhaling slowly and opened her eyes. She pulled the helmet on, put the bike in gear, and accelerated forward, turning left.

The rain had subsided but an occasional bolt of lightning off in the distance lit up the night sky. Bending low, Jaden accelerated, flying over the wet, black pavement.

Rounding a bend, a bolt of lightning lit up the night sky. Jaden spotted his truck parked in front of a small white farm cottage.

Jaden turned right onto his gravel driveway and parked beside his Ford. Sliding off the Ducati, she tucked the key into her jeans pocket, removed the helmet and shook her hair out. She walked to the door, trying to ignore the butterflies fluttering in her stomach. She knocked.

The door opened and before her stood Jonathan King, wearing lightweight black cargo trousers, his shirt unbuttoned and open, his muscular chest partially exposed. He ran his hand through his disheveled dark hair.

"What brings you to my doorstep on this stormy Saturday night?" he said, his voice hoarse from sleep, his lips quirking upward in a charming smile.

"Our power is out—I need to use your phone," Jaden blurted anxiously.

"Sure." Jonathan stepped aside to let her pass.

Jaden stepped over the threshold into a sparsely decorated living room. The walls were painted a sandy shade, the curtains echoing the same hue. A 50-inch flat screen mounted above the fireplace served as the focal point for a black leather sofa.

"Why are you on the Ducati?" Jonathan asked curiously.

"A tree was down across our driveway." Jaden laid the helmet down, slipped out of her rain slicker. Her eyes met his.

"I *really* need a phone, Jonathan!"

Jonathan nodded. "Follow me," he said leading the way towards the kitchen.

"What's wrong with your mobile?" he asked over his shoulder.

"I don't know. It's not working," Jaden said hurriedly. "And you can't exactly text the *police*!"

"Police?"

"Joe Martin's gone crazy—he's kidnapped Hannah!"

Jonathan stopped abruptly and pivoted around, his expression dark, fierce, his eyes blazing.

"*What did you say*?" he demanded, steel in his voice.

Startled by his extreme demeanor, Jaden froze. The realization that she truly knew nothing about Jonathan King washed over, filling her with icy fear. She turned to leave, but Jonathan grabbed her arm, his reflexes cat-like.

"Hold on, you're not going anywhere," he growled.

Jaden tried jerking her arm away but his grip was like iron.

"LET ME GO!" She hit him in the chest with her free hand. It was like hitting a marble statue.

Jonathan reached for her other wrist, pulling her closer. She raised her knee, but he was quick and he shifted, pinning her up against the wall with his body, her arms over her head.

"*Please trust me, Jaden,*" he said in a husky whisper, his face inches from hers. "I need you to come with me."

Feeling his strong, hard body pressing against hers, Jaden struggled to focus. She took a long, deep calming breath and scrutinized him. His expression was severe but his eyes were trustworthy.

The eye is the lamp of the body. If your eyes are good, your whole body will be full of light.

"I trust you," she said sincerely and relaxed.

Jonathan nodded and stepped back, releasing her. Turning, he marched briskly across the kitchen and out the back door.

Jaden trotted after him down a narrow dirt path to an old garage. He swung the double doors open, and flicked on a light switch. The area was immediately flooded with fluorescent light. A silver-colored motorcycle was parked in the center of the room.

Jaden stared in wonder at the motorcycle. "What kind of bike is that? It looks like something from a Sci-Fi movie."

"It's a MTT Turbine Superbike." Jonathan pushed the motorcycle forward.

Jaden ran her hand across its futuristic lines. "How fast does this thing go?"

"I've gone over two hundred miles per hour on it," Jonathan said nonchalantly. He bent over a hatch in the floor where the bike had been parked, and flung open the door, revealing stairs leading below ground.

Jaden looked at him with apprehension, questioning.

"It's an old fallout shelter," he said, taking two steps down. "During the Eisenhower administration when anxiety about the cold war was high, a lot of American's built them." He descended, disappearing from sight.

Staring down the stairs, Jaden saw a light flicker on. She hesitated and then descended slowly down the staircase which curved to the left. The small square-shaped room was no longer stocked with the necessities for prolonged habitation, but was instead packed with equipment the likes she'd never seen before. A massive mounted flat screen spanned the length of one wall. Running parallel to the screen sat two long, rectangular tables filled with computers, flat screen monitors, a radio transmitter and other electronic equipment. Sitting in a leather executive chair in front of one of the tables, wearing a black shirt, was Jonathan.

"Welcome to the crib. Satellite will be coming up shortly," he said, his manner formal, his accent unfamiliar and not-American.

Jaden stood paralyzed, unable to move while her brain unscrambled itself. "WHO—ARE—YOU?"

Jonathan put on a headset and said, casually, without looking at her, "My name is Caleb Reynolds," and then he was speaking commandingly into a microphone in a foreign language she didn't recognize.

Jaden glanced around. She spotted a large board covered in pictures and her mouth dropped open. In the center of the board, there were two 8 x 10 photos—of Joe Martin and Hannah Butler.

Jaden walked over to the board and stared at the photographs. All but two were in black and white. There was a head shot of a thin lipped man with a skull and crossbones cap on his head; another of a man dressed in a Nazi uniform sitting in a chair with his hands folded; and several pictures of people in all manner of dress. The photographs of Hannah and Joe Martin were the only two in color. Staring in shocked bewilderment, she didn't realize that Caleb was standing beside her until he spoke.

"I'm with an agency called HaMossad leModi'in uleTafkidim Meyuchadim."

"In English—*please*," Jaden implored.

"I'm Mossad," answered Caleb, stepping to the board. Pointing at the picture of Joe Martin, he said, "Joe Martin's real name is Josef Reinhard Eichmann. He's a Nazi war criminal."

Jaden stared horrified at the black and white photograph of a good-looking young man in a Nazi uniform.

"This is Joe's older half brother, Adolf Eichmann," Caleb said pointing to the black and white head shot of the man wearing the skull and crossbones cap. "Adolf Eichmann was the coordinator of the final solution."

Jaden gasped.

Caleb nodded. "This is Klaus Barbie, better known as the Butcher of Lyon," he said, pointing to the photograph of the man dressed in a Nazi uniform sitting in a chair. His finger tapped on the photograph of a much younger Joe Martin.

"In his early twenties, Josef Eichmann served under Klaus Barbie when Barbie was head of the Gestapo in Lyon, France. Barbie had six sub-sections that answered to him, and Eichmann headed one of them."

Caleb was standing before a photograph of Hannah taken at the Champagne Run horse show, but he was pointing to a black and white picture of young woman resembling Hannah. "These people were members of the French Resistance that died by Josef Eichmann's hand."

"*But what does Hannah have to do with this*?" Jaden screamed.

"Everything," Caleb said flatly. He was standing at military parade rest with his feet shoulder width apart, his hands clasped behind his back, and his chest out. His black shirt clung to him perfectly, accentuating his shoulder and arm muscles.

"It's a long story. I don't have time to explain it right now." Caleb stepped over to stand in front of Jaden.

"Don't worry, Jaden," he said reassuringly, squeezing her arms. "Joe's not going to hurt Hannah. He needs her alive and I've got a team in the area that will keep him from fleeing."

Jaden's green eyes widened in horror as it instantly dawned on her that she hadn't told him about her brother.

"Jonathan—I—mean—Caleb," she sputtered in utter panic. "Jacob's on his way there right now!"

Caleb's smiling eyes immediately turned intensely serious. He touched his headset and began speaking authoritatively. Walking to the chair, he sat down and pushed several keys on a keyboard. The massive mounted flat screen before them filled with a green glow that slowly grew until it was clearly recognizable as a house and the area surrounding it.

"Is that Joe's house?" asked Jaden coming up behind him. "It's like I'm directly above it."

"Yes," said Caleb, swiveling the chair around. He stood up and walked to a portable cabinet against the short wall behind them, and he opened the door. He began removing tactical gear and equipment, putting it on methodically.

Jaden's eyes remained glued to the mounted flat screen, hoping to catch a glimpse of Jacob and Armani. It was fascinating, looking down on Joe's house. She could see everything with unbelievable clarity, thanks to some satellite orbiting above the Earth.

Caleb returned to where Jaden was standing. She looked at him and gulped. He resembled a guerilla-gladiator. He was dressed in all-black military fatigues, wearing an armored vest, knee pads, laced up combat boots and tactical weapons belt. His dark hair was in disarray and his muscular frame evident through his form-fitting clothes.

"I could use your help," Caleb said, putting his hand on the small of her back. He steered her to the chair.

Jaden sat.

Caleb pointed to the computers and monitors before her on the table.

"This equipment is state-of-the-art and monitors all forms of communication including television and radio," he said, looking at her, his expression business-like. "I need for you to sit here and watch the monitors and I need to know immediately if local law enforcement is alerted."

"You don't want their help?"

Caleb shook his head. "No, Jaden, I don't. We prefer to operate covertly."

Jaden looked up at the screen and then at Caleb.

"Show me what you want me to do," she said confidently.

Caleb explained what each monitor was for, what he wanted her to focus on and how to work several pieces of equipment. "Any questions," he asked.

"No—I've got it," murmured Jaden shaking her head, her wide eyes on Caleb. She watched him in awe as he leaned over and strapped a semi-automatic pistol to his right thigh and placed a fixed-blade knife on the back of his assault belt. He put on a black helmet with night vision goggles and mounted camera, adjusted his radio transmitter headset and picked up his assault rifle.

"See you soon," he said, winking, he pivoted and bound up the stairs.

Jaden watched Caleb's quick ascent and her gaze returned to the screen. All of a sudden, the image shimmied and disappeared, then immediately returned with two different views; the left view was of the house and grounds from the satellite, the right view were video images transmitted from the camera attached to Caleb's helmet.

Jaden stared at the right view, the road flashing by in a fuzzy blur—Caleb was traveling on his Superbike at a phenomenal speed. Her gaze flicked back to the satellite view on the left. Spotting movement at the top of the screen, it took her a second to realize it was Jacob on Armani. She fumbled for the headset in her lap, putting it on hastily. She pressed a button and yelled into the microphone, "CALEB."

"Yes, Jaden," he said, his voice flat and emotionless.

"I SEE JACOB!" she shouted.

"Jaden," said Caleb, his voice warmer, a whisper of amusement in his tone. "Speak as if I were standing beside you," and before she had time to apologize he asked, "What direction is he coming in from?"

"Umm...," said Jaden staring at the screen trying to get her bearings. "It looks like he's passing Joe's barn."

"Okay," Caleb said, and then he began speaking in a foreign language, his voice flat again. Jaden heard the voices of men answering in the same language and on the left screen she saw obscure figures emerging from the surrounding trees. She heard Caleb's voice call her name again.

"Jaden," he said, in the same level voice. "Remember what I said, remain silent, no matter what you see."

"Yes, I will."

"And I mean, no matter what you see," Caleb said, steel in his voice. "Contact should only be made under the two conditions I specified," and not waiting for her response, he returned to speaking in another language.

Jaden sat back in the chair, staring at the screens. On the satellite view, she watched as Armani carried Jacob closer to Joe Martin's house, a Nazi, and a true monster. She feared she might lose Jacob or Hannah or both of them—the pain pierced her heart. She pressed her lips together refusing to cry.

Jaden saw Jacob dismount. He quickly pulled off the western saddle and removed the bridle, dropping both on the ground. He patted Armani on the neck, and then turned and started running, his red Nike shoes clearly visible with each ground-covering stride. He rounded the northwest corner of the house, slowing when he reached the stone terrace outside of Joe's office. He crossed the terrace and he disappeared into the house.

Jaden felt her stomach knot in terror when he vanished from view. She cradled her head in her hands, her heart pounding, taking deep breaths, reminding herself to have faith and to trust in God. When she lifted her gaze, she could tell by the video image from Caleb's helmet that he was there. She heaved a sigh of relief.

She watched as Caleb got off the motorcycle and he walked around the front of the house. The view from the helmet camera was bobbing up and down with his steps.

She heard a male voice that she didn't recognize, and then another, and then Caleb's voice answered. On the screen she saw armed men working in pairs, moving out from behind the trees, moving stealthily through the darkness towards the house.

Two figures were moving along the backside of the house. Two others entered the garage on the east side of the house and disappeared from view. The last two rounded the southwest corner of the house and stopped. Caleb was one of the motionless figures.

Minutes ticked by in dead silence. The waiting gnawed at Jaden's insides. She closed her eyes, clenched her hands together and prayed. When she opened her eyes, the screen remained still and silent. The view from the helmet camera remained motionless, Caleb frozen like a statue. Minutes ticked by.

Suddenly, Armani spun to the right and galloped away. An immense cloud of dust rose from the ground washing the darkness. Within seconds, she was looking down at the swirling blades of a large helicopter. It landed on the west side of the house. Two figures emerged from the side of the helicopter closest to the house, and sprinted towards the house. She watched them run by the bushes where two of Caleb's men crotched behind bushes. The two men stepped onto the terrace and then disappeared into the house.

The view from Caleb's helmet camera remained motionless, unmoving. The minutes ticked by. The helicopter blades began spinning faster and five figures emerged from the door to Joe's office. They moved across the terrace. The view from the helmet camera came into focus and Jaden saw a large, burly man with dark hair, dressed in a T-shirt and jeans, dragging Hannah by the arm towards the helicopter. Hannah was twisting and thrashing, trying to break free of the burly man's grasp.

Caleb's helmet camera image began bobbing up and

down with each long stride he took. He was moving swiftly, covering ground quickly when Hannah spotted him. The stunned expression on her face caused the big man to glance around. Seeing Caleb, the man pulled Hannah to him, holding a large, shiny blade to her throat. Jaden could see stark terror etched on Hannah's face as the knife tip pushed into her skin. She heard Caleb speak in a foreign language, his voice soft and calming. She heard Hannah speaking the same language, the fear in her voice palpable.

Caleb and Hannah exchanged several sentences before the big man ordered them to stop. Caleb stood fixed. From his helmet camera Jaden saw two men in the distance, clad exactly like Caleb, running in semi-crouch positions. The big man, his back to them, didn't see them. Looking at the satellite view, Jaden saw two figures drawing near to the helicopter's rotor tail. She heard the crack of a gunshot. Glancing frantically at the screen, she saw that Caleb and Hannah were unharmed.

Jaden heard Caleb's voice. He said something and Hannah immediately twisted around, swinging her arm, connecting with the man's groin, his face contorted in agony. Hannah turned, and gimped towards the house, the big man chasing her. Caleb yelled at her, his tone commanding and angry. The big man caught her by the arm, threw her over his shoulder, and turned towards the helicopter. Jaden saw Hannah beating her arms against him but he just kept walking. From the helicopter door, a man started firing an assault rifle.

The view from the helmet camera abruptly turned sideways—Caleb crashed to the ground. Jaden reached to turn on her microphone when the view suddenly changed as Caleb rolled onto his stomach. He was speaking again and she heard several voices answer him. The big man was now almost to the helicopter with Hannah over his shoulder when Jaden heard another gunshot and the big man fell over frontwards, dropping Hannah to the ground.

Caleb was up, sprinting towards the helicopter, shouting. Hannah scrambled to her feet and started towards him. A thickset man with pale blonde hair, his arms covered in tattoos, jumped down from the helicopter, sprinting after Hannah. The satellite image showed the man closing the distance at an alarmingly rate. He grabbed Hannah and wrapped a thick, tattoo-covered arm around her waist. Reaching behind his back, his free hand reappeared clutching a handgun. He held the gun to Hannah's head. Caleb stopped in his tracks. He spoke again, in a soft, calming voice when into view of the camera appeared Joe Martin.

Jaden recoiled, the hair on her arms and neck prickling in genuine fright. He looked sinister, his face seething with unadulterated hatred, chilling her like an icy wind. He spoke in German, his voice full of contempt. Jaden heard Caleb answer him in German, his voice measured and calm.

Moving quickly for an old man, Joe grabbed the handgun from the tattooed man, and aimed it at Caleb's head. Suddenly, Joe bent over bellowing in pain, both hands clutching his eye, his gun dropped to the ground. The helmet camera swung right. Jacob was standing 50-feet away, his feet spread apart, his stance awkward and unsteady.

His face and body was bruised and bloody. In his left hand, he was holding his old hunting slingshot.

Caleb sprang forward, sprinting towards Joe, the helmet camera bouncing up and down rapidly; Jacob was no longer in view.

Jaden saw Joe had recovered his gun and he was holding it to Hannah's head. He faced Jacob and he snarled, "Am I a dog that you should come at me with a slingshot?"

Jaden heard Jacob's stern voice.

"Let her go, Joe!"

"Think your God's going to help you rescue your Jew girlfriend," Joe sneered with disdain.

"I trust God. I'm not worried about dying," Jacob said in an unwavering voice. "Now—let her go!" he demanded defiantly.

The sudden crack of gunshots made Jaden jump again. She heard Hannah shriek Jacob's name. Looking at the satellite image, she saw a figure crumbled on the ground. Jaden screamed and fumbled for the microphone. Turning it on, she shouted into it, "*What's happened to Jacob?*"

"Jaden, get off now," barked Caleb.

"No," she said. Her tone was fierce. "Not until you turn your head so I can see my brother." She watched as the view panned quickly to the right and Jacob came into view. He was moving.

"He's alive," said Caleb, he was breathing hard from running.

"Now get off!" he commanded.

Jaden turned the microphone off just as Caleb's right fist smashed into Joe Martin's jaw. The old man spun, swayed and collapsed to the ground. The helmet camera swung instantly around to the left, the thickset blonde man had a large blade in his right hand and he was holding Hannah by the arm with his left. Jaden heard Caleb say something in a foreign language, and Hannah immediately reacted, stabbing the man in the eye with her fingers. The man growled angrily and released his grip on Hannah's arm. On Caleb's command, she shuffled quickly away.

The pale blonde-haired man spun to his right, switching the knife to his left hand, thrusting it at Caleb who deflected it. Looking at the satellite view, Jaden saw Caleb crab walking, slowly, confidently, his arms crossed with a knife in each hand. The man switched the knife from his left hand back to his right, lifting his right arm up and down in an arch, slashing Caleb's forearm.

Caleb laughed, his tone utterly fearless. She watched

as the blonde-haired man charged at Caleb. Caleb sprang backwards, dropped his right shoulder, raised his left arm, swinging his knife. The blade cut across the blonde man's chest, blood oozed across his shirt and down his jeans.

The blonde-haired man brought his right arm up and around, but Caleb lifted his left arm straight up, blocking the blow. Then the big man shifted his weight to his right foot, kicking up and out with his left leg. His foot connected with Caleb's arm knocking the knife from his hand. Caleb spun clockwise towards the blonde-haired man, dropped his left shoulder, bringing his fist up with speed and strength, connecting under the man's jaw with a forceful whap. The man stumbled back several steps before righting himself, and then he lunged at Caleb. Caleb ducked low and spun underneath, plunging his knife into the man's side.

Jaden heard the man howl. She saw his lips curl back, his face contorted in pain. Before the blonde-haired man could right himself, Caleb spun around and kicked, his foot smashing into the man's face with a loud whack, sending him flying backwards.

Jaden looked at the satellite view and saw a flurry of movement. Caleb barked orders. Figures emerged from the east side of the house; others moved around the helicopter. She heard voices yelling in a strange language. She looked at the view from Caleb's helmet camera and she saw that he was walking towards the terrace. Hannah was on the ground beside Jacob, her hands and arms covered in blood. She was wailing.

Jaden screamed, reached up, yanked off the headset, and flung it onto the table. Turning, she sprinted up the stairs, out the garage door, and around the outside of the house to where she'd parked the Ducati.

CHAPTER 26

H ANNAH ADJUSTED THE HOSPITAL BED. To keep her mind from exploding with worry, she picked up the remote and flipped haphazardly through the TV channels. There was nothing worth watching and her finger pushed the off button.

Fear was clawing at her thoughts. She knew the way to conquer the fear and closed her eyes. She began speaking the words out loud in a low voice.

> *Whenever I am afraid, I will trust in You. In God, I will praise His word, In God I have put my trust; I will not fear. What can flesh do to me?*

The door creaked open. Hannah looked over to see Jaden and Cory, walking into the room.

"I'm so glad to see you. I've been going crazy," cried Hannah. "What's happening with Jacob?"

"I just spoke with Dr. Martindale. Jacob is out of surgery," said Jaden in a firm and calm voice. "The bullet in his femur has been removed. He has some broken bones, but he's going to be just fine."

"The nurses . . . wouldn't tell me . . . ," stammered Hannah, her eyes filling with tears. The feelings of shock and relief brimming over.

"Everything's going to be alright, Han," promised Jaden in a soft voice, walking over to the hospital bed.

"Jacob—"

"*Hush*," urged Jaden soothingly, stroking her on the head. "*He's alright.*"

"There was . . . so much . . . blood," whimpered Hannah, her face in her hands. "I thought Jacob . . . was going . . . to die."

Jaden climbed onto the bed.

"Shush," she said softly, wrapping her arms around Hannah. "Jacob's going to be okay."

"I heard glass breaking—I thought a tree had fallen on the house. I went to investigate and saw Joe Martin and this other man," sobbed Hannah into Jaden's shoulder. "Next thing I remember, I wake up and I'm in Joe's office with my legs and arms taped to a chair and Joe's talking in German." She wiped her eyes and stared at Jaden.

"How did Jacob know I was at Joe's?"

"He found your phone. We listened to the recording," said Jaden. "What happened when Jacob got there?"

"I looked up and there's Jacob standing in the door way. Joe and the other man had their back to the door and didn't see him," said Hannah. "He cut my leg bindings and was working on my wrist bindings when Joe heard the helicopter and looked around. That's when he saw Jacob. The burly man marched over, grabbed Jacob, and slugged him. Then Joe started beating him with this ghastly looking walking cane." The image of Jacob lying on the hardwood floor being repeatedly beaten flashed in her mind and she started crying again. Tears spilled out of her eyes, trickling down her lovely face.

"I thought Joe was going to beat Jacob to death. I don't understand why—"

"Joe Martin's real name is Josef Eichmann," blurted Jaden, pulling back to look at her. "He's a Nazi—"

"*What?*" Hannah stared disbelievingly at Jaden, her eyes wide in shock.

Jaden nodded. "Joe was an SS officer and he served under the chief of Gestapo in Lyon, France during—"

"*A Nazi,*" repeated Hannah. She shuddered. "The walking cane Joe was using looked like it had been made from human femur bones."

"*It probably was made of femur bones!*" cried Jaden, her face twisting in horror. "Adolf Eichmann was Joe's older half-brother."

"No . . . it's not possible," croaked Hannah, shaking her head. "This is all like . . . a horrible, surreal nightmare."

"I know," agreed Jaden with a sarcastic laugh. "Like something from a Hollywood movie."

"Han," interjected Cory, stepping closer to the bedside. "I called your grandparent's and they're on the way home."

Hannah nodded appreciatively.

"Mom's trying to get an earlier plane home from Virginia," added Jaden. "How's your leg feeling? The nurse told us they redid your cast."

"I'm not in any pain," said Hannah, shaking her head slowly. She felt suddenly drowsy. The pain medication they'd given her was starting to take effect.

At the sound of the door opening, everyone looked up to see a pretty woman with blonde hair and large, soft brown eyes wearing a hospital badge, walking in.

"My name's Tabatha." She smiled warmly. "I'm a friend of your mom's," she said, looking at Jaden.

"Ms. Tabatha," exclaimed Jaden surprised. "I remember you!"

"Your Mom called and asked me to check on all of you."

Jaden introduced Hannah and Cory.

"I've been down to recovery and Jacob is doing just fine," said Tabatha, her voice was calming.

"When can we see 'im?" prodded Hannah, her voice barely audible, her eyes heavy with drowsiness.

"When he gets into a room," said Tabatha

"When 'ill that 'e?" murmured Hannah, slurring her words.

Tabatha smiled tenderly at Hannah. "Soon."

Hannah closed her eyes.

"Get some rest, Han," whispered Jaden, stroking Hannah's hair. Hannah drifted into an exhausted sleep.

"They're going to keep Hannah over night," informed Tabatha, patting Jaden on the shoulder. "The nurses know how to get in touch with me. Feel free to call me if you need anything."

"Thanks, Ms. Tabatha," said Jaden, flashing her a grateful smile.

HANNAH PICKED AT HER BREAKFAST on the hospital tray. She pulled apart the muffin and plucked a piece into her mouth. At the sound of a soft rap on the door, Hannah looked up. It swung open and into the room walked Bethany Shevar. She was wearing a white dress with wedge heels, her long, lightly curled hair falling loosely down her back. She approached slowly, apprehensively, stopping beside the bed.

"Hi, how are you feeling?" she asked in a soft voice.

"I feel okay," said Hannah, staring at Bethany in disbelief.

"I'm so ashamed of my behavior, Hannah," insisted Bethany, her head down, a tormented expression on her face.

"I want to apologize to you for everything—for the way I acted, for calling you a gutter-slut, and most especially for starting that rumor about you and Jacob sleeping together," she said remorsefully, her blue eyes pleading."Can you ever forgive me?"

"I was angry for a long time," said Hannah coolly. "But I've forgiven you."

"Hannah—thank you," whispered Bethany, her eyes full of tears.

"Why did you do it? Why did you say the things you did?" asked Hannah in a voice of forced calm.

"The Thursday before you all left for Rolex, Jacob told me that he wasn't attracted to me. He said he would be my friend, but that's all. *No one's ever said that to me!*" Bethany said, brushing tears away with her long, elegant fingers. "After he left, I was *so* angry—at you. All I could think about was hurting you."

"Why?"

"I wanted Jacob—even though I knew he would *never* feel for me the way he does about you. My pride was wounded. I blamed you," said Bethany, her voice soft and even. "I'm so sorry, Han. *Please believe me.*"

"Jacob and I have been friends since we were children," insisted Hannah, meeting her gaze. "There was no need for you to be jealous."

Bethany rolled her eyes.

"It was in his voice when he'd talk about you and in his eyes whenever you would walk into the room," she said frankly. "I could see how it was between the two of you, even though neither of you could see it. You and Jacob are meant to be together. I'm truly happy for you."

The door creaked open and in walked a doctor wearing a white coat.

"Well, I'd better be going," said Bethany, turning to leave.

"Bethany," called Hannah. "What caused—"

"Me to change."

Hannah nodded.

"I started using God's Word as my manual on how I needed to live," said Bethany brandishing a radiant, genuine smile. She turned and strolled from the room.

CHAPTER 27

———◆·•·◆———

H ANNAH SHIFTED, TRYING TO FIND a measure of comfort in the uncomfortable hospital chair. She read the paragraph again.

Have you given the horse his might? Have you clothed his neck with quivering and a shaking mane?

It was pointless. She put the book down unable to focus when she could watch Jacob sleep. The pump beside his hospital bed gurgled, automatically dispensing medication. She could see the rise and fall of his chest with every breath he took. His face was hideously discolored in purple and black bruises—but not disfigured. White gauze covered two lacerations on his forehead and his cheek. The plaster cast on his forearm stopped just below the elbow. The cast encasing his right leg ended at mid-thigh. Slowly, he opened his eyes, smiled and asked in a hoarse voice, "Is there any water?"

"Yes, your Mom dropped off bottled water." Hannah laid her book down, reached into a red cooler, and removed a bottle of water and untwisted the cap.

"Where's Mom?"

"She'll be back," said Hannah, handing him the bottle of water. "She had to go meet Jim Honeycutt." Seeing Jacob's concern, she added quickly in a soft voice, "Armani only has a stone bruise, don't worry."

Jacob drank greedily.

"How are you feeling?" Hannah smiled.

"I've felt better. What day is it?"

"It's Tuesday." Hannah kissed his battered face tenderly. "Are you in pain?"

Jacob smiled a lopsided smile. "More like intense discomfort." His eyes flicked down to the bulky walking cast on Hannah's left leg and he asked, "How does your leg feel?"

Hannah shrugged. "Better—want me to read some more?"

Jacob nodded.

Hannah retrieved the book she'd put down and climbed carefully onto the bed next to Jacob, snuggling up against him. "Anything in particular you want me to read?"

Jacob shook his head. "You pick."

Hannah opened the book and began to read.

Have you given the horse his might? Have you clothed his neck with quivering and shaking mane? Was it you who made him to leap like a locust? The majesty of his snorting nostrils is terrible. He paws in the valley and exults in his strength; he goes out to meet the weapons of armed men. He mocks at fear and is not dismayed or terrified; neither does he turn back in battle from the sword. The quiver rattles upon him, as do the glittering spear and the lance of his rider.

There was a knock on the door, Hannah stopped reading.

"Come in," said Jacob and the door swung open. Into the room walked Cory Price wearing a broad smile on his attractive face, a short sleeve polo shirt that hugged his muscular frame, and khaki shorts.

Eyeing Jacob, Cory asked sympathetically, "Are you in pain?"

A grin spread slowly across Jacob's bruised and swollen face.

"Not at the moment," he said eyeing the pain pump beside the bed. "Thanks to that."

Cory laughed. "Seriously, man, you look like you collided with a train."

"So, I've been told." Jacob smirked.

Cory's eyes flicked from the cast on Jacob's right leg to Hannah's left leg. "You two really are perfect together. Even broken you make a matched set!" he said, stopping beside the bed. "The story about Joe Martin is getting international attention. The media is camped outside the hospital and outside your house."

"Glad I'm in here," confessed Jacob in a tone of mild sarcasm.

"Any idea when you get to go home?" Cory asked.

Jacob shook his head. His glazed eyes shifted to Hannah. Picking up her hand, he pressed it to his lips, then placed it over his heart and closed his eyes.

"They've got him on strong pain meds," declared Hannah, brushing her lips against Jacob's temple. "From what the doctor says, he'll probably be released on Saturday."

"He looks like he's about to go to sleep," admitted Cory.

Leaning in, Hannah whispered in Jacob's ear, "Sweet dreams, baby."

Jacob's face and body relaxed and he drifted off.

HANNAH, CURLED UP NEXT to Jacob on the bed reading, looked up when the door creaked open and was shocked to see her father. Arthur Butler looked handsome, chicly dressed in dark silk slacks and white cotton button down shirt with the sleeves rolled up. His black hair, peppered lightly with gray at his temples, was short and parted on the right. Seeing Hannah, his large, dark eyes moistened.

"*Dad*," Hannah squealed in happy surprise. "What are you doing here?" She hobbled into his outstretched arms.

Arthur wrapped his arms around his daughter, engulfing her in a hug with all his strength.

"Dad, I can't breathe," Hannah cried into his chest.

Arthur kissed the top of her head.

"I've been a *really* neglectful dad," he said, his voice ringing with guilt. He pulled back, placing his hands on her shoulders. "Can you forgive me?"

"Of course," muttered Hannah, her voice choked with tears. She fell against his chest and Arthur hugged her tightly.

"*Hush*," he pleaded. "Please don't cry. You look like an abandoned puppy and I can't stand it."

"She knows this is a no-cry zone," croaked Jacob, his voice gravely hoarse from sleep.

Hannah laughed.

Arthur smiled appreciatively, looking down at Jacob. "How are you feeling, son?"

"Not too bad," said Jacob, wiping the sleep from his eyes. "It's good to see you, sir. I'm glad you're here."

"Jacob," said Arthur, his composure on the brink of crumbling. "Thank you," he whispered. He opened his mouth to say more, but Jacob waved him off.

"No worries, sir," he said. "Did Mrs. Butler come with you?"

"Diane, Tristan, Edmund and Maria will be arriving Friday afternoon." Arthur looked down at Hannah, his dark brown eyes radiating with intensity.

"Your mother believed the safest, best place for you was here with my parents in Jackson," he said sincerely. "She made me *promise* that if something happened to her before you came of age, I would send you to live with my parents."

Hannah looked at her father puzzled. "Dad, what are you talking about?"

"It's time you knew the truth about your mothers family and *who you are*," said Arthur straightforwardly.

"What truth?" Hannah prodded worriedly.

"You come from an ancient family of extraordinary women dating back to Biblical times, directly to Achsah—a daughter of Caleb."

"Caleb—one of the chosen spies sent into Canaan by Moses?" asked Hannah in disbelief, her eyes wide in astonishment.

Arthur nodded. "Yes." His eyes flicked from Hannah to the book with gold embossed initials, H.L.B., lying on the bedside table.

"Your mother's Bible," he said, smiling wistfully. Picking up the Bible, he opened it to the book of Joshua. "Read chapter fifteen, verse sixteen to verse twenty," he instructed, handing the Bible to Hannah.

Hannah shot an incredulous look at her father. She took the Bible from him and returned to the spot on the bed where she'd been sitting. She glanced down at the page and began reading aloud.

Caleb said, 'He who smites Kiriath-sepher and takes it, to him will I give Achsah my daughter as wife.'

And Othniel son of Kenaz, Caleb's brother, took it; and he gave him Achsah his daughter as wife.

When Achsah came to Othniel, she got his consent to ask her father for a field. Then she returned to Caleb and when she alighted her donkey, Caleb said, 'What do you wish?'

Achsah answered, 'Give me a present. Since you have set me in the dry Negeb, give me also springs of water.' And he gave her the sloping field with upper and lower springs.

This is the inheritance of the tribe of Judah according to their families.

"Now look in the book of Judges," said her father, pulling a chair close to the bed and sitting down. "Read chapter one, verse twelve through verse fifteen."

Hannah turned to the chapter and read silently. Finished, she closed the book and stared wide-eyed at her father.

Arthur cleared his throat.

"Achsah, like her father, Caleb, had a fearless resolve to serve God and she recognized the great responsibility of her inheritance," he said. "And so she began the Legacy which has been passed down through the female line from Achsah all the way to you."

He paused, took a deep breath and continued, "The Legacy was meant to pass to your Aunt Miriam. When Miriam died, it passed to your mother and her biggest concern was protecting you."

"What is the Legacy?" asked Hannah. "Is it money?"

A half smile appeared on Arthur's lips.

"The enormity of the Legacy is indescribable," he said emphatically. "It is money, property and much, much more. Every generation added something to the Legacy from ancient scrolls and books to gold, precious stones and jewels to artifacts and knowledge."

Hannah blinked. "When do I come into this Legacy?"

Arthur leaned forward, his elbows resting on his thighs. "On your twentieth birthday, you'll receive your trust fund, a codex and twelve keys."

"What is a codex?" Jacob asked, frowning.

"A codex is an ancient handwritten manuscript," answered Arthur. "Around the time of Christ it became a popular writing surface because it could be folded and stitched together."

"An early form of a book," interrupted Jacob.

"Yes," answered Arthur. "The codex replaced Papyrus scrolls and is associated with the rise of Christianity."

Jacob looked at Hannah and asked, "Have you seen this codex?"

Hannah nodded affirmatively.

"When I turned ten, Mom showed me two codices," she said simply. "She told me there were others and that they were stored in special, concealed locations."

"Stored where?" Jacob asked.

"She didn't tell me that." Hannah's gaze shifted to her father. "Do you know where they are?"

"No," answered Arthur, shaking his head. "The *Key Keepers*—"

"Oh, wow, I remember," Hannah cried, her hands flying to her face. "It just came to me. I remember hearing about the Key Keepers."

"I had no idea that you'd been told," said Arthur with a touch of annoyance in his voice.

"I wasn't told, Dad," Hannah insisted. "At our last family gathering at the Chateau de Vignon, I was playing hide and seek with my cousins and I hid in the kitchen pantry. I overheard Aunt Miriam and Mom talking about the codex collection and the role of the Key Keepers."

"What are Key Keepers?" questioned Jacob.

"The Achsah codex collection and the Legacy treasures

are stored in separate locations around the world," said Arthur. "The Key Keepers are responsible for keeping those locations secret."

"Who are the Key Keepers?" asked Hannah.

Arthur shrugged. "I've no idea."

CHAPTER 28

H ANNAH, DRESSED IN SHORTS AND a white top, her silky dark hair falling down her back, was sitting in a hospital chair with a game of Battleship open on her lap. She looked at Jacob, and smiled a sly smile.

"B2."

Jacob glanced down at his board.

"Miss," he said, humor in his voice. His eyes shifted back to hers. "H9."

"Hit," muttered Hannah, pretending to scowl.

"Obviously, it's not your sub."

Hannah shook her head and said, "C2."

Jacob smiled crookedly. "Hit."

"I hope you're hungry," announced Paige, walking into the hospital room carrying a pizza box from Picasso Pizzeria.

"Hi, Mom," replied Jacob.

"Your timing is perfect, Paige." Hannah laughed. "Jacob was about to sink my battleship."

Paige laid the pizza box down on a small table.

"You look much better today," she said to Jacob, rolling

the hospital table over to the bedside.

"How are you feeling?"

"Ready to get out of this place," grumbled Jacob, adjusting the bed. He flipped the box lid open. "Today's only Thursday—"

"You're going home in thirty-six hours," chided Paige tenderly, sitting down in a chair.

"I had breakfast at The Baker's Rack," Paige said. "I ran into Martin Jelinek, Diane Abbott and Tawyna Moore—they said to tell you hello."

Jacob nodded. "What about school?"

"The school knows you're going to be out for a little while," replied Paige.

"*Dad*," yelled Hannah happily.

Arthur Butler walked into the hospital room, followed by a gray-haired man with pleasant smiling brown eyes, and Jonathan King.

Arthur cleared his throat. "Hannah, do you remember your grandfather, Isaac?"

Hannah stood up slowly, staring incredulously at her grandfather. At eighty-five, he projected a vivacity that flowed through him like sparks of static electricity. He stopped in front of Hannah, put his hands on her forearms and asked lovingly, "Do you remember me?"

Hannah bit her lip to keep from crying.

"Yes, Grundy," she whispered.

Isaac kissed her forehead and embraced her.

"You were ten-years-old the last time I saw you. I've missed you so much. Caleb was right—you're resemblance to Angelina is striking," he said in a quiet voice, his eyes flicking to Jonathan.

Hannah's head snapped up and she looked around at Jonathan, standing with his arms folded, and questioned disbelievingly, "*Caleb*?"

Jonathan nodded and he smiled affectionately.

Hannah slowly shook her head, her expression shifting

211

from shock and disbelief to anger as the information sank in. She rounded on her father, glaring at him.

"Why did you let me believe all these years that Caleb was dead?" she hollered, her eyes flashing in resentful fury. *"How could you lie to me?"*

"Hannah," said Isaac, his deep voice soft and calm. "Your mother didn't want anyone in the family to have *any* communication with you. We gave her our word that we would abide by her request to protect you."

The expression on Hannah's face changed to bewilderment.

"But why?" she demanded.

"Your mother was terrified that someone would learn where you were and come after you," replied her grandfather in a level voice.

"And that is *exactly* what happened," Caleb interjected, stepping forward. He wrapped his strong arms around her.

Hannah felt her anger dissolve, the combination of shock, disbelief, and elation overwhelmed her and her eyes filled with tears. She stifled a cry into his chest.

Caleb pulled back to look at her.

"I always knew where you were and what you were doing. We've kept an eye on you, Cousin," he said protectively.

"Cousin?" questioned Jacob and Paige in unison, staring at Jonathan in bewilderment.

"My real name is Caleb Reynolds. Jaden didn't tell you?" he asked, surprise in his voice.

Isaac stepped forward.

"Mrs. Winston," he said warmly, his eyes crinkling, extending his hand. "I'm Isaac Leitner—Hannah's and Caleb's grandfather."

"It's nice to meet you," replied Paige, smiling, shaking his hand. "Please call me Paige."

"Why don't we all get comfortable," suggested Arthur.

Isaac settled into a chair. Caleb disappeared into the hall and returned carrying an additional chair. He put it down next to his grandfather. Arthur and Paige sat down. Hannah climbed onto the hospital bed beside Jacob.

"Okay, *someone* needs to start talking," demanded Hannah impatiently, looking around at her father, her cousin and her grandfather.

Isaac wavered, seemingly torn by some internal dilemma.

"The need for secrecy is over, Isaac!" stated Arthur, steel in his voice. "There are others outside the family who know about the Achsah codex collection and the Legacy treasures."

"I agree," said Caleb meeting his grandfather's gaze.

Isaac nodded slightly and fixed his gentle brown eyes on Hannah.

"Josef Eichmann, or as you've known him, Joe Martin, had a history with your grandmother and her two older sisters, Angelina and Gabrielle Bonet," Isaac said. "Joe Eichmann served under Klaus Barbie, head of Gestapo, when the Germans occupied France during the war. Angelina, Gabrielle and Zara were in the French Resistance. For reasons unknown, Angelina took one of the ancient codices with her to a meeting at her boyfriend's. When the Nazis raided his apartment, they found the codex. Angelina was taken to Lyon and interrogated by Gestapo. That is how Joe Eichmann learned about your family's Biblical lineage and that is why he kidnapped you."

"But I didn't know anything about my Biblical ancestry, or anything about the Achsah Legacy," Hannah said heatedly.

"I know my dear," replied her grandfather. "But Joe didn't know that."

"Joe Martin has known Hannah for years," protested Paige with a slight shake of her head. "Why now?"

"Joe didn't know who Hannah really was," replied Isaac. "He became suspicious when he realized that someone—"

"I found his secret Nazi room in his house," confessed

213

Caleb. "I got clumsy and he noticed."

Isaac turned his appraising brown eyes on Caleb.

"You were clumsy twice. That's not like you," he said and he smiled warmly.

Caleb nodded, his expression hardened in evident annoyance.

Hannah looked at Caleb. "So—that's why you stopped coming around after we got back from the Champagne Run horse show," she said confidently.

Caleb nodded again. "I was afraid you'd figure out who I was."

"How did Joe discover that I was related to Angelina and Zara," asked Hannah.

"Most likely through your DNA," offered Caleb. "The man had unlimited resources so there's no telling. He had your house bugged, Hannah." Seeing the concern on the faces of Hannah, Jacob and Paige, he held up his hands and added, "The FBI swept the house. Everything has been removed."

Hannah stifled a shiver. She stared wide-eyed at Caleb and asked, "Why did you come to Jackson when you did?"

"Remember when Gabriel attacked Joe and ripped his shirt off of him? You posted the pictures on Facebook. Adah saw your post," said Caleb. "She recognized Joe's arm tattoo for what it was and—"

"Why would my childhood nanny recognize his tattoo? I don't understand!" Hannah cried, her gaze shifting between Caleb and her father.

"Adah Winters was no ordinary nanny—she was your bodyguard," answered Arthur. "She possessed the skills your mother desired. Your mother entrusted your life to Adah—more importantly, she was family."

"Adah is family?" repeated Hannah eagerly.

"She's your mother's cousin," said Arthur, nodding.

"Caleb," said Paige, looking at him. "What did you mean about the tattoo—'for what it was'?"

"It's called a blood tattoo and it was worn by members of the Waffen-SS."

"I always knew Gabriel had a gut dislike for Joe Martin," exclaimed Paige proudly.

"Grundy, if Joe Eichmann had the codex," said Hannah, casting a curious look at her grandfather. "Why did he want me?"

"He didn't have it. Your grandmother stole it back," said Isaac with a satisfied grin.

"What was my grandmother Zara like?" asked Hannah.

"Your grandmother was a remarkable woman," said Isaac lovingly. "She was intelligent, brave, and feisty. Foreign languages were easy for her. She spoke Italian and German perfectly and mixed easily with the Germans. With her blonde hair and blue eyes, they never suspected that she wasn't Aryan. She worked at Gestapo headquarters. That's how she was able to steal the codex back."

The door swung open and Jaden walked in. She was wearing a short sleeve top and western boots with old jean shorts that showed off her toned, tan legs. Seeing Caleb, she stopped and stared at him, utterly thrown by the sight of him. Her mouth opened but nothing came out.

Caleb sprang up and was instantly at her side. Putting his hand on the small of her back, he gently steered her over to Isaac.

"Jaden this is my grandfather, Isaac Leitner."

Isaac, already on his feet, hugged her.

"Thank you for helping to rescue my granddaughter," he said, releasing her.

Jaden blinked, still dazed and stared at Isaac wide-eyed. Her green eyes slid slowly to Caleb and she murmured, "You're . . . *that* . . . Caleb?"

Caleb nodded, brandishing a dazzling smile.

"Jaden," said Jacob. "Why didn't you tell us that Jonathan's real name was Caleb Reynolds?"

Jaden rounded on her brother, her hand on her hip.

"*Seriously?*"

Jacob grinned sideways at her.

"Well, let's see," said Jaden sarcastically, rolling her eyes. She extended her thumb. "First, my best friend gets kidnapped by our neighbor who turns out to be a Nazi war criminal." She extended her index finger.

"Second, you get beat up, almost to death, and shot." Jaden extended her middle finger.

"Third, I've been teaching riding lessons all week." She extended her ring finger and pinkie finger.

"We start school tomorrow and the media is camped out at the end of our driveway." She put her hand up and said, "Five reasons why it slipped my mind, Jacob."

"I was just curious," said Jacob with a shrug.

"Grundy, what happened to my great-aunt Angelina?" asked Hannah.

After a long pause, Isaac turned his brown eyes to Hannah and said in a soft voice, "She was beaten to death by Joe Eichmann."

CHAPTER 29

ISAAC PUSHED HIMSELF UP AND out of the hospital chair, announcing, "I don't know about the rest of you but my stomach won't let me ignore it any longer."

"There's cold pizza," joked Paige.

Isaac smiled politely and shook his head.

"The hospital has a good food court," declared Arthur, rising to his feet.

"Sounds good," said Isaac. He looked at Hannah, Jacob and Jaden and announced. "At some point, there is a financial matter to discuss. There is a reward for providing information that led to the capture of Josef Eichmann."

Jaden glanced impatiently at the wall clock, anxious to escape. She had no appetite. She was struggling with the rush of tangled emotions she felt every time Caleb Reynolds looked her way. His blue eyes, free of the dark contacts, were breathtaking—the kind of eyes you could melt into.

"I have horses to feed," announced Jaden.

Suddenly, Caleb was standing beside her, his eyes questioning. "You're not going to eat?"

Jaden shook her head.

Caleb smiled invitingly. "How about I go with you to the barn and we can talk?"

"Okay," agreed Jaden, trying to sound casual.

"We're going to feed the horses," said Caleb to no one in particular, as he followed Jaden out of Jacob's hospital room. They strolled down the hall in silence and stepped into a very crowded elevator. The large man standing beside Jaden shifted abruptly, knocking her into Caleb who chivalrously caught her, his arm wrapping protectively around her waist. The feel of his muscular arm made her heart thump hyperactively.

The elevator stopped, the doors opened and the crowd shuffled out.

"I didn't think I'd ever see you again," Jaden confessed quietly, stepping off the elevator into the bustling hospital lobby.

"I told you the night Hannah was kidnapped that I'd see you again," said Caleb.

"You did," agreed Jaden, without looking at him, trying to keep her voice even. "But I thought you were kidding."

Caleb laughed.

They headed through the lobby and down a short hallway and out through a pair of sliding glass doors into the parking garage.

"Over there," said Jaden pointing to the next row. They walked in silence to her Jeep. Jaden pulled the key from her jeans pocket and slid behind the wheel. Caleb climbed into the passenger seat.

Jaden put her Maui Jim sunglasses on and started the Jeep. Easing out of the parking space, she asked "When did you and grandfather arrive in America?"

"We flew into the Memphis airport last night," replied Caleb. "We drove over to Jackson this morning."

Jaden drove out of the garage into the bright July sunshine, and turned left onto Forest Avenue. She heard a Mat Kearney song start playing and she turned up the volume. She felt Caleb's eyes on her, and she looked over. He was staring at her intently.

"*What?*" she asked questioningly.

"I was just wondering what you're thinking?" said Caleb casually.

Jaden focused intently on the road, and on not hitting anything. After an extended silence, she said shyly, "I'm thinking the person I got to know isn't who you are—I don't know anything about you."

Caleb's sensuous mouth curled into a lopsided smile. "I'll tell you *anything* you want to know . . . all you have to do is ask."

"Well . . ." stammered Jaden, trying to think of what to ask. "Where were you born?"

"I was born in Jerusalem, but I grew up in New Zealand and France."

"Where's home?"

"I don't really have one," replied Caleb, indifference in his voice. "My job keeps me moving around."

"Don't you have a house or an apartment somewhere?" questioned Jaden, an expression of incredulity flashing across her pretty face.

"I've got a flat in Tel Aviv and a set of apartments at the Chateau de Vignon in Grenoble, France."

"That night . . . what language were you and Hannah speaking?" Jaden turned left onto Campbell Street.

"Hebrew."

Jaden glanced over. "How many languages can you speak?"

Caleb shrugged. "A bunch" he said nonchalantly.

"How did Joe Martin—I mean, Joe Eichmann, kill Angelina?"

"Trust me, Jaden," replied Caleb with a sardonic laugh. "You don't want those morbid details in your head."

"That night, in the crib, was that Angelina Bonet's picture I saw on the board?"

"Yes."

The sun was setting in the western horizon. Jaden drove, questioning Caleb steadily about his life, places he'd been, and things he'd seen and done. When they arrived at the farm, the sky was glowing with the red and orange colors of the impending sunset. Approaching the barn, they heard a chorus of nickers and a hee-haw. Opening the feed room door, Jaden flicked on the light. On a shelf above the built-in feed bins, Jaden lined up six silver metal pails and filled them with the dietary needs of each horse. She handed Caleb three feed pails and said, "The bucket on top goes to Black Tie."

Caleb followed her out.

"How many of the Bonet sisters are still alive?" asked Jaden, stopping outside of Lyre's stall.

"Three— Caroline, Chloe and Lydia."

"They must be *ancient*."

Caleb laughed heartily.

"Caroline and Chloe are eighty-one and Lydia is seventy-nine," he said over his shoulder, emptying feed into Gabriel's bucket.

"Who has the keys now?"

"There are no physical keys, Jaden," said Caleb smiling. "After World War II ended, my great-great-grandmother, Edmae Chavel, made the decision to separate the codex collection and the treasures in locations around the world. The Key Keepers are responsible for keeping those locations secret."

"Will you tell me who the Key Keepers are?"

Caleb wavered and after a long pause, he said, "Caroline, and her twin sister, Chloe."

They finished feeding the horses in silence. Jaden clicked off the feed room light and pulled the door closed behind her. They strolled side by side slowly down the aisle and out of the barn. Jaden directed Caleb to a bench and they sat down. They stared at the horizon and the ever-changing hues of the setting sun.

"Have you ever been shot?" asked Jaden curiously.

"Unfortunately—yes."

Jaden's eyes widened. "More than once?"

"Yes."

Jaden cast an intrigued look at Caleb and said, "Show me."

Caleb removed his shirt, showing her a bullet scar on his side.

Jaden gulped. His body was powerfully built, each muscle group gloriously chiseled and well-defined—the personification of a warrior. She pointed to a tattoo on his shoulder blade and said, "What's that?"

"It's a Bohemian Waxwing . . . the Achsah family symbol," said Caleb simply. "It's in the bird's DNA to pass on what it collects."

Jaden eyed the number of scars on his body. Reaching out, she slowly, delicately traced an odd-shaped, jagged scar on his side with the tip of her finger. "What's this from?" she asked, meeting his gaze.

"Shrapnel." Caleb stared back, amused, studying her reaction. "I was in the military. I saw combat."

Caleb hastily pulled his shirt back on. "Are you done asking me questions?" he asked, humor in his deep, husky voice.

"No, I still have plenty to ask you, Jonathan -King-Caleb-Reynolds."

Caleb laughed.

"How did you learn to fight the way you do?" prompted Jaden.

"My mom hired people to teach me?"

"How old were you when your training began?"

"I was just a boy. I started with fencing lessons, martial arts and boxing," Caleb said. "As I got older, the techniques I was taught expanded to include Pankration, stick fighting, Japanese marital art sword-fighting, and

Brazilian Jiu-Jitsu—among others."

"Let's see—stick-fighting, sword-fighting and boxing—what else are you good at?"

A roguish grin unfurled on Caleb's face.

"I'd be happy to demonstrate," he boasted, his eyes glimmering playfully.

"Obviously, insecurity isn't something you struggle with," Jaden chided sarcastically in a low voice, her face reddening, and she quickly asked, "Why the heck did your Mom want you to know so many combat fighting techniques?"

"We *are* all trained," Caleb said in a straightforward, casual manner.

Jaden looked at him mystified. "*We*?"

Caleb nodded. "All of us in the Achsah line—my aunts and uncles, my cousins."

"*Why*?"

"To protect the Legacy—its treasures and its secrets."

"As the legatee, is Hannah in danger?" Jaden asked worriedly. She stared at Caleb, an expression of apprehension on her face.

"There are people who know about the Legacy. So—yes, dangers do exist," said Caleb calmly. "Starting next week, Hannah will have bodyguards."

"Bodyguards? Who—"

"They will be family."

"How big is your family?"

Caleb grinned. "*Big*."

Jaden smiled. "Hannah said the Legacy passes down to female family members," said Jaden. "What happens if Hannah doesn't have any daughters?"

"I don't know," said Caleb, shrugging. "In our family, having a lot of girls has always been paramount. The family's never had to face the question before."

"What question?"

"That there wouldn't be a female to inherit," replied

Caleb. "Gabrielle Bonet only had boys, so the Legacy passed to Zara, and she had two children . . . my mom and Henda."

"What if you got married and had a daughter—could the Legacy go to her?"

"I'm *not* husband material," said Caleb candidly. "I don't plan to marry so that's not a possibility."

"You don't want a family?"

Caleb shook his head.

"I prefer to keep my life simple with no intimate entanglements," he said emphatically.

Jaden threw a questioning, sideways glance at Caleb.

"You've never been in love?" she asked, trying to sound casual.

"No, I've never been in love."

Jaden looked quickly away from Caleb's scrutinizing gaze, pondering her next question.

"How old was your sister when she died?" she asked in a low voice.

Caleb's expression darkened.

"I'm *sorry*, Caleb," said Jaden apologetically. "I shouldn't have asked that."

"Don't apologize, Jaden," insisted Caleb sincerely, meeting her gaze. "Lily turned fifteen the day she died . . . it was her birthday."

Jaden gasped, her eyes widened in horror.

"We were at a restaurant celebrating her birthday. I went to the restroom and was on my way back to the table when a suicide bomber entered the restaurant. The bomb went off and the blast blew me backwards into the hallway," said Caleb, sadness in his voice. "I survived. My parents died instantly. By the time I reached Lily, she was losing consciousness. She died . . . in my arms . . . minutes later."

"I can't imagine how horrific that must have been," said Jaden, squeezing his arm, her voice soft and tender. "I understand things better now."

Looking at her curiously, Caleb asked, "Such as?"

"Why Hannah's crash at the Champagne Run horse show freaked you out so badly."

"When Black Tie crashed down on her, I thought for sure he had killed her," groaned Caleb. "I was unprepared for that."

"Wait a minute," cried Jaden, staring knowingly at Caleb. "You were on duty the entire weekend—you *lied* about spending the night with those girls."

Caleb nodded. "I lied."

"You were so convincing," quipped Jaden, her lips parting in a smile.

Caleb shrugged.

"It was a job requirement," he said in a resigned voice. "So . . . *where* were you?"

"In the room next to you and Hannah." Caleb smirked.

Jaden turned scarlet.

"Were you listening to us?"

"Yes," Caleb said, sounding amused. "You like to sing, '*More of Us*', in the shower."

Jaden nodded, grinning proudly. "I love that Trace Adkins song."

Caleb laughed.

They sat in silence watching the darkening twilight.

After an extended pause, Caleb turned to Jaden, his gaze intense, an expression of torment on his chiseled features.

"I've seen way too many horrific things, Jaden. Being around you and your family is like coming into the light from the dark—it's *highly* intoxicating," he said, his voice emphatic.

Jaden quickly turned her eyes away, her heart swelling with elation.

"My turn for questions," announced Caleb.

"Okay."

"That night—why did you come to *me* instead of riding to Jackson for the police?"

Jaden stared into his eyes. "I trust God *completely* and when I had to decide which road to take, I asked Him to guide me and He did."

Caleb smiled, his eyes shining with evident respect. "Winston Churchill said, 'There is something about the outside of a horse that is good for—"

"The inside of man!" Jaden said with an approving nod.

"Will you teach me to ride?"

"Of all the things you were taught, you weren't taught to ride?" said Jaden surprised.

"Growing up in Queenstown, New Zealand, my family was into climbing, fly fishing, and especially skiing," replied Caleb. "My mother was an Olympic skier. She had no interest in learning to ride."

"Your mom went to the Olympics?" asked Jaden, admiration in her voice.

Caleb nodded. "Three times actually . . . twice in skiing. She broke her leg and then she switched to Fencing."

"As your teacher, I'll expect you to do exactly what I tell you to do!" said Jaden staring at Caleb with an expression of playful sassiness.

Caleb's lips parted in a suave, impish grin. "I like the sound of this!"

Jaden punched his arm hard.

"Okay, I surrender. Do with me what you will," laughed Caleb, lifting his tan, muscular arms in mock surrender.

CHAPTER 30

O N THE FIRST SATURDAY MORNING in August, after a week in the hospital, Jacob arrived home. He was sprawled out lengthwise on the right end of an L-shaped beige leather sofa in the large, open family room, his right leg elevated by pillows.

"Glad to be home?" asked Hannah, sinking down beside him.

Jacob pulled her close, crushing her against him, his nose in her hair and whispered, "Very."

"Are you in any pain?"

"No," Jacob murmured, his lips brushing against her neck, his mouth running a steady trail of kisses from behind her ear down her neck.

Hannah shivered, the feel of his lips against her skin sent a rush of sweet sensations through her body. She nestled closer against him.

"Everything's going to be different, Jacob," she whispered.

Jacob lifted his head.

"What are you talking about?" he asked, frowning.

"Dad told me the family's wealth is obscene. He's going

to resign from the bank and take over one of the family's holding companies. Last night, he and Grundy told me that I'm going to have *bodyguards*. They'll be with me at all times," groaned Hannah. "Caleb told me he's designing a combat training program—"

"I'll be your *bodyguard*," muttered Jacob, smiling a kiss-me smile.

Hannah grabbed his face between her hands and pulled him to her, her mouth closing on his.

———————————

FIVE HOURS LATER, Paige, sitting on a stool at the kitchen island, was cutting up strawberries. She glanced up, "Can I get you anything, Jacob?"

Jacob, propped up by a pile of pillows, rolled his head back. "No thanks, Mom," he said, grinning. "But I'm curious when we'll be eating?"

Sheila, standing at the stove stirring a sauce, answered over her shoulder, "Arthur, Diana, Tristan, Edmund and Maria should be back from Memphis around the time Isaac and William are finished playing golf."

The back door squeaked open, Jaden and Caleb walked in.

Paige looked Caleb up and down. She frowned. "Why . . . is your T-shirt so dirty?"

"I fell off," answered Caleb, cool and unruffled, his usual composed self.

Paige's eyes flicked questioningly to Jaden. "Who was Caleb riding when he fell off?"

Jaden flushed a deep scarlet. "Lyre."

"*Lyre?*" repeated Paige, giving her daughter a reproving look.

"My lesson was on Sophie," Caleb interjected. "We were riding Lyre double and she bucked."

Paige cast an anxious look at him.

"Caleb, you weren't hurt?" she asked worriedly.

"No," promised Caleb, his eyes alight with humor, a devil-may-care expression on his face.

"Jaden—get Caleb a clean shirt from the utility room," said Paige.

Turning on her heel, Jaden marched to the utility room, returning with an orange Tennessee T-shirt.

"Bathroom is on the right," she said, handing the shirt to Caleb.

"Thanks." Caleb sauntered out of the room.

"Jacob," said Paige without looking at him, her eyes on what she was doing, cutting up strawberries. "I saw your Bible teacher, Ms. Myers, at the grocery store yesterday. She told me you have an assignment due on Monday."

"School only started yesterday!" grumbled Jacob.

Paige slid off the stool, walked across the room, picked up Jacob's backpack, carried it back to the sofa, and handing it to Hannah said, "Mind finding it?"

Hannah rummaged through the backpack until she found Jacob's Bible notebook. She pulled it out and laid the three-ring binder aside, dropping the backpack on the floor with a thud.

Hannah opened the three-ring binder, and removed the worksheet.

"This assignment requires participation from family and friends," she said in a level voice, her eyes scanning the instructions. "Participants are to name a person from the Bible that Jacob shares personality traits with or physical similarities to."

"King David," blurted Jaden, collapsing down on the sofa.

"Yes, a young David—before he was King," gushed Hannah.

"Do we just tell you or how does it work?" asked Jaden, staring at Hannah.

Hannah slipped her fingers down between the folder flaps and withdrew a stack of index cards bound together with a rubber band.

"I think we're supposed to use these," she said, waving the white 4-inch by 6-inch cards in the air. She peeled off the rubber band.

Paige walked to a drawer by the refrigerator, pulled it open, and grabbed a handful of pens. She walked to the sofa, handing a pen to Hannah with one hand, taking the index cards from her with the other. She settled on the sectional beside Jaden.

For a few minutes, there was silence as everyone wrote. Jaden, who had finished first, peered over at her mother's index card and laughed.

"That's what I said too," she whispered loudly.

Hannah passed her index card to Jaden. "Here pass this to your mom."

Jaden passed both cards to her mother.

"I'll start with Jaden's," said Paige, her eyes on the card. "Like King David, Jacob is brave and courageous, loves God, and begins each day with devotional." She shuffled the cards.

"Hannah's next," she said, staring down at the white index card. "Jacob trusts God, never hesitates to stand up for his beliefs, and like David, he has beautiful eyes."

Jacob looked embarrassed, the color rising in his cheeks.

Caleb swaggered back into the room. Jaden looked up and felt her heart flip-flop. The T-shirt fit him snugly. The fabric clung to his muscular frame. The orange color of the shirt set off his blue eyes, reminding her of the blue-colored waters of the Blue Grotto sea cave she had visited in Capri. Suddenly, memories of Tristan Wakefield fluttered alive. He would be arriving soon. She wondered what it was going to be like to see him again. Snapping back from her reverie, she heard her mother's voice telling

Caleb about the Bible assignment.

"If I may add something," said Caleb, sitting down next to Jaden. "At seventeen, David used a slingshot to defeat Goliath."

"Joe Eichmann certainly qualifies as a Goliath," said Hannah sharply.

"I didn't exactly defeat Eichmann, Caleb," argued Jacob.

"I beg to differ," retorted Caleb. "Eichmann would have shot me in the head if your rock hadn't hit him at the moment it did."

"I just thought of something," said Jaden, her emerald green eyes laughing gaily. "Michal, Saul's daughter, was in love with David and she became his wife."

Hannah blushed and looked at Jacob. He was grinning broadly.

William Butler and Isaac Leitner, their faces flushed from the hot summer day, strolled into the great room.

"Hello everyone," said William cheerfully. Walking over to Sheila, he kissed his wife on the cheek.

"Did you have a good game of golf, dear?" asked Sheila.

"Yes," answered William.

"It's been a glorious day," declared Isaac, ambling over to the sofa. He stopped behind Hannah, bent and kissed the top of her head.

Hannah glanced up. "Grundy—did you meet Gabriel?"

"I did," said Isaac smiling with pleasure. "Gabriel has soft, intelligent eyes and he talks with his ears. He reminds me very much of a burro the Bonet's had named Parable."

"I saw a family picture of three little girls in a cart pulled by a burro—was that Parable?" Paige asked keenly.

"I'd have to see the picture to tell you," said Isaac with a velvety laugh. "There were over a dozen donkeys at the Chateau de Vignon."

"Why so many? Did they breed donkeys?" Paige questioned.

Isaac shook his head.

"Edmae Cheval and her daughter, Monique, *loved* donkeys," he said, meeting her gaze. "They believed any donkey marked with the cross was a descendant of the donkey that carried Jesus into Jerusalem on Palm Sunday, and was therefore—special."

Paige stared at Isaac in astonishment.

"The Jerusalem Donkey Legend—I think Gabriel is a descendant of *that* donkey," she said with honest conviction.

"I believe it was an Angel that guided Gabriel to that sink-hole Hannah was in," injected Sheila from the kitchen with a firm nod.

"Divine intervention, I'd say!" William said loudly from across the room.

"Without a doubt!" agreed Paige.

"God used a donkey in the book of Numbers to send a message," Jaden added.

"God works in supernatural, unconventional ways," Isaac stated, settling himself into an oversized club chair facing the sofa.

"Are you familiar with horses, Isaac?" Paige asked.

"Somewhat," Isaac said, nodding slightly.

"Grundy's great-grandfather and great-great-grandfather were both Choctaw Lighthorsemen," beamed Hannah. "Grundy was riding by the age of four."

"Cool!" exclaimed Jacob.

"*Seriously cool*," agreed Jaden.

Isaac grinned.

"Hi, we're here!" A cheerful girl, her heart-shaped face framed by long silky pale blonde hair, walked into the room followed a tall, lean youth with a round face and wavy blonde hair, a pretty woman and Arthur Butler.

Rising to her feet, Paige went to greet the new arrivals.

"Paige, this is Diana," said Arthur, his arm circling around his wife's waist. Shorter than Paige, Diana had shoulder length honey-blonde hair and creamy translucent skin.

Paige embraced Diana warmly. "Welcome to our home, Diana."

"Thank you. Please excuse my son, Tristan," said Diana, in a tone of mild exasperation. "He's outside on the phone. One of his hotels needed his immediate attention."

"This is Maria and Edmund," Arthur said gesturing with a slight nod.

"Did you enjoy Memphis?" inquired Paige, her gaze flicking from Maria to Edmund.

Edmund shrugged. "I'm glad Mom got to see Graceland."

"Mom is a big Elvis fan," quipped Maria. "She's wanted to see Graceland for a long time."

"Maria," called Hannah affectionately. "Where's my hug!"

Maria hurried to Hannah, throwing her arms around Hannah's neck, hugging her warmly. She turned her large expressive eyes to Jacob, and said in a sweet voice, "I'm Maria."

"Hi, Maria," he said smiling. "I'm Jacob. It's nice to meet you."

Maria looked at Jacob from underneath her lashes and her cheeks blushed pink. "When are you getting that off?" she asked, eyeing the cast on his arm.

"In several weeks," replied Jacob. "Why?"

Maria blushed again.

"Because I really want to see you vault up onto a horse," she said looking at him shyly.

"Don't I get a hug?" cried Jaden.

Maria spun, took three big steps and launched herself into Jaden's arms. Jaden laughed and engulfed her in a bear hug. Maria smiled, stepped back and looked at Caleb, eyeing him inquisitively. Extending her small, delicate hand she said boldly, "I'm Hannah's step-sister, Maria."

"I'm Caleb. I'm Hannah's cousin," he said smiling tenderly at Maria. He pointed to Isaac and said, "This is our grandfather, Isaac."

Maria's eyes widened and she threw a quick look at Isaac.

"Nice to meet you, Maria," said Isaac with a nod and he smiled fondly.

Lord Wakefield, known to his family and friends as Tristan, strolled confidently into the crowded room. He was dressed casually in a white shirt, open at the neck, and jeans. His messy bronze-colored hair, parted on the left, was short on the sides, and long on top. He was sporting a neatly trimmed beard and mustache popular with the young Hollywood stars. He walked directly to Paige.

"Mrs. Winston, I'm Tristan," he said in a cultured Brit accent. His facial hair enhanced the sculpted plains of his face, making him look older and more handsome.

"Thank you for inviting us into your home," he said extending a golden-brown tan forearm.

"We're delighted you could come," replied Paige. "Please, call me Paige."

Tristan nodded politely and walked over to the sofa, extending his hand to Jacob.

"Hi, Jacob," he said casually. "You look better than what I was expecting."

He turned to Hannah, leaned over, and kissed Hannah chastely on both checks and said, "Glad you're okay."

"Tristan," cried Maria, hurrying over to him. She grabbed his hand. "This is Hannah's grandfather, Isaac," she said, pulling him after her.

"Nice to meet you," said Tristan courteously, shaking Isaac's outstretched hand.

"This is Hannah's cousin, Caleb," said Maria.

"I didn't know Hannah had a cousin," said Tristan, extending his hand, his eyes wide in surprise.

Caleb shook his outstretched hand.

"She does," he said coolly with a smile that didn't reach his eyes.

"Hi, Tristan," said Jaden.

"Hi, Jaden," replied Tristan, turning towards her, his voice laced with fondness.

Maria tugged his hand. "Tell Jaden about Man O'War."

"Why don't you tell her?" suggested Tristan, ruffling his sister's blonde hair.

Maria smiled adoringly up at her brother. She stepped over to the sofa and flopped down beside Jaden, announcing in her sugar-sweet voice, "Lyre has Man O'War in her bloodline."

"I didn't know that," said Jaden, her questioning gaze shifting to Tristan.

"I'm familiar with Lyre's bloodline. My father had a broodmare by Olden Times, the sire of Two Davids," explained Tristan, settling himself in an oversized club chair. "War Relic, who was sired by Man O'War, was Olden Times grandfather."

Jaden looked at him startled. "How did you know who Lyre's sire was?"

"Hannah told me," declared Tristan with a shrug.

"Can I please meet Gabriel?" Maria interrupted.

"You sure can." Jaden grinned at her. "Would you like to go on a trail ride tomorrow?"

"I'd *love* to!" Maria cried eagerly, clapping her hands together. "Edmund, do you want to go riding with us tomorrow?"

Edmund swiveled his blond head around. "Nahh, I'd rather stay here and watch sports with Jacob."

Maria looked at Caleb. "Want to—"

"I don't know how to ride," said Caleb.

Maria cocked her head to the side and looked at him as if he had just told her he was an alien from outer space.

"You don't know how to ride?"

Caleb laughed.

"I'm learning," he said, smiling warmly at her. "Does that count?"

"I suppose," said Maria with a shrug. Looking at Tristan, she asked, "You'll go won't you?"

"I'd love to go," said Tristan, his eyes fixed on Jaden.

Jaden looked away from Tristan's fervent gaze. She winked at Maria. "We'll have fun."

"Dinner is ready," announced Sheila. "There is Penne pasta with five cheeses, green beans with honey cashew sauce, squash casserole, grilled asparagus, beef Wellington and a salad of mixed greens and strawberries with balsamic vinaigrette."

"Sheila, you've clearly out done yourself," remarked Diana.

"With so many of us, I think its best that we just serve ourselves," said Paige. "Everyone please sit wherever you can find a spot. The table in here sits six and the dining room table can seat ten of us."

When no one moved, Sheila handed plates to William, Arthur and Isaac, instructing them to start. They filled their plates, and Sheila directed them towards the dining room.

Caleb stood, and stretched out his hand to Jaden.

"I love chaotic family meals," he said lifting her easily to her feet, an expression of boyish delight on his handsome face. Leaning down, he whispered in her ear, "Family *is everything*."

AFTER DINNER, Isaac, William, Arthur and Diana were in the dining room playing cards. Paige and Sheila were cleaning up the kitchen. Edmund, Caleb and Jacob were sitting on the sectional fixated, watching ESPN. Jaden, Hannah Tristan, and Maria were sitting at the kitchen table playing UNO.

"It just came to me," blurted Jaden excitedly, springing to her feet. "I know what I want to do with my share of the reward money."

All eyes turned her way.

"After graduation next year," Jaden said. "I want to take Lyre to England for the summer to train."

Jacob's head jerked around, his attention no longer on the television.

"That's an awesome idea," he hollered. "Hannah and I have been talking about going to England next summer."

Paige looked at Jacob and then Jaden but didn't say anything. Taking her silence as a sign of consideration, Jacob continued.

"We could find a place to lease for the summer, something centrally located that is big enough for all of us, including a couple of horses," he said.

"Why not just stay at my place in Hertfordshire?" suggested Tristan, his gaze on Paige. "There is plenty of room at Ashland Hall."

Paige shook her head in protest. "Tristan that is a very generous—"

"Seriously, Paige, it wouldn't be an imposition," insisted Tristan, his tone adamant. "I'll be offended if you don't take me up on my offer."

Maria turned her big saucer blue eyes on Paige.

"*Please,* Ms. Paige, I keep my pony there and I'd love to be able to ride everyday with Jaden," she pleaded.

"Tristan's not kidding about there being plenty of room," said Edmund pointedly. "Ashland Hall has over two hundred rooms."

"And an Olympic size covered Dressage ring, jumper ring and its own cross country course," interjected Maria, with an affirmative nod. "The cross country jumps go up to advanced."

"You should see the barn," Edmund smirked.

"Mom," said Jacob, meeting his mother's gaze. "Ever heard of The Donkey Sanctuary in Devon, England?"

"No."

"Over fourteen thousand donkeys have passed through

the Donkey Sanctuary's gates," said Jacob. "You've been talking about starting a donkey rescue. Just imagine how much you could learn from them."

"By the way, William and I are planning on spending several weeks in England next summer while he does research for his next book," Sheila announced, standing beside Paige.

"I must admit that I've always wanted to live in England," Paige mused. "I *adore* the country."

"Paige," said Sheila, resting her hand on Paige's arm. She whispered in her ear, "You're clearly outnumbered, dear."

Paige stared at her children, then smiled and excused herself. She walked down the hall and into her bedroom. On her nightstand was the leather bound book that Robert had given her on the day the twins were born—the one she'd dug out of the box last spring. She picked up the book and sat down on the edge of her bed. She ran her fingers slowly over the embossing on the spine of the book—*Amplified Bible*—and thought back to the morning in April when she began reading her Bible. Reading His Word had opened her stony heart, eliminating the rage and malice she felt toward the man who had shot and killed her husband 7 years ago.

Her eyes flicked to a 4-inch by 6-inch photograph of Gabriel lying on her nightstand. Her heart swelled with love. Grateful tears pooled in her brown eyes. She grinned at God's sense of humor—using a little blushed-colored burro to steer her to the Bible. She knew she believed unquestioningly in the power of His Word. Her shattered heart was healing, her faith was restored. She had peace and joy.

Paige, picked up the picture of Gabriel, kissed it and tucked it between the pages of her Bible. She ran her hand lovingly over the soft, smooth leather, closed her eyes and whispered, *"England—here we come!"*

THE KEY KEEPERS

BOOK TWO OF THE
ACHSAH LEGACY

BY ANNE CHURCHILL

Read on for a preview.

PROLOGUE

APRIL
2012

THE PALATIAL OFFICE IN MANHATTAN, with a wall of floor-to-ceiling windows with views of the Hudson River, was shrouded in darkness except for the muted glow from a desk lamp and a computer monitor. Vitor Lessard squinted at the computer screen and silently cursed his old age. He took off his eye glasses and cleaned them slowly, replacing them on his nose. It didn't help. At eighty-nine, his eyes were tired from six hours of unrelenting reading. He heard his office door open and glanced up to see his younger brother, Gideon.

Vitor's eyes flicked to the clock on his computer screen.

"It's almost ten on a Friday, what are you still doing here?"

"I have something for you." Gideon flicked on the overhead lights. He was wearing a dark suit, white shirt and red tie, carrying a brown folder. He laid the brown folder down on the massive nineteenth-century mahogany partners' desk, turned, and walked to an antique cabinet against the wall.

"Care for a drink," he said, without looking around. It wasn't a question. He withdrew two crystal glasses and a bottle of twenty-year old Pappy-Van-Winkle bourbon, carrying all of it back to the desk. "Caleb Reynolds is back in the country. His private jet landed this afternoon at McKellar-Sipes Regional airport in Jackson, Tennessee."

Vitor's head snapped around.

Gideon poured, handing his brother a crystal tumbler.

"Is Isaac with him?" asked Vitor contemptuously, taking the glass from his brother. His mouth tightened into a hard line, the fingers of his left hand reflexively brushing his hair over the old scar, carved into his flesh by Isaac Leitner in 1945. Upon learning that he had collaborated with the Nazi's, Isaac had tracked him down, branding him a traitor by carving a large T into his forehead.

"No," said Gideon. "Isaac is in Israel."

"Why is Caleb Reynolds in Jackson?"

"There's a birthday party tomorrow night for the Winston twins, Jacob and Jaden," replied Gideon. "My guess is he's here for that."

"I can't afford guesses," said Vitor tersely, a hint of concern in his voice. "Not while Eichmann is still alive and there's a chance he might tell the Mossad about me." As the war was drawing to a close, Vitor had assumed the identity of a dead Jewish man matching his height and body type, teeth and eye color —all thanks to his good friend, Josef Eichmann. With aid from Bishop Alois Hudal, he had escaped Europe to South America, then Canada, finally settling in America. With his new identity, he had become a well-respected business man and philanthropist. He was on Forbes list of Billionaire's. Among his powerful allies and friends, was the President of the United States.

"What does Eichmann know about Meridian?" asked

Gideon, his eyes staring down into the glass at the deep burnt-amber liquid. Meridian was a secretive, transnational organization with a globalist agenda.

"He knows enough to expose us. He'll have no problem betraying me or the others if he thinks it will save his life," Vitor said acidly. "There's a possibility that Joe's son, Andrew, knows something about me. I want eyes and ears on Dr. Martin and his ex-wife, Rebecca." He sipped his drink.

"I want to know if Caleb Reynolds has any communication with them," he said firmly. "Caleb is like his grandfather, he tracks like a blood-hound. If he picks up any scent about me or Meridian—"

"I thought Meridian had someone on the inside that was taking care of the Eichmann issue?"

"It will be done, but when the time is right," said Vitor assuredly. "In the meantime, I want an insurance policy—Hannah Butler."

Gideon leaned over and pushed the brown folder towards his brother.

"The latest surveillance reports on Hannah Butler are on top. She never goes anywhere alone," he said. "She has two body guards that we know of and Jacob Winston is always at her side."

"You say the boy's name as if he can make a difference," Vitor sneered.

"Don't underestimate that boy. Jacob has excelled in his combat training and he is turning into a skilled fighter," admonished Gideon. "More importantly, he's in love with Hannah Butler and he would die to protect her. . . and that, *brother,* makes him formidable!"

Vitor opened the file and stared at the eight by ten photograph of Michal Hannah Butler. Her resemblance to Angelina Bonet was striking. Like Angelina, she had the same bone structure, the same lovely brown eyes, the same long graceful neck and pink, pouting lips.

"One of her bodyguards, Kaden Bennett, is a cousin. He's a grandson of Caroline Bonet," said Gideon, pausing. "He's *Richard Bennett's son.*"

Vitor scowled in displeasure. Richard Bennett had gotten close to discovering his assumed identity and he had him killed for it. Killing to protect his identity was not something he shrank from.

"This is Kaden Bennett?" he asked, reaching for two pictures of a powerfully built, handsome man with black wavy hair. He had the high cheek bones and sculpted jaw line common in the Bonet family. He laid both photographs of Kaden Bennett down and he picked up the eight by ten picture of a young girl with long, straight dark hair, bangs that hung to big, round brown eyes.

Vitor shot his brother a look of astonishment, and blurted, "This little girl is the one who fought off the two men—"

"I know Aaliyah Myers looks like she's fourteen—she's really twenty-two and highly trained!" protested Gideon.

Vitor slammed the picture on the desk, fuming.

"*I warned you—never underestimate anyone in that family!*" he barked. "They're trained, skilled fighters!" He reached for his drink and froze. He sat up abruptly, his eyes on the photographs spread out in front of him. He studied the eight by ten photograph of Kaden Bennett, shirtless, busy digging a fence post. There was a tattoo of a bird on his left shoulder. In the second picture of Kaden, he was lifting a bale of hay, his muscular bareback glistening with sweat.

"The Bohemian Waxwing tattoo is on his right shoulder. They're identical twins!" cried Vitor, flashing the pictures at his brother. "This has Isaac Leitner stamped all over it. I'll never forget how Isaac used Chloe and Caroline Bonet's identicalness to his advantage when he rescued Zara from the Gestapo."

"I'll find out the name of the twin," said Gideon, staring

into his drink. After a long pause, he said grudgingly, his voice low, "Caleb Reynolds wasn't alone. He had two of his cousins with him."

Vitor glared at his younger brother, his brown eyes narrowed. "Which two?"

"Reece Myers and Quentin Picard."

Vitor reached for his drink, gulping what bourbon remained in his glass. The news disturbed him.

"I don't like this . . . Mossad, British Special Forces and Interpol . . . it's not to attend some birthday party . . . I can assure you!" he snarled, pushing his empty glass towards Gideon.

Gideon leaned over and refilled his brother's glass. "We've got eyes on them."

"Get me the Bonet files."

Gideon put his drink down, stood, and walked to the wall where a Gustav Klimt painting hung. He slipped his fingers behind the frame. There was a faint click and the painting swung out on cleverly concealed hinges, revealing a front loading black wall safe. He punched in the six digit code. He opened the door and removed a stack of thick, stuffed folders and returned to Vitor's desk.

"I'm going home," Gideon said, laying the pile before his older brother.

Vitor nodded and reached for the file on top. It was marked: Chloe Bonet Belmont. He opened it and stared at the picture of Chloe Bonet, taken on her wedding day in 1953 when she married Samuel Belmont, heir to an Australian metals and mining Empire. He thumbed through the pages until he found what he was looking for, withdrawing the profile on her grandson, Reece Myers. His eyes scanned the profile. Raised on an eighteen-thousand acre cattle station in Queensland, Australia and in England, Reece attended Eton College before entering the Royal Military Academy Sandhurst. While at Eton he excelled in sports, particularly rugby and polo, foreign languages and mathematics. Trained by the United Kingdom Special Forces, he was currently with the Special Reconnaissance Regiment.

Vitor studied an eight by ten photograph of the fine-looking twenty-eight-year- old, leaning against a fence, a gray horse at his side. He was tall and broad-shouldered, the sleeves of his dark blue shirt rolled up to his elbows, revealing strong, muscular forearms. He was looking out from underneath a black cowboy hat, his burnished-copper hair swept across his forehead, grazing large, serious eyes, his full lips parted in a cocky grin.

Vitor replaced the photograph and closed the folder. He reached for the next file. It was marked: Gabrielle Bonet Picard. He opened it and stared at the picture of Gabrielle and her husband, Charles Picard, heir to Picard Dynamics, taken at the Paris Opera. He shuffled through the pages until he found the profile on her grandson, Quentin Picard. At thirty-five, Quentin was the oldest of the current generation. Born in Jerusalem, he had grown up in Grenoble, France. He entered the École Spéciale Militaire as a cadet at twenty-one, then the French Air Force. He was now an Interpol agent assigned to the Millennium Project.

Vitor reached for his drink, lifting the crystal glass to his lips. His mind whirled with memories from the past. Isaac Leitner had done more than track him down. He dragged him home and publicly branded him. His seething shame had swelled into a consuming hatred for Isaac that had blazed intensely for sixty-seven years, swirling through him like a voracious wild fire, devouring his soul.

"Isaac—I'm going to turn your joy to ash," he said in a low, menacing voice to the empty room. He put the glass down, reached for the phone, and dialed Gideon's cell phone.

"When are the Winston's leaving for England?" he asked impatiently.

"Paige, Jacob and Jaden Winston, Hannah Butler, Aaliyah Myers and Kaden Bennett are booked on a Delta flight leaving Nashville on Monday, May twenty-eighth at six-twenty p.m. with a short-layover in Detroit, arriving—"

"We grab Hannah Butler during the layover in Detroit," announced Vitor.

"In front of airport cameras, her bodyguards—"

"*Yes*, it's the perfect setting," bragged Vitor. "I've an idea for a distraction—something right out of Isaac Leitner's playbook."

RESOURCE NOTES

Prologue
1. Psalm 23:1-4 (New King James Version)
2. Psalm 27:1 (New King James Version)
3. Philippians 4:13 (New King James Version)

Chapter 4
1. John 1:1 (New King James Version)
2. Psalm 33:6 (New King James Version)
3. Romans 10:10 (Thompson Chain-Reference Bible, New International Version)
4. Proverbs 30:5 (New King James Version)
5. Hebrews 4:12 (Thompson Chain-Reference Bible, New International Version)
6. Psalm 119:105 (New King James Version &Amplified Topical Reference Bible)

Chapter 9
1. Ephesians 6:11 (Thompson Chain-Reference Bible, New International Version)
2. Ephesians 6:14-15 (Thompson Chain-Reference Bible, New International Version)
3. Ephesians 6:17 (New King James Version)
4. Hebrews 4:12 (New King James Version)
5. Luke 11:4 (Amplified Topical Reference Bible)

Chapter 25
1. Matthew 6:22 (Thompson Chain-Reference Bible, New International Version)

Chapter 26
1. Psalm 56:3-4 (New King James Version)

Chapter 27
1. Job 39:19 (Amplified Topical Reference Bible)
2. Job 39:19-23 (Amplified Topical Reference Bible)
3. Joshua 15:16-20 (Amplified Topical Reference Bible)

ACKNOWLEDGMENTS

Much love and thanks to my husband, son, and step-children for their patience and understanding these past two years.

A special thank you to my aunt Pat for believing in me.

I am in your debt, Gary and Becky, for your blunt, honest criticism which pushed me forward.

Love and gratitude to my editor, Nancy, without whom, I couldn't have pulled this together.

A big thank you to Trish and Gary Stanfill, Tom and Mary Reed, Danielle and Brad Tursky, Mark and Kathy Brooks, and Martin and Shelley Jelinek.

And a gargantuan thank-you to Jonathan Cain, Mary Nell Sparks, Samantha Jelinek, Dillon Tull, Tanner Chapman, Joey Hanson, Payton Stanfill, Saundra and Rachel Carrington, Glendon Haddix, Jeremy Woods, Shawn Wyatt, Lonnie Cobb, Paris Parkins, David Dray, Tyreece Miller, David and Tabatha Tremblay, my sister, Geeta Churchill and my parents.

ABOUT THE AUTHOR

Anne Churchill has been riding horses since the age of five. She lives in west Tennessee with her family.

CPSIA information can be obtained at www.ICGtesting.com
Printed in the USA
LVOW081307150413

329133LV00002B/5/P